Praise for

Touch of Death

"HOLY MEDUSA AND HADES! … Come along for the greatest ride of a lifetime. You will love the mythology retelling and the cast of characters who will become family to Jodi… I am sure this series will be one people will talk about for years to come."

— Diary Of A Book Addict

"I Hereby Award This Book 5 Wings, but I would gladly award it a thousand times that… It is a MUST read. If you like zombies, necromancers, mythology, gorgeous men and fantastic writing, then you need to add this to your own TBR pile. NOW!"

— Gothic Angel Book Reviews

"I adored this book. Right from the start I found this positively one of the coolest books I've ever read… *Touch of Death* is phenomenal and it completely and utterly took my breath away. I am dying to read more and I cannot wait to find out what happens next. Kelly Hashaway is an author to look out for in the future. She is amazing and *Touch of Death* is one book that is not to be missed."

— K-Books

"*Touch of Death* was everything I expected it to be and so much more. It had a gripping story line, young romance, a fierce heroine, evil villains, and a swoon worthy hero. To put it simply, I really loved this book… *Touch of Death* is deadly addictive and I dare you to put it down."

— Readers Live A Thousand Lives

"Devastating truths, compelling characters and a brilliantly unique storyline, *Touch of Death* was unlike anything I've read before and I enjoyed it so, so much. It's going to be Hades waiting to read *Stalked by Death*… I rate *Touch of Death* Five out of Five!!!"

— BookSavvy

Spencer Hill Press

Contact: Spencer Hill Press, PO Box 247, Contoocook, NH 03229, USA

Please visit our website at www.spencerhillpress.com

First Edition: July 2013.

Kelly Hashway
Stalked by Death : a novel / by Kelly Hashway – 1st ed.
p. cm.
Summary:
A teenage necromancer must train her kind to follow Hades' rules, but with a new guy messing with her powers, she might become the biggest threat of all.

The author acknowledges the copyrighted or trademarked status and trademark owners of the following wordmarks mentioned in this fiction:
Band-Aid, PowerPoint

Cover design by Kate Kaynak
Necklace by Stained Glass Creations & Beyond
Interior layout by Marie Romero

ISBN 978-1-937053-51-2 (paperback)
ISBN 978-1-937053-52-9 (e-book)

Printed in the United States of America

Stalked by Death

Death

Kelly Hashway

SPENCER HILL PRESS

Also By Kelly Hashway

Touch of Death
(Touch of Death #1)

Stalked by Death
(Touch of Death #2)

Face by Death
(Touch of Death #3, Spring 2014, Spencer Hill Press)

The Monster Within
(April 2014, Spencer Hill Press)

The Darkness Within
(2014, Spencer Hill Press)

Love All
(Game. Set. Match. Heartbreak #1, Swoon Romance)

Advantage: Heartbreak
(Game. Set. Match. Heartbreak #2, Swoon Romance)

Perfect Match
(Game. Set. Match. Heartbreak #3, Swoon Romance)

Into the Fire
(Spring 2014, Month9Books)

Curse of the Granville Fortune
(August 2014, Month9Books)

To Ayla, with love

Chapter 1

Most people didn't spend every waking minute thinking about death, but when most of your day consisted of raising corpses, what else could you really focus on? The guy in front of me was vicious. His skin hung off his bones, and he looked like he was ready to tear me to pieces. Sure, I'd raised him from the depths of Hell, but I would've thought the guy would welcome a break from eternal torture.

"See, the second you raise them, they'll come right at you." I stared the guy down, not taking my focus off him for a second. The last thing I wanted was to lose control of the soul and have it attack me—or worse, poor Leticia, who still wasn't used to her necromancer powers. She cowered behind Randy, peeking one eye out at the corpse.

"Have a command ready, because if you give the soul time to turn on you, it will." The guy reached for me, but I was already mixing my blood in my veins, letting my Gorgon blood do its magic. I locked eyes with the corpse. "Don't move." He froze, his bony fingers extended toward my neck. His eyes showed nothing but hatred for me.

"How come they listen to you?" Leticia broke me out of my trance. "I mean, *I* raised the guy. My blood brought him here, so why is he only listening to you?"

Being able to command any soul, whether I'd summoned it or not, was one of my special powers, an added perk that came with being a direct descendent of Medusa. Usually Ophi were able to do it once they became adults, but I'd been able to do it from the start. "He *will* listen to you, Leticia. You just have to show him you are in charge. You are the one with the power."

"I don't feel like I'm in charge." She stepped out from behind Randy and moved closer to the corpse. "He came right at me and tried to bite me."

"That would've been the end of him if he did bite you." Alex moved to my side. "Your blood would've sent him straight back to Hell."

Leticia's eyes widened in horror. "Great, so I have to get bit every time I raise a soul?"

"No." I elbowed Alex for teasing Leticia. She was a sweet girl, and even though Alex wasn't trying to freak her out, he'd managed to. "Alex just means that the corpses really can't hurt us. They'd end up hurting themselves." Okay, now that wasn't entirely true. The corpses could hurt us plenty, as long as we didn't bleed on them in the process, but Leticia was very sensitive right now, so I needed to raise her spirits.

"Come on." I walked over to her and positioned her two feet in front of the frozen corpse. Leticia was by no means intimidating. She was only five foot four, like me, but she had a tendency to cower behind her long blonde hair, making her look even smaller. "Try releasing his soul. Send him back to where he came from."

Alex laughed. "Yeah, Leticia, tell him to go to Hell."

I turned around and gave him a look, but he knew I wasn't really mad. I couldn't get mad at him. He'd chosen me over his family, even after I'd sentenced them to servitude in the underworld. Well, that and he was gorgeous. Like all Ophi, he had green eyes. His dirty blond hair was a little unruly in an "I-just-got-out-of-bed" kind of way. Not true bed head, just… sexy. He winked at me, and before I knew it I was smiling.

"Jodi?" Leticia had apparently been talking to me, asking for instructions.

"Right. Okay, tell the soul that you are releasing him and that he should go back to where he was before you summoned him. Be firm. *Make* him listen to you."

Leticia nodded, but her bottom lip quivered. The April air still had a chill, but I knew that wasn't the problem. She was scared. Unsure of herself. And that was going to get her hurt. She needed confidence to control the dead.

"Okay, I think we need a break." I put my hand on Leticia's shoulder. "Why don't you and Randy go inside and help set up for dinner?"

"No." Leticia shrugged my hand away. "I'm tired of being the weak link here. I have to figure out how to do this. Unfreeze him, Jodi."

"Leticia, I was—"

"Just do it!"

I'd never seen Leticia this angry. I didn't know what I'd said to make her get so upset. Still, I hesitated. I didn't want her getting hurt because she was determined to prove a point. Truthfully, I wasn't sure she was ready to control this soul.

"Forget it!" She broke into sobs. "You don't even believe in me. Some teacher you are, Jodi." She turned and ran for the mansion that we used as a school. Randy shook his head and followed her.

"Leticia!" I yelled after her, but she ignored me.

Alex wrapped his arms around me. "She'll get over it. She's been overly sensitive lately. It'll pass."

I nuzzled my head against Alex's neck, breathing in his scent. I'd had to give up everything to come here—my home, my friends, my mom. I was completely cut off from my old life. Alex was home to me now.

"Hey, none of that." He pulled me back and looked into my eyes.

I hadn't even realized I was crying. "Sorry." I wiped the tears from my cheeks.

"Can I help?" Not waiting for a response, he leaned down and kissed me.

I lost myself in him. No thoughts of corpses, Hades, or Ophi. Just Alex. The kiss went on forever—at least it could have if Tony hadn't interrupted.

"Ahem." He cleared his throat. I pulled away from Alex to see Tony looking out past the mausoleum. "Sorry to interrupt. I thought you were training Leticia and Randy."

"I gave them a break. Leticia needed it."

Tony nodded. "She has been very sensitive lately."

It was understandable. Two months ago, Victoria had raised Leticia's parents, and they came back horribly wrong. Nothing more than zombies. That was a lot to ask Leticia to put behind her. I had no doubt she saw her parents' faces every time she raised a corpse. I knew what that was like.

"She's been distant in class," Tony continued. I might be the one teaching about the actual raising of the dead, but Tony taught us all about our race, our powers, and where we came from. I couldn't run this school without him.

"She needs more time," I said.

"I know, but the reason I came to get you is that you have a call from Mason."

My eyes widened, and I smiled. "Great! I've been waiting for his call." Mason ran Serpentarius, an Ophi club back in my hometown. I was trying to convince him to bring his group to the school. I'd promised Hades I would teach all the remaining Ophi to use their powers in a way that wouldn't disrupt the underworld too much. I was trying to end a war, but so far, just about every Ophi I'd talked to wasn't listening. No one was worried about Hades coming after them anymore. Because Hades wasn't coming after *them*. He was coming after me. Or at least he would be if anyone got out of line.

"Let's go," I said to Alex.

"What about him?" Tony pointed to the corpse standing behind us.

I'd completely forgotten about him. "Right." I faced the body, allowing my blood to bubble under my skin, combining the powers of both sides of my body—the right side with the power to restore life, and the left side with the power to kill. The sensation was still a rush, even though I'd done it so many times now. The only bad part was that using too much power gave me headaches and left me drained of energy. But releasing souls was easy. They didn't fight you because they wanted to be released.

"Go back to where you were before Leticia called you. Go now." My tone was serious, commanding. The corpse's eyes flickered slightly, and I felt his soul release. A second later, the body slumped to the ground.

Back when Victoria and Troy ran the school, there were servants to clean up after messes like this. But the servants had all been raised souls, and I'd promised Hades we wouldn't use his dead for our own purposes anymore. That meant I'd be digging up a grave this evening.

"I'll take care of the body after my call with Mason," I said.

Alex and I ran back to the school, leaving Tony way behind. I'd already kept Mason waiting, and I couldn't have him in a bad mood when I needed a favor. I went straight to Victoria's old office. My office now. The phone was lying on the desk. I threw myself into the chair and grabbed the phone. Alex stood behind me with his hands on my shoulders for support.

"Hello, Mason? I'm so glad you called. I—"

"Yeah, listen, Jodi, before you get too excited, I'm only calling to tell you that we're happy where we are. We don't see the need to come out there. We're all responsible with our powers. We aren't causing any trouble."

"I know, but—"

"I'm sorry, Jodi, but I really need to get back to work."

"If you'd just hear me out. I need more Ophi on my side. It's the only way to keep Hades off our backs."

"We're not against you. We just don't want to join you. We've got a good thing going on here." Mason sighed. "Look, this is my business. I have a family to support. I can't just walk away. I'll have nothing to come back to."

My face fell. "I understand. But listen, if you hear of anyone doing anything they shouldn't be, would you at least let me know? Give me a heads-up?"

"You got it, kid. I wouldn't want Hades breathing down my neck, either. I'll do what I can."

"Thanks, Mason." I hung up the phone feeling completely defeated. How was I supposed to lead the Ophi if I couldn't even get them here? I put my head down on the desk.

Alex knelt down beside me. "Hey, you need to get some rest. You can't fix everything in a day."

I raised my head to meet his eyes. "In a day? Alex, it's been two months, and all I've accomplished is getting one new student."

He rolled his eyes. "When's good old Chester getting here anyway?"

I shook my head at him. He knew the guy's name wasn't Chester.

"Chase," I pronounced the word slowly, "will be here in the morning." I stood up, pulling Alex to his feet with me. "And you're going to be nice to him. He's Mason's nephew, which means he'll be reporting back to Mason about what's going on here."

"Tell you what—I'll be really nice to Chester if you stay away from him."

I sighed. Ever since Alex saw the picture Chase had emailed me, he'd been worried. Chase looked like a male model. Tall and well toned, with dark hair and green eyes. The green eyes were to be expected, but the rest of him—well, I understood why Alex would feel a little intimidated. Not that Alex was lacking in the looks department, but still.

"What makes you think Chase will show any interest in me?"

Alex turned away, pretending to look out the window. "Jodi, stop fishing for compliments. We've been through this before. I'm not going to tell you how hot you are, but aside from that, you are the most powerful Ophi. You're our leader now. What Ophi wouldn't show an interest in you?"

"Okay, fine, but it doesn't matter anyway." I stepped between him and the window so I was inches from his face. "There's only one Ophi I've ever been interested in." I tugged on his arm, making him face me again. I reached up on my toes and pressed my lips against his. He wrapped his arms around me, pulling me closer to him. His kiss was hungry, like he didn't want to let go. Finally, I pulled away, completely breathless. Alex just smiled, clearly impressed with himself.

"I bet you weren't thinking about Chase at all during that."

"Don't you think it's kind of odd that the first thought in *your* mind after a kiss like that is Chase?" I playfully swatted at his arm, but I was hit with a wave of dizziness. My legs gave out, and I fell forward. Alex caught me and lowered me to the floor. I was in his lap, barely conscious. The only thing I was really aware of was my blood mixing in my veins.

I tried to speak, but I couldn't. Alex was talking, but I didn't hear a sound. I only saw his lips moving. My eyes rolled back and everything went black.

I heard someone calling my name, and I realized it was Medusa. I was used to seeing her image and talking to her in my mind, but I was usually connected to the Medusa statue in the foyer when it happened. The statue contained Medusa's spirit.

"Jodi, your power is unstable. You must not put so much pressure on yourself. You are splitting your focus and allowing your abilities to get out of control. Find yourself." Medusa's image faded, and I felt Alex tapping my cheek.

"Jodi? Can you hear me?"

I opened my eyes. My blood had stopped mixing, and I felt a little more normal. "I hear you."

"What happened?"

"I don't know. I got dizzy, and then my blood was mixing. But I don't know why."

"How do you feel now?"

"Like I used up too much energy. I need to connect with the statue." The statue always gave me a boost of energy. It would help me make it through the evening, at least until bedtime.

Alex helped me up and walked me to the statue. I didn't want to tell him I'd seen Medusa or that she'd said I was putting too much pressure on myself. I knew that already. Alex had been saying it for months, but what else was I supposed to do? I had to make all the other Ophi follow me, do things my way. Hades' way.

The second I reached the statue, I joined hands with Medusa, feeling her power surge through me. I hadn't needed to connect to the statue since drinking Medusa's blood from the bloodstone locket she'd given me. I hadn't thought I'd need power boosts like this anymore, but that was just one more thing I'd been wrong about.

I was careful not to stay connected to the statue for too long. Otherwise it would have the reverse effect, draining me completely. I took only what I needed and let go. "Thank you." I knew Medusa's spirit would hear me.

"Any better?" Alex asked.

"Much. Let's go bury a corpse."

Alex grabbed my arm. "You go have some dinner. You should eat something to get your strength up. I'll take care of the body."

I shook my head. "Really, I'm fine. Good as new, and the corpse is my problem. If I hadn't been such an awful teacher to Leticia, I would've had more help digging the grave."

"Hey, you're not an awful teacher. You're doing a great job. Leticia is just having a tough time. Randy's really shown improvement over the past two months, and that's thanks to you."

I walked outside and started for the cemetery. "He is getting better. He's a hard worker."

"It's not all him, Jodi. Take the credit you deserve."

We walked through the cemetery gate, and I stopped to smile at Alex. "You're good for the ego, you know that?"

"Nah. I'm honest."

That was true. He was the first person to call me out when I was wrong. Not in a mean way. He just kept me firmly grounded in reality.

We paused at the mausoleum. It had become our spot. Plus, we kept some shovels leaning against it. The shed was at the other end of the cemetery, and this way we had access to shovels no matter where we raised the bodies. Alex pulled me to him and kissed me. His stomach rumbled loudly, making me pull back with laughter.

"I guess we better hurry up and dig this grave before we miss dinner."

He smiled, looking a little embarrassed.

We walked around the mausoleum to where we'd left the body. The ground was bare. I looked all around. "Where's the body?" Alex didn't answer, but he didn't need to. It was obvious. The body was gone.

Chapter 2

I bent down, inspecting the ground. Looking for marks to show the body had been dragged off somewhere. Nothing. Everything looked the way I'd left it. All except for the body lying on the ground.

"Where is it?"

"Don't panic." Alex spoke calmly, though his eyes furiously scanned the entire graveyard. "Maybe Tony took it somewhere."

"Why would he take it somewhere? If Tony moved the body, it would've been to rebury it." I pointed to the ground in front of the headstone. "The dirt wasn't dug up."

Alex walked to the mausoleum. "Maybe he put the body in here. You know, to keep it safe until we reburied it."

Keep it safe? It was a corpse, not a lost puppy. I knew Alex was only trying to help and keep me calm, but there was no explanation for a missing body.

Alex opened the mausoleum and stepped inside. The window was still broken from when he and I had been trapped in there by zombies Victoria sent after us. I peeked in after him, knowing I wasn't going to find a body.

"Nothing." He stepped back outside.

"So, now what?"

"We talk to Tony."

A weird feeling came over me, sending shivers down my back. "Alex, what if Tony decided to make his own living dead servant, like the ones Victoria had?"

Alex shook his head. "No way. Tony wouldn't do that."

What other explanation was there? "Let's not ask him about it."

"Jodi, you're being silly. He'd never—"

"Humor me, okay? If Tony just moved the body, then he'll tell us at dinner. He knows we have to bury it tonight."

"And if he doesn't say anything?"

Then, we had a problem. I didn't want to question Tony or think he would do something as evil as use the living dead to serve him. But he used to follow Victoria, and as an adult he could easily control one dead body. I couldn't rule out the possibility, no matter how much I liked Tony.

Alex raised his eyebrows.

"Then we'll keep searching for the body." I left off the part where the first place I planned to look was in Tony's room.

"I don't think we should mention this to Leticia or Randy," Alex said.

"Definitely not." I started for the mansion. "Leticia can't handle anything else right now."

"Are you going to talk to her about what happened this afternoon?"

I knew I had to, but it wouldn't be easy. I wasn't sure how to make her believe that I had faith in her. That I was only trying to protect her.

"I don't want to say anything at dinner where Tony and Randy will hear us. I thought I'd invite her to watch a movie with me in my room later."

Alex lowered his head, staring at his feet as we walked. "I guess that means we're not hanging out tonight?"

"You could come by after the movie. I heard Arianna talking about this devil's food cake she made." Arianna had been a cook at Serpentarius, but she'd gotten tired of the club scene. When I first called all the Ophi two months ago, she jumped at the chance to come help us out. She wasn't the most skilled necromancer, but she cooked for us and even did a little cleaning, so I was happy to have her. "How's a little dessert before bed sound?"

Alex raised an eyebrow and gave me a sly grin.

"I was talking about the cake." I couldn't keep from laughing.

"Okay, fine." He stopped at the front door and spun me around to face him. "Just promise me that nothing is going to change tomorrow."

"Tomorrow? Why would things change tomorrow?"

He wrapped his arms loosely around my waist and shrugged.

The insecure look instantly gave him away. This was about Chase. I raised my hands to his face. "Nothing will change between us." I kissed him, and without knowing why, Chase's picture came into my mind. I jumped, pulling away from Alex.

"What?"

"Um…" I couldn't tell him the truth. I wasn't even sure what the truth was. Why did Chase's picture come to mind? "I bit my cheek," I lied, raising my hand to my face.

Alex leaned forward and kissed my cheek. "Better?"

"Much." I forced a smile and went inside. I barely looked at Alex on the way to the dining room.

We were the last ones there. Tony and Randy were in the middle of a conversation over spaghetti and meatballs, and Arianna was trying to convince Leticia to eat something. A bowl of mac and cheese was on the table in front of Alex's seat. In all the time I'd known him, he'd had mac and cheese at every meal. He ate other things, too, but he had to have his mac and cheese. And now that I knew it was because Victoria used to make it for him as a child, it broke my heart every time he ate it.

As Alex and I sat down, Arianna greeted us with a smile. "You both must be starving. Eat, eat." She placed a plate in front of me.

"It smells delicious, Arianna. Thank you." Arianna was amazing. She kept us all fed and clothed. In a way, she made up for not being able to see or talk to my mom. That was the hardest part about being Ophi. I couldn't be around my human mom. Not if I didn't want to poison her with my blood. Again. Luckily, Alex had been there to bring her back before her soul left her body. Arianna had assumed the role of "mom" from the minute she came to the school. She loved us all, and we loved her in return.

Arianna sat down in Troy's old seat at one end of the table. Victoria's seat remained empty. No one seemed to want it, even if it was at the head of the table. "What's on the agenda for this evening? A lesson? Some more training?"

"Actually, I think we all could use a night off." I twirled spaghetti onto my fork.

"Really?" Randy asked. "That's awesome."

Leticia didn't even raise her eyes.

"Yeah, and, Leticia, I was wondering if you'd like to watch a movie with me in my room after dinner."

"Oh, a girl's night," Arianna said. "How nice. I'm sure Leticia would love to."

That was another reason I loved Arianna. She somehow knew everything, and she used that knowledge to help each one of us. She was aware of Leticia's fragile state and what had happened during training today, too, I was sure. Arianna wanted us to work through this.

Leticia sighed. "Fine, but I get to pick the movie."

"Great." I smiled and ate my spaghetti.

Everyone chatted about pretty much nothing for the rest of the meal. I kept waiting for Tony to say something—anything—about the body in the cemetery, but he didn't. As we were clearing our plates, I gave Alex a look. He understood it immediately and shrugged. I knew he thought Tony's silence meant he was innocent, but I wasn't so easily convinced.

Alex and I were on clean-up duty tonight. I'd created a schedule so Arianna didn't get stuck doing all the household stuff. There was no reason for her to have to clean up after all of us. We each cleaned our own rooms and bathrooms, and we took turns setting the table and doing the dishes. Arianna did the cooking, laundry, and vacuuming, and she never complained. She liked being around family, and that's what we were to her.

"You look cute in rubber gloves," Alex said.

"You look cute with soapsuds on your nose." I reached one glove up and dabbed soap on his nose.

Instead of wiping it off, he pulled me to him and kissed me, getting soapsuds on *my* nose in the process.

"Ugh, come on," Randy said.

Alex and I separated.

Randy turned his head away from us. "Can't you two ever stop with all the cute couple stuff? It's nauseating."

Alex used the dishtowel to wipe the soapsuds from his nose. "Admit it. You're completely jealous that Jodi's into me."

"Whatever, man. Just wait until I'm out of here before you two start going at it again." Randy put his plate on the counter and practically ran from the kitchen.

"What's up with him?"

"Who cares?" Alex reached for me again.

"Alex." I swatted at him with my wet gloves. "I have to meet Leticia in my room in ten minutes. We have to get this cleaned up."

"Fine." He grabbed another dish to dry, pouting in the process.

Man, he was even cute when he was pouting. I tried not to notice. If I was late for meeting Leticia in my own room, it would look bad. Like I didn't really care about her. I had to let her know I wanted to help her and that I understood what she was going through.

We finished the dishes, and Alex walked me to my room. Luckily, I had two minutes to spare, and Leticia wasn't in sight.

"See, plenty of time." Alex leaned in to kiss me again.

"Am I early?" Leticia came out of the bathroom.

"No." I pushed Alex back. "Right on time." I turned to Alex. "See you later."

He smiled, said a quick hello to Leticia, and headed for his room.

"Do you have any idea how lucky you are?" Leticia followed me into my room.

Actually I did. At least when it came to Alex. The rest of my life? That I wasn't so sure about.

"What movie did you pick?" I looked down at her hands, realizing she hadn't brought a movie.

"I was wondering if we could just talk instead."

"Okay." We did need to talk, so maybe this was better. I sat down on my bed, leaning my back against the pillows. Leticia stood at the end of my bed. "Have a seat. Make yourself comfortable."

She sat down on the edge, looking anything but comfortable.

"Was there something in particular you wanted to talk about?" I asked, since she wasn't saying a word.

She nodded. "My parents."

Good. She wanted to get right to what was bothering her. That was a good sign.

"Why did you hand them over to Hades like that, Jodi?"

What? I jerked back as if she'd slapped me across the face. I wasn't expecting that.

"They were innocent. They weren't like Victoria. She made them into zombies. Tortured them. And then, instead of helping them, you let Hades take them again. Why did you do that?"

She wasn't yelling. It was worse. She was heartbroken, and it was because of me.

"Leticia, I'm sorry. I had no idea you felt this way. That you were angry with me."

"I'm not angry. I know Victoria was controlling them. She made them do awful things, but that was her. You have to know that."

"I do."

"Then why did you give them over to Hades like that?" Her eyes were red and swollen from holding back tears.

"I didn't know what else to do. I was trying to save us. Stop Hades from taking us all. I knew I had to make a deal with Hades. He responds to deals, and all I had to bargain with was Victoria and her army of—" I didn't want to finish my sentence. I didn't want to risk hurting Leticia's feelings any more than I already had.

"I know, and you saved Randy and me. I'm grateful for that. But my parents didn't deserve what happened to them." She lowered her head, giving in to the tears. They poured down her face, falling onto my lavender bedspread.

I got a tissue from my bathroom and brought it to her, sitting down beside her. "I know your parents didn't deserve what happened to them. Believe me, if I could fix it, I would."

She lifted her head and looked at me. "Can you do something for me?"

"Sure. Name it. If there's something I can do to make you feel at least a little better, I'll be happy to do it."

"You can bring Ophi back to life. I want you to bring my parents back. The right way."

My breath caught in my throat. "Leticia, I'm sorry, but I can't do that."

"Yes, you can. I saw you bring Alex back after Troy killed him. You have all this power. Please, Jodi, you're the only one who can help them." She started sobbing all over again.

I leaned her head against my shoulder, letting her cry on me. I wished I could do what she wanted, but the truth was, it was impossible. Alex had explained it all to me after I'd accidentally killed my human boyfriend, Matt, and turned him into a zombie.

"Leticia, when a soul is summoned correctly, it returns exactly as it was before it died. Do you understand what I'm saying?"

She lifted her head, looking up at me.

"Victoria brought them back wrong. They were zombies. Hades took them to the underworld as zombies. If I brought them back now, they'd still be zombies. I can't change that."

"So, you're saying there's no way to make them the way they used to be?"

I couldn't bear to answer her. My heart shattered for her and the pain she was feeling.

"Do you know anything about me? I mean, before I came here?"

Her body shook as she cried. I wasn't even sure she was listening to me anymore, but I had to continue. I had to explain.

"I killed my boyfriend. He was human, and I kissed him. My blood brought him back to life. As a zombie. I watched him eat a bunny. I watched the guy I was crazy about lose all sense of who he was, and it was my fault."

Leticia stopped crying and stared at me.

"You made him a zombie?"

"I didn't know what I was doing. I didn't have control of my powers yet."

"And your mom…" her voice trailed off, and I knew what she was going to say.

"I accidentally killed her."

She nodded.

"I cut myself with a kitchen knife. She tried to help me." I choked on the words.

"Alex saved her for you."

"Yeah." I took a deep breath. "I know what it's like to miss your parents. To feel like you got cheated out of having parents. You met my dad that day in the cemetery when Victoria raised him. You know what they did to him."

"I'm sorry," Leticia said. "I shouldn't have asked you."

I bit my lip and blinked tears from my eyes. It was a lot to relive in one night.

Leticia blew her nose. "It's just hard, you know?"

"Yeah, I know. Believe me, if I could help you, bring your parents back the way they used to be, I'd do it in a second. But I know what happened to you when you saw what Victoria had made your parents become. I won't do that to you. I will never bring a zombie back again."

Someone pounded on the door. Not a normal knock. Not a "hurry up and open the door" kind of pounding either. It was clumsy, awkward. I got up to answer it when a fist slammed through the wood. The hand was bluish and covered in dirt, and that could only mean one thing. I'd found the corpse from the graveyard—or he'd found me. And he wasn't dead anymore.

Chapter 3

I went for the door and opened it, not wanting to see how much this corpse was willing to destroy to get into my bedroom. His body probably would've crumbled to pieces before he got in, and I had no clue how to get dead guy out of the carpet. I swung the door open and faced the guy Leticia had raised in the cemetery. Normally, a corpse honed in on the person who had summoned them. It was a revenge thing, a desire to rip apart the one who pulled them out of wherever they were. But this guy was staring right at me.

Leticia whimpered on my bed. "What do we do?"

"We have to release him."

"I thought you already did that. Did you leave him in the cemetery or something?"

"No. I released him, but when I went back to bury his body, he was gone."

"Yeah, well, you found him. Now get rid of him."

I knew I could easily send him back to Hell—I was quickly becoming convinced that's where he'd come from—but I glanced back at Leticia. "You want to give it a try?"

"What? No! Get rid of him." She squeezed my pillow in front of her, like that was going to stop a zombie from ripping her heart out.

"Come on, Leticia. You summoned him. You need to release him."

"But I didn't summon him. You said you released his soul. Someone else must have summoned him."

I looked at the guy. He glared at me, waiting for a command.

"What's he doing? Why is he just standing there?" Leticia's voice cracked.

"I think he's waiting for orders." This had never happened before, but he was waiting for me to tell him what to do. How was I controlling him without knowing it?

"Then *you* raised him?" Leticia got up from the bed and walked over to me. "What's going on, Jodi?"

"I'm not sure. I didn't raise him. At least, I don't remember raising him."

"You don't remember?" Leticia looked back and forth between the corpse and me. "That's impossible."

"Jodi!" Alex rushed into the doorway, stopping short of the zombie. He looked at me with wide eyes. "Whoa, is that—"

"In the living dead flesh. The question is, how did he get here?"

"We know how." Leticia was looking at me like she wanted to scream in my face. So much for our heart-to-heart. "You told me you would never raise a zombie again, but here's one now. Did you plan this?"

"Leticia, no!" How could she even think that?

"Leticia, go to your room and calm down. Jodi and I will figure this out." Alex stepped aside so she could leave.

"Wait." I reached for Leticia, but she sidestepped me. "I swear I didn't do this. You have to believe me. Everything I told you tonight was the truth."

She paused, considering what I said. I silently pleaded with her to believe me. To stay and hear me out. I had to get her to listen. To stop running away from me.

Without warning, the corpse reached out and grabbed Leticia. She shrieked as he locked his arms around her. Alex tried to pull Leticia from the guy's grasp, but all he succeeded in doing was breaking chunks of flesh from the corpse's arm.

"Stop!" I yelled. "Let her go! Now!" The guy let go of Leticia, and she ran for her room without looking back.

Alex stared at me, and I knew exactly what he was thinking. This guy thought I was the one who'd raised him. Was that possible? I had to know. The thing about zombies was, they didn't talk until you told them to. They were pretty much mindless beings unless an Ophi commanded them. They followed directions, and if there were no directions to follow, well, they'd try to eat the thing nearest to them.

I took a deep breath and looked the zombie in the eyes. His pupils were a pale blue color and one eyeball oozed a greenish liquid. I swallowed hard, trying to keep my dinner from resurfacing. "Tell me who raised you after I released your soul."

He pointed a bruised finger at me. "You." His voice was scratchy, like—well, like someone who'd been dead for a while.

"This can't be happening. I didn't raise you. I didn't raise anyone." My body was shaking, and I felt the blood in my veins mixing.

"Jodi, calm down." Alex put his arm around my shoulder, but he practically jumped back the second he made contact with me. "You're burning up."

"I'll be fine. I just have to relax, but that's hard to do when I have no idea what's going on." I turned to Alex, looking for help. "I didn't summon anyone."

Alex wrinkled his forehead. "Maybe you did it when you blacked out earlier. Can you raise souls when you're only semi-conscious?"

I shook my head. "I don't know." Nothing was making sense. All I knew was I had to get this zombie back in the ground. I faced him. "I release your soul. Go back to wherever you were before…" I stumbled on the words, "before I raised you."

The corpse shuddered as his soul left, and the body fell limp to the floor.

Alex reached for the guy's arms. "I'll get him out of here."

"I'll help. If what he said was true, and I brought him here, then I should be the one to put him back in the ground."

Alex let go of the body and took my hands. "Jodi, you have to stop taking on all the responsibilities yourself. Look what it's doing to you. You're stressed out. You blacked out earlier, and now this. You're summoning souls without knowing it. That's dangerous."

He didn't need to tell me how dangerous it was. I knew. If I could raise this guy when I wasn't aware of it, I could raise more souls, and that would send Hades straight to me.

"I'll talk to Medusa. See if she can help me sort all this out."

"That's great, but you still need to let the rest of us help you more."

"You do help me. Tony is teaching classes. Arianna is cooking and cleaning. You're keeping me sane." I gave him a weak smile.

"What about Leticia and Randy? You're treating them like they can't handle anything. All you let them do is train and go to classes."

I didn't think Leticia could handle much more right now. I wasn't even sure she could handle training with me anymore. Not after what had happened today—or tonight. And Randy? His father was taken to the underworld with the others, too. He wasn't exactly emotionally stable either.

Alex wrapped his arms around me. "Stop trying to protect them, Jodi. They'll never learn to handle all this if you don't give them the chance to."

I nodded and looked up at him. "I couldn't do any of this without you."

"You don't have to." He smiled and gave me a quick kiss.

"But I do have to bury this body, and this time, he's staying buried."

It took an hour to dig up the grave. We didn't bother burying the bodies too deep. With our training every day, it was easier if the corpses didn't have to dig too far to get out of the ground after we raised them, and reburying them was easier if we didn't have to dig six feet down. Still, it was hard work. By the time we were finished, I was sweaty and covered in dirt.

"That's a nice look on you." Alex playfully bumped me with his shoulder as we headed back to the mansion.

"Yeah, I'm thinking about bottling some of the stuff and selling it as an alternative to perfume. I'm sure the smell of the dead would be a big seller."

"Sorry our night together had to be spent digging a grave. I was hoping—" He stopped. I knew what he was hoping, but I wasn't exactly ready to have that conversation. It had only been a couple months. In his mind, that probably equated to years.

"I'm going to take a really hot shower and go to bed. Chase should be here for breakfast, and I want to have enough time to show him around a little before training starts."

We climbed the stairs and turned left toward my bedroom. I could tell Alex was fighting the urge to make a comment about Chase. I didn't understand how he could hate a guy he'd never even met. Was he really that jealous? That insecure? He'd always seemed so confident, even when we'd first met and I was completely freaked out by him. He knew I would end up liking him, and he'd been right.

"Goodnight." He kissed first my lips and then my cheek. "Sleep well."

"Night." I watched him walk to his room before I went inside. I didn't want things with Alex to get complicated. Everything else in my life was complicated. I wanted one thing that was perfect. Alex and I could be perfect. I knew we could.

After a hot shower that steamed up the entire bathroom and part of my room, I crawled into bed. My head sank into the pillow, and I was off in dreamland.

Only the dream felt so real. It was morning, and I was late waking up. I hurried to get ready before Chase arrived. I had to be there to greet him, to look like I had a clue what I was doing at this school. But when I got downstairs, Chase was already there, waiting for me. His olive skin and dark hair looking absolutely stunning next to the golden Medusa statue. He winked at me and reached one hand out. I took it, without saying a word. I was fixed in a sort of trance, unable to look away from his green eyes. He pulled me closer to him and leaned down, pressing his lips against mine. My blood surged through my veins until he finally pulled away.

That was when I gasped. It wasn't Chase. It was Alex.

I sat up in bed, breathing heavily. Why had I dreamt that? My arms tingled, and I realized my blood was settling, returning to normal.

A heavy hand knocked on my door. Tony had already patched it up for me. He wasn't exactly a carpenter, but it would do. I turned to the alarm clock on the nightstand. Breakfast was already being served. I was late. Just like in the dream. I threw the covers off. "Just a second!" It had to be Alex at the door, wondering where I was. I threw on clean clothes and ran a brush through my hair, before flinging open the door.

"Oh!" The word escaped without my control. The person knocking on the door wasn't Alex. It was the same corpse I'd reburied last night. Was I still dreaming? "No. This isn't happening. It can't be real."

"Jodi?" Alex called up the stairs. "Everything okay?"

Nothing was okay. I'd done it again. I'd raised a soul without meaning to, this time while I was asleep. Part of me wanted to hide this from Alex. He'd freak if he knew I was messing up like this, but how could I hide a zombie?

"Jodi?"

I heard Alex's footsteps on the stairs, and I panicked. "Come in," I told the corpse. "Hide in the bathroom, and don't come out until I call you." He did as I said. The second he disappeared in the bathroom, I rushed into the hallway and shut my door behind me.

"Hey, I know I'm late. I overslept. I guess I didn't set my alarm last night. Is Chase here?"

"Whoa, slow down." Alex blocked my path. "You look... Did something happen?"

"No." I shook my head to avoid his eyes. "I overslept, and I wanted to be there when Chase got here. It doesn't look good that I wasn't there to greet him. I'm in charge. I should've been there."

"Jodi, you need to take a deep breath. Chase isn't even here yet."

"He's not?" I sighed. "Okay, good."

"If you call being late your very first day 'good.'"

"It's good for me. He won't know I screwed up. The last thing I need is him telling the other Ophi at Serpentarius what a flake I am."

Alex put his arm around me, and we headed to breakfast. "Who cares what he thinks of you?"

"*I* care. I'm supposed to be the leader of the Ophi. No one is going to follow me if they think I can't handle the job."

Arianna greeted us as we walked into the dining room. "Good morning. Eggs and bacon all around today."

"Thank you, Arianna. It smells great, as usual."

I said good morning to everyone, even though Leticia wouldn't look at me, and took my seat. Alex dug into his mac and cheese while I fended off questions about why Chase was late.

"I don't know what's holding him up, but I'm sure he'll be here in time for training."

He wasn't. I was in the middle of helping Randy raise two souls at once when a flashy red sports car pulled up the driveway.

"Wow," Leticia said. "Now, that is a hot car."

The driver's side door opened, and Chase stepped out.

"And that is one seriously hot Ophi." She grabbed my arm as if she was steadying herself. Who knew all it would take was one hot guy to make Leticia forget she was mad at me?

Randy and Alex exchanged eyerolls as Leticia continued to drool. I had to pry her fingers off my arm to go greet Chase. And surprise, surprise, when I reached Chase, Alex was by my side. I gave him a quick "Be nice" look.

"Hi, Chase. I'm Jodi." Alex cleared his throat. "And this is Alex."

"Her boyfriend," Alex added without missing a beat.

I turned to glare at him quickly before directing my attention back to Chase. He was even better looking than his picture. His eyes were a really deep green, almost like emeralds. And he had a scar above his left eyebrow. A small one that seemed to give his face more character—as if he needed it. His smile was slightly crooked in a way that made me keep staring at his mouth. I worried he'd get the wrong idea, like I wanted to kiss him or something. I definitely didn't want to come off looking like a love-stuck girl. Leticia was doing a good enough job of that for the both of us.

"Did you have trouble finding the place?" I managed to get out.

Chase looked me up and down, and I swore I heard Alex give a low growl. I felt really self-conscious, so I started blabbing like an idiot.

"We thought you were coming earlier. I had a plate set for you at breakfast, but no worries. We can still get you set up in your room and have you back down here for the end of the lesson."

Chase continued to stare at me, but now his eyes were locked on mine. I couldn't turn away, couldn't blink. It was exactly like my dream. I silently pleaded that he wouldn't reach for my hand, because I knew in that instant I would take it, even with Alex standing there.

"Is there a problem?" Alex asked. "You're staring pretty intently at my girlfriend."

"You're even more beautiful than I thought you'd be." Chase ignored Alex.

My cheeks burned, and I knew I was turning red. "Um, thanks. That's nice of you to say."

Alex put his arm around my waist and pulled me toward him. "Jodi, why don't I show Chase to his room so you can keep working with Randy?" Before I could answer, he leaned down and kissed me. Not a quick "I'll-be-right-back" kind of kiss. A passionate "get-a-room" kind of kiss. I pulled back, completely embarrassed, and widened my eyes at him. "Don't worry. We'll be quick." Alex squeezed my hand before nodding at Chase.

Chase smirked and grabbed a bag from his trunk. He kept his eyes on me as he followed Alex into the mansion. It was a wonder he didn't trip up the steps. I tried to turn away, pretend I didn't care if Chase was still watching me, but I couldn't. It was like a car wreck. If a car wreck looked like a gorgeous guy.

Leticia was at my side again. "Since you already have Alex, can I get dibs on Chase?"

I gave a nervous laugh, but I could feel my blood bubbling in my veins. Leticia might want dibs on Chase, and I was happy with Alex, but it was obvious Chase was already eyeing me. And no matter how much I thought things between Alex and me were great, I couldn't deny what Chase's presence had done to me.

"Um, Jodi." Randy sounded worried. "I didn't do that." I turned to see him pointing at the two graves in front of him. Pale, discolored fingers were clawing their way through the dirt.

Leticia looked at me and backed away. "Did you do that?"

That's when I realized my blood was still boiling.

Maybe Alex had a reason to be worried after all.

Chapter 4

Randy and Leticia stared at me, looking for an explanation. I tried to come up with something—something clever to make them think I'd done it on purpose to try to teach them to always be ready, but it didn't make sense. Ophi didn't raise souls without knowing it. At least no Ophi other than me.

"I—"

"Hey, nice work, Randy. You did it!" Alex said, running over to join us.

"What are you doing here? I thought you were showing Chase to his room."

"Yeah, yeah. I did. I told him to go up the steps to the right. Fourth door on the right. He'll find it." Alex shrugged. "Besides, I got back just in time to see Randy's raising. That's awesome, man." He smacked Randy on the back.

Randy shook his head. "I didn't do it. I was standing here, watching the girls go gaga over pretty boy, and these two started coming out of the ground."

Alex immediately turned to me. "Did you do this?"

At least he'd missed the part about me going gaga over Chase. "I don't know." I lowered my head, not wanting to meet anyone's eyes or look at the zombies crawling out of the earth.

"Jodi, this is serious." How Alex could go from caring to stone cold serious so quickly had always been a mystery to me. "If you don't get control of your powers, you're going to get us all killed."

Leticia gasped. "Do you think Hades is going to come after us?"

"That, or Jodi's zombies are going to eat us in our sleep," Randy said.

I rolled my eyes. "Thank you, Randy. That's really helpful."

Alex grabbed my arm. "He's not wrong."

I looked at Alex, feeling completely alone. He was supposed to be on my side, defend me, but he was attacking me like everyone else. I pushed past him and walked over to the corpses.

"Don't bother getting up. I release your souls. Go back to where you came from." I didn't even wait for their souls to leave. I turned and headed for the mansion. I needed to have a talk with Medusa. She would understand. She would listen to me.

I climbed the steps and pushed through the door in a hurry. My head collided with something hard, and I fell back, landing on the floor. "Ouch!"

"You can say that again." Chase was on the floor in front of me. "Anyone ever tell you that you have a hard head?"

"I could ask you the same thing." I rubbed the front of my head, which felt like it was the size of a basketball.

"Here." Chase got to his feet and extended his hand to me. I stared at his hand and then his eyes, noticing the way they sparkled with confidence. Now, it was too much like my dream.

"I'm good." I used the doorway to help me up.

Chase lowered his hand, shoving it in his pocket. Just great. He was the new guy who didn't know anyone, and I was making him feel unwelcome by not even taking his hand.

"Did you find your room okay? I'm sorry Alex didn't give you a real tour. He was eager to get back to the training, I guess."

Chase smirked. "Yeah, I'm sure that was it."

"He's a good guy. He just—"

"Doesn't want to let you out of his sight."

I was hoping Alex's behavior wasn't as obvious to everyone else as it was to me. Apparently I was wrong.

"Anyway, I found my room and my bag's unpacked. I was coming back out to join you guys when I ran into you. Or should I say you ran into me?"

"Yeah, sorry about that. I needed a break."

"And in a hurry. Something wrong?"

I felt like someone was always asking me that. "Nothing to worry about. Tell me about you. How long have you been training?"

"Mason's been teaching me basic stuff. You know—raising, releasing, being careful around humans. Nothing major. You know how the Serpentarius Ophi feel about using their powers to raise souls." He leaned against the Medusa statue.

"Uh, could you not do that?" I tugged him away from Medusa.

"Oh, sorry. Is it valuable?"

"More than you know, but we'll get to that later. Did you spend a lot of time around humans?"

Chase nodded. "Yeah, I was usually in charge of helping the bands set up every Friday when they let humans into the club. Never had a problem being around humans." He lowered his eyes. "Until three weeks ago."

I stepped closer to him. "What happened?"

"The bass player wasn't happy with the sound quality on his amp, so he took out a knife and tried to adjust the wire. I should've gotten out of there as soon as the knife came out of his pocket—that's what I was taught to do, but I was sure I could handle it. I mean, I wasn't the one using the knife."

"Did he slip and get you with the blade?" My eyes flew to the scar above his eye.

"No, he didn't slip. He started going off about this show he played and how the crowd wasn't that into it because the sound wasn't right. I made a comment about how maybe the sound quality wasn't the problem. He didn't like that very much."

My eyes widened. "He attacked you?"

"Nah, he wasn't tough enough to actually pick a fight with me. He yelled at me. Told me I was tone-deaf, and he was flailing his arms. The knife nicked me." He raised his hand to his scar. "It really wasn't bad, but instead of getting out of there, I yelled back at the guy and took a swing. Only I'd touched the wound first."

"So, your punch was deadly."

"You got it." He frowned. "I didn't mean to do it. I got careless."

"I'm starting to think Ophi don't belong around humans. I know my experiences with humans were awful after I came into my powers."

"Should I pull up a chair? Are we going to compare horror stories?" He said it with a smile, and I realized he was trying to break the tension. All this talk about killing wasn't exactly uplifting.

"You're right. That's enough reminiscing." I pointed to the statue. "You want to meet Medusa?"

"I think the statue and I have already met. Remember? You told me to stop leaning on her."

"I did. Because she's not just a statue."

He raised an eyebrow. "You guys don't join hands around it and chant, do you?"

I laughed. "You know I kind of thought the same thing when I first got here. But no. We're not a cult. We don't worship the statue." I tugged his arm. "Come stand here, facing her."

He listened, but he kept looking at me like I was crazy.

"Okay, take Medusa's right hand in yours."

"You want me to hold hands with a statue? Really? I mean, if I'm going to hold someone's hand, I'd rather hold yours."

I felt my face flush. "Just do it."

"Okay." He took my hand in his.

"That's not what I meant," I said.

He squeezed my hand. "I don't see you letting go."

"Am I interrupting anything?" Alex asked, walking through the door behind us. His eyes immediately flew to our hands.

My entire body felt like it was on fire. I took my hand away and walked toward Alex. "I was about to introduce Chase to Medusa, but he misunderstood me when I told him to take her hand."

"Misunderstood you? Yeah, I'm sure that's all it was." Alex took my hand in his, and we walked back to the statue.

"Go ahead," Alex said. "Take Medusa's hand." He said Medusa's name slowly, like Chase might get confused. "In fact, why don't you take both her hands?"

"No!" I reached for Chase, our fingers touching.

"What?" Chase asked.

"The last person who held both Medusa's hands at once ended up dead on the floor." I realized I was still touching Chase. I lowered my hand and turned away.

"They died?"

"For a little while, but I was able to bring her back."

"Wow, you brought back an Ophi? You really are something, aren't you?"

Alex reached for my hand, clearly not liking the way Chase was looking at me.

"Only one hand at a time, okay?" I said.

"What's this about, anyway?" Chase asked.

"You'll see. It's something every Ophi who comes here does. Believe me, you'll like it."

He smiled at me and took Medusa's right hand in his. His eyes closed, and I knew he was feeling Medusa's power breathing life into every inch of him. While he enjoyed the connection, I turned back to Alex.

"What were you trying to do, kill him?" I kept my voice a whisper, hoping Chase would be too involved in the connection with Medusa to hear me.

"I wouldn't have really let him do it," Alex said. "But the guy needs to be put in his place."

"Yeah, well, killing him isn't the way to do it." I stepped closer to him. "When you do stuff like that, you make me think you're—I don't want you to end up like Victoria and Troy." I'd never held it against Alex that his parents were evil Ophi who had tried to kill me. Alex wasn't like them, but he was their son, and it made me wonder if he had that same evil buried somewhere inside him. If he did, I was determined not to let it come out. I owed him that for helping me face his parents and for saving my life.

Alex was silent, and I had no clue what was going on in his head. "You think I'm going to turn into them? Do you really have such little faith in me?"

"No. I'm worried about you. That's all." I wished he would look at me, but he was staring past me at Chase. I leaned forward, resting my hands against his chest. "Alex, I care about you. A lot. I don't want to lose you."

The coldness evaporated from his face, and he lowered his eyes to meet mine. "You won't lose me." He gave one last look at Chase before taking my face in his hands and kissing me.

Chase cleared his throat, making me jump. "Sorry, was I supposed to stay connected to the statue until you two were through making out?"

I spun around, but Alex didn't let me step away from him. He put his hands down heavily on my shoulders, grounding me in my spot. If I wasn't so embarrassed, I would've been annoyed by Alex's little attempt to claim his territory.

"You can try holding her left hand now." I pointed to the statue, trying to get Chase's attention off me.

Chase's eyes lingered on me for a few more seconds before he reached for Medusa's left hand. His face twisted in a worried expression.

"It's okay," I said. "The blood in the left side of her body is only poisonous to humans. What you're feeling is the power of that blood flowing through your veins. It can't hurt you, though."

"It feels like—"

"Snakes, I know, but trust me, you'll get used to it." I watched Chase give in to the sensation and become oblivious to us.

"Shall we pick up where we left off?" Alex asked.

I shrugged his hands from my shoulders and glared at him. "Don't treat me like I'm this prize you've won. I saw you look at Chase before you kissed me. You knew he was watching us."

"So? Do you have a problem with him knowing you're my girlfriend?"

"No. I have a problem with you groping me every time Chase is near. You're not a dog, and I'm not a tree. So, stop trying to piss around me."

Chase started laughing, and I turned to see he was no longer connected to Medusa.

"It's nice to see a girl who isn't afraid to stand up for herself."

I stared at Chase, not liking the way he was looking at me any more than I liked the way Alex was acting. I spun on my heel and headed toward the kitchen to help Arianna with lunch, and more importantly to put some distance between both guys and me.

"Jodi," Alex called after me.

"See you at lunch." I waved my hand, not looking at either of them, and kept walking. I turned the corner, almost smacking into Arianna.

"Jodi, what's gotten into you?" She shook her head at me. "I've only known you for a couple months, but I've never heard you talk like that. Especially to Alex."

She was right. I didn't talk like that. I had no idea where it was coming from, all this anger. Before Chase came, things with Alex had been great. I'd never minded when he kissed me out of the blue. I thought it was romantic. But now…

"It feels like the only reason Alex is acting like this is because he doesn't like the way Chase looks at me."

"The only reason?" Arianna tsked. "Honey, that boy is in love with you. If you can't see that, well, you need to get those pretty green eyes of yours checked."

In love with me? No. No way. We'd been together less than three months. Alex couldn't be in love with me.

"And Chase definitely has a crush on you. I saw the way he was looking at you. Holding your hand."

My eyes widened. "Arianna, were you spying on me?"

"Sweetheart, please. I was dusting in the living room. It's not like you and Chase were behind closed doors. I have eyes and ears, and they work just fine."

"Well, since you know what's going on, maybe you can help me. I really care about Alex. I do. But Chase is different. I'm annoyed by his cockiness, but drawn to him at the same time. It's so much like the way I felt when I first met Alex." I hung my head. "What should I do?"

"Okay, here's one way to find out where your heart really is." She brought me over to a couch in the living room, and we sat down. "Close your eyes."

I took a deep breath and did what she said.

"Now clear your mind completely." She paused. "Is it clear?"

Clearing my mind wasn't easy these days. I had too much going on in there. "Not really."

"Different question then. Whose face do you see?"

Whose face? I didn't see a face. Wait! Yes, I did. But it wasn't Alex or Chase. It was Matt. My ex-boyfriend, Matt. My human boyfriend I'd killed and brought back as a zombie, Matt. What did that mean? And did I really want Arianna to know I was this boy-crazed?

"Jodi? Do you see a face?"

"No," I lied, opening my eyes.

"All right. Let's try something else."

I didn't want to try anything else. I wanted to forget I was a complete headcase right now.

"Hades is coming."

"What? Where?" I whipped my head around.

"Relax." Arianna grabbed my arm, gently rubbing it. "It's another method of figuring out what's really in your heart. *Pretend* Hades is coming. He's determined to take one of the boys. Either Alex or Chase. You can't bargain with him. You can't get out of making a decision. Who do you save?"

"Alex," I said, without hesitation. "I've known him longer. I don't really know anything about Chase."

Arianna cocked her head to the side. "Is that the only reason you're choosing Alex?"

"No. I really like Alex."

"So, you don't like Chase?"

"I don't know. I haven't gotten to know him yet."

"But you want to get to know him?"

"Yes."

"Even if it hurts Alex?"

"I don't know." All this was doing was confusing me more. I felt like I should be lying on a couch in the middle of a therapy session while a shrink analyzed all my thoughts.

"So, if you could get to know Chase without hurting Alex, you would?"

"Yes."

"And what if getting to know Chase means losing Alex?"

"I don't know."

"You don't know?" Alex asked.

I spun around on the couch to see the twisted expression on his face. "No, that's not what I meant." I reached out to him, but he was already taking off upstairs.

Chapter 5

"Alex, wait!" I jumped up and ran after him. "Let me explain!"

At the top of the stairs, Chase grabbed my arm. "Explain what?"

"Let go of me, Chase. I need to talk to Alex."

"Don't tell me you two are fighting again." His expression was unreadable. Not quite concern, but not quite wishful thinking.

"We're not fighting. Things are fine. Let me go."

He released his grip, letting his fingers lightly trail down my arm until he reached my hand. He laced his fingers through mine, and a tingling sensation soared through me. I couldn't deny the effect he had on me, but I didn't want to feel this way. I wanted Alex. I dropped Chase's hand and walked around him, careful not to touch him in the process.

"See you at lunch," he called after me.

I rushed to Alex's door and knocked. "Alex, please let me in. I need to talk to you."

For a moment there was only silence, but then I heard footsteps coming toward the door. "Go away, Jodi. I have nothing to say to you."

"Well, I have something to say to you. Please, Alex." My voice quivered as I struggled to hold back tears. Emotions welled up inside me. Emotions I hadn't realized I had. Arianna's words echoed in my brain. *Honey, that boy is in love with you.* I pressed my palms against the door and let the tears spill from my eyes. "Alex...I love you."

Time seemed to freeze as I waited for some sort of reaction, but all I got was silence. My throat constricted. If Alex didn't listen to me after I'd said the L-word, there was nothing I could do to save our relationship. I was about to walk away when the lock clicked, and the door swung open. Alex stared at my tear-streaked face.

"I'm sorry if I said that too soon. If it freaked you out. I just had to tell you."

His arms were around me before I could blink. He pulled me close and kissed me. He didn't have to say it. I knew Arianna was right. He loved me. Alex pulled away slightly. "Do you want to come in?"

I nodded, and he stepped back so I could follow him into the room. Before I made it through the doorway, I saw Chase still standing in the hall. Staring at me. He'd seen and heard everything. My blood bubbled under my skin, but I looked away and walked into Alex's room, shutting the door behind me.

Alex and I hung out until lunch. I let myself forget about everything else and focused on him. It was exactly like it was before Chase had gotten here. The only problem was that once we left this room, Chase would be there, and what would happen the next time he touched me?

I tried not to think about it while we walked to the dining room. Arianna smiled at me when she saw Alex holding my hand. I smiled back at her and mouthed the words, "Thank you." She had helped me realize how I felt about Alex. I was still confused about Chase and why he affected me the way he did, but at least I had a handle on Alex.

We took our seats and dug right into the meatball subs Arianna had made us. I even had a side of mac and cheese with Alex. Chase still hadn't shown up for lunch, but I pretended not to notice. Finally, I heard footsteps and looked up, expecting to see Chase, but instead I saw the corpse. The one I'd left in my bathroom with instructions not to leave unless I told him to.

Leticia screamed and everyone else pushed their chairs back away from the table, ready to spring into action if the zombie tried to attack us.

"That's the guy from the cemetery," Leticia said. "The one Jodi raised and brought to her room."

"I didn't bring him to my room," I said. "At least not on purpose."

Tony stared at me. "What's he doing back here?"

"I don't know." It wasn't a complete lie. I didn't know why the zombie had left my bathroom. I hadn't called him.

Chase walked into the room. "What did I miss?" His gaze fell on the zombie, and he stopped. "Do you guys always invite the dead to eat with you? 'Cause it's a little gross, don't you think?"

I shook my head. "No one invited him. He just showed up."

Alex stared at me. He knew I was hiding something.

Tony walked over to the zombie but kept a safe distance. His face fell completely still and focused. He was calling on the power in his blood to control the corpse. "Who brought you here?"

The zombie looked past Tony at me. "Her."

All eyes were on me. No way could I hide this anymore. "Okay, okay." I put my hands up in defense. "I sort of summoned him this morning…in a dream."

A chorus of "What?" rang through the room.

"I didn't know I'd done it. I had this dream and—"

"About what?" Randy asked.

"I can't remember." I played dumb. I couldn't admit I'd been dreaming about Chase. "I only remember I was dreaming, and then someone was knocking on my door. I forgot to set my alarm, and when I saw what time it was, I figured it was Alex knocking, trying to wake me up." I paused, but everyone was silent, waiting for me to continue. "It wasn't Alex. It was him." I turned toward the corpse. "I didn't know I'd summoned him."

"Why didn't you tell me about this?" Alex asked. "I came to get you when you were late for breakfast. Why didn't you tell me then? And what did you do with the guy? He wasn't in your room when I got there."

"I told him to hide in the bathroom." My voice was barely a whisper.

Alex threw his head back and ran his fingers through his hair.

"I was freaked out. You have to understand that. I'm raising souls in my sleep now. Do you know how dangerous that can be for us?"

"Exactly, Jodi," Alex said. "That's why you should have told me."

"Lay off," Chase said. "She panicked. Big deal."

I looked at Chase, thankful for his support. I felt like I was up against a firing squad, so it was nice to have one person on my side.

Alex was seething at this point. He slammed his hand down, knocking over his meatball sub. "Don't try to play the hero here. You have no idea what you're talking about or what Jodi has been going through."

"Alex, I think Chase was only trying to help everyone calm down." Tony put a hand on Chase's shoulder.

I lightly touched Alex's arm. "I was going to tell you."

"When?"

I shrugged. "I sort of forgot he was in my bathroom. I haven't been to my room all day, and so much has happened since this morning. It slipped my mind, but honestly, the second I saw him again, I was going to come to you for help."

Alex closed his eyes, processing everything. I wasn't sure if he believed me or not. All I knew was he was mad.

The room fell silent. I was supposed to be the leader. The one to make the decisions and keep us safe. But instead I was clueless about how to do my job, and I was putting us all in danger. I wasn't cut out for this, and somehow I had a feeling Hades knew that when he'd agreed to my deal.

Alex sighed. "Release his soul, and Tony and I will go bury him."

"I'll help you." I stood up. I needed to get out of this room. Away from all the judgmental stares.

Alex put his hand on my shoulder, stopping me. "No. We got it. You eat." There was a small hint of warmth in his voice. Yes, he was angry, but that didn't change the fact that he cared about me.

I released the soul and watched Tony and Alex carry the body out of the room. The rest of the day was pretty much a blur. Tony lectured about Ophi history. Arianna made something for dinner. It wasn't my turn to help with the dishes, so I headed to my room to lie down. I wasn't up for interacting with everyone. Not that anyone really wanted to interact with me. They weren't being mean or anything, but they weren't going out of their way to talk to me either.

I flopped facedown on my bed and tried to let the awfulness of the day melt away. It might have helped a little if someone hadn't knocked on my door.

I sighed and got up to answer it. Chase was standing in the hall with a big bowl of popcorn and a movie in his hands. Oh, this wasn't going to be good.

"Um, what's up?" I asked, fully aware of how dumb that sounded.

"Thought you could use a good horror movie to forget your troubles." He shook the DVD, and I saw it was a zombie flick. How appropriate.

"You're kidding, right? My life is pretty much a horror movie. How would this make me forget about it?" I couldn't help it. I laughed. Chase smiled, and I realized that was his exact reason for choosing the horror movie. The sheer irony of it.

"So, what do you say?" His eyes were hopeful, and I didn't want to crush him by saying no. After all, he was the only one talking to me right now. Still, being alone in my room with Chase could only add up to trouble. There was only one thing to do.

"Tell you what, let's invite the others. I know Arianna and Tony won't go for it, but Alex, Leticia, and Randy might want to watch." So much for not wanting to interact with people tonight.

Chase's face fell. It wasn't what he was hoping for.

"Go on in." I opened the door more. "I'll go get the others." I hurried down the hall before he could protest. Leticia's room was the closest, so I started there.

"Leticia." I lightly tapped on the door. "We're all going to watch a movie in my room. Want to come?" I figured I'd have better luck if I made it seem like everyone else had already agreed to it.

She opened the door and shrugged. "I guess."

"Great, go on in my room. Chase is setting it up now. I'll be there in a second." I continued down the hall to Randy's room. It didn't take much to convince him. The mention of popcorn was enough. I'd saved Alex for last because I knew he'd be the most difficult to convince.

"Alex?" I called through the door. "It's Jodi."

He opened the door. "You think I don't know your voice by now?"

I smiled. He didn't look angry with me anymore. "I missed you."

"You saw me at lessons and dinner."

"Yeah, but it's not the same." I leaned forward and kissed him.

"What was that for?"

"For understanding about the corpse and cleaning up my mess for me. I seem to be needing a lot of help lately, and you're always there for me."

"Want to come in?" he asked.

"Actually, I want you to come to my room."

He raised an eyebrow. "Okay." He didn't hesitate. He closed his door and wrapped one arm around my waist as we headed to my room.

Okay, so I'd purposely misled him, but I had to get him to come with me. It was the only way I was going to make it through the group movie. The only way I'd be able to keep myself from staring at Chase. As we got to my open door, Alex heard and saw the group inside.

"What's going on?" He stopped short, hooking his finger through my belt loop so I had to stop, too.

"Movie night." I tried to sound all innocent. "Come on. Things have been tense lately. I think it would do everyone good to hang out and watch a zombie flick."

"A zombie flick? What moron decided that would be a good movie choice for a bunch of stressed out necromancers?"

"I did." Chase stepped into the doorway. "This was my idea, only I was hoping—"

"That everyone would think the zombie thing was funny," I blurted out before Chase could tell Alex what his real plan had been. To get me alone.

"Funny?" Alex asked.

"You know, in an ironic kind of way." I forced a laugh and reached for his hand, lacing my fingers through his.

Chase's eyes dropped to our hands before he gave me a look that clearly meant "What are you trying to prove?"

"Shall we?" I motioned toward my room.

As we went inside, Alex whispered in my ear, "You owe me. Big."

I reached up and kissed his cheek. He gave me a small smile, and we sat down on the bed. I kind of thought the bed would give out under the weight of all five of us, but it held strong. The movie was every bit as cheesy as I'd expected it to be. We were all cracking up five minutes into it.

"Oh, yeah, as if a zombie would really walk around with its arms out all the time," Randy said.

Leticia laughed. "Or yelling, 'Braaaaiiins,'" she said in her best Hollywood zombie voice.

I smiled at Alex, happy to see everyone having a good time. Well, almost everyone. Chase was sitting by my feet, and he spent most of the movie staring at me instead of the screen. I ignored him as best as I could, trying to keep my attention on the movie.

I must have been tired because, at one point, I dozed off to the sounds of everyone talking and getting along. I woke up to a tingling in my foot. It started very lightly and crept up my leg. The sensation was electrifying, and after all the stress I'd been under, it felt amazing. I opened my eyes and rolled over slightly, resting my head on Alex's chest.

"Thanks, that feels great."

"What does?" he asked.

I saw Alex's hands behind his head. I discreetly looked down at his feet, thinking maybe he was rubbing my foot with one of his, but his legs were crossed. My gaze met Chase's, and he smiled.

Oh, God!

"Jodi, what feels great?" Alex asked again.

"Being here with you." I tried to keep my voice steady. "Thanks again for agreeing to this."

He smiled. "I don't really have a choice when it comes to you."

I put my head back down on his chest and stared at Chase. He was still rubbing my foot, sending waves of this strange tingling sensation throughout my body. Why wasn't I stopping him? I willed my foot to move away from Chase's hand, but it wouldn't. I was paralyzed by this feeling. I didn't want it to stop. Not really.

I closed my eyes, giving in to it. My blood surged with power I'd never felt before. It was sort of like the power I used to raise souls, but there was something different about it. Something stronger. Something that felt almost wrong. Yet, I couldn't stop it. Wrong felt right.

I felt Chase's fingers on my other foot now too, and the power welling up inside me doubled. I didn't know what was happening. Only that I didn't want it to end.

"Jodi?" Alex's weight shifted under me. "Are you okay?"

I couldn't answer. Couldn't open my eyes. I was lost in the power. Lost in Chase's touch. The energy in my body was overwhelming.

"Leticia?" Randy said. "What's wrong?"

"She's choking," Alex said. He sat up, and my head fell onto the pillow. "And something's wrong with Jodi, too. She isn't moving."

I heard Leticia gasping, and suddenly the feeling in my feet stopped. The power slowly drained from my body, leaving me feeling like I had pins and needles all over.

Something fell to the floor with a thud just as I managed to open my eyes. I sat up, feeling wobbly all over.

Randy reached for Leticia's body, resting in a heap on the floor. "I think she's dead!"

Chapter 6

I tried to get up, but I collapsed back on the bed. My head was spinning, and sweat dripped down my forehead. Alex wiped my face.

"Oh, God, Jodi, you're burning up."

"What about Leticia?" Randy asked, panic in his voice.

"Check her pulse," Chase said.

I was vaguely aware of Randy checking on Leticia. "I can't feel anything! Jodi, do something. You're the only one who can raise an Ophi."

Alex shook his head. "Look at her. She's sick or something. I don't think she's strong enough to try raising anyone."

"So, what, we let Leticia die?"

"She's already dead," Chase said. The coldness in his tone brought me to attention.

"But why?" I croaked.

"Shh, don't try to talk. I'm going to get you some water, okay?" Alex kissed my head and headed for the bathroom.

"We have to do something!" Randy insisted.

"Jodi." Chase slid into Alex's spot. "I can help you. Mason said Ophi can combine their powers to make them stronger. It's dangerous, but it's possible. I'd guess, with you being the Chosen One, you have a better chance than anyone at figuring it out. Let me help you raise Leticia. Before her soul leaves her body."

Combining powers. Victoria had told me that the Ophi had had to combine their powers to raise Medusa's soul and put it in the statue. Many of them had died in the process. This was more than a little risky, but I had to try for Leticia's sake. I glanced toward the bathroom. "Okay, but we have to hurry. Alex won't let me try this without knowing what's wrong with me."

Chase scooped me into his arms and carried me to the floor near Leticia. He held my hand, and we touched Leticia's forehead. I didn't normally need blood to raise things anymore. Other Ophi did, but since I'd drunk Medusa's blood I no longer had to bleed on the body of the person I was raising. Chase didn't know that though. He took a needle from the sewing kit on my dresser and poked both our fingers. Drops of blood dotted Leticia's forehead.

"Ready?" Chase asked.

I nodded and willed my blood to mix. I felt it working, and Chase was right about combining powers. I could feel his blood flowing through the veins in his hand. I focused all my strength on Leticia's soul. Sweat poured down my cheeks, and I started shaking. Still, I concentrated on bringing Leticia back. Her soul was still in her body, so I only had to wake it. "Breathe," I commanded. There was a sudden intake of air as Leticia's eyes and mouth opened. She was alive.

"What are you doing?" Alex yelled. I could barely see. My vision was cloudy. He rushed to me and pulled me away from Chase. "Why did you let her do that?" He buried my face in his shirt.

"Alex, calm down," Randy said. "They brought Leticia back. They saved her."

"And it nearly killed Jodi." Alex's chest heaved, and he let go of me. I pulled back and saw his shirt was covered in blood.

"What happened to you?" I asked.

"It's not my blood." He wiped my cheek with his thumb and showed it to me. It was covered in a deep red liquid. "It's yours."

I brought my hands to my eyes. Blood was pouring out of them. I'd gotten headaches and nosebleeds from using my powers, but never anything like this. At least not from raising souls. My eyes had bled after I drank Medusa's blood, though. I turned to Chase, and he looked as horrified as I was.

"Jodi, I had no idea combining our powers would do this."

"It didn't do anything to you," Alex snarled.

Chase shook his head. "You have to believe me. I didn't know. I was only trying to help Leticia."

Leticia sat up and gasped. "Jodi? Are you okay?"

I was burning up from the power inside me. My blood wouldn't stop boiling. "It's too much. It's trying to find a way out."

"What is?" Alex asked.

"My blood. There's too much power in it." My body shook, jolting with every surge of power running through my veins.

"Alex, we should take her to Arianna and Tony," Randy said. "They might be able to help her and explain what happened.

"No," I said. "Take me to Medusa. She'll know."

Alex carried me downstairs and held me up while I joined hands with Medusa. The second the connection was made, I started to feel better, and before long I was standing on my own. Medusa's spirit appeared in my mind like usual.

"My child, what's happened? Who did this to you?"

"I'm not sure. It happened when I brought Leticia back from the dead." Luckily, my conversations with Medusa were completely private. We spoke only in my mind, so Alex couldn't overhear anything.

"How did Leticia die?"

"I don't know. I was sort of out of it when it happened. I heard her choking and gasping for air. Then she fell to the floor. Randy checked for a pulse and said she was dead."

"Why were you out of it, Jodi?" Medusa eyed me suspiciously. She knew I was holding back.

"There's a new student at the school."

"Yes, I met him earlier today." Medusa only ever appeared to me, but when another Ophi connected with her statue they felt her power and Medusa could tap into their emotions.

"Right. Well, we were all watching a movie in my room." I swallowed hard before continuing. "Chase started touching my feet. It was weird at first, like a tingling in my feet and legs, but then I recognized it was power I was feeling. Only it wasn't like the power I feel when I raise souls. I don't think this power came from you."

Medusa nodded, like she understood. "Jodi, when you arrived here you were told that the blood in the left side of my body could not harm you, but that was not entirely true."

"What do you mean? I thought it was only poisonous to humans?"

"It is highly poisonous to humans, but in its purest form it's poisonous to Ophi as well."

I shook my head. "In its purest form? What does that mean?"

"It means you weren't mixing your blood, Jodi. You were pushing all the blood with the power to restore life to a very concentrated part of your body and allowing the poisonous blood to spread throughout the rest of you."

I started to feel dizzy again, but this time it was from information overload. "How is that possible?"

"How much do you know about Chase?"

"Just that he's from Serpentarius. He studied with Mason, but he wanted to learn more about his power, so he came here. They don't actively train there. They don't believe in it."

"Keep him close, Jodi. I sense he isn't like the others."

"Do you mean he's like me? He has more power than other Ophi?"

"More power, yes." Medusa looked down at our hands. "That's enough for now. You don't want to indulge in too much of my power at once."

I wanted to know more, but Medusa was right. Connecting with her for too long drained my energy completely. "Thank you." I let go of her hands.

"Well?" Alex asked the moment I opened my eyes. I'd only been connected to Medusa for a few minutes, ten tops, but he looked like he'd been waiting an eternity. "What did she say?"

He wasn't going to like this. "She said Chase isn't like the other Ophi. He's more like me. He has more power."

"You're kidding, right?" His voice was full of disgust.

"No." I conveniently left off the part about Chase touching my feet, the incident that had started all this power overload. "When we combined my power and his, it was too much for my body to contain."

"So, now we know not to let you work with Chase anymore."

"Actually, I think I need to work with him more."

He folded his arms in front of him. "How do you figure?"

"We need all the power we can get. Hades is breathing down my neck, and my power alone isn't enough to keep him away. Maybe if I can figure out how to work with Chase, then—I don't know. But if it might help us, it's worth a shot."

"What about before you raised Leticia? You were acting really weird. What was that about?"

"Stress, I think." I turned away so he wouldn't be able to read my face. I was sure it had "big fat liar" written across it.

He stepped forward and hugged me. "We'll figure it out. But just so you know, whenever you train with Chase, I'm going to be there to make sure nothing like this happens again."

I nodded. I'd expected as much.

"Let's get you cleaned up. The blood-streaked face is very last season."

I smiled. He always could make me feel better.

The movie party was definitely over, so I said goodnight to Alex and took a long, hot shower. Nothing calmed me down better. I was looking forward to crawling under the covers and sleeping my problems away. I couldn't deal with another thing today. Before I shut my eyes for the night, I said a little prayer—that I wouldn't have a single dream.

I woke up still feeling slightly exhausted from the previous day, but I didn't have any dead guys pounding on my door, so I was content. I couldn't remember dreaming at all, so I took that as another sign that today would be a better day. In fact, I started to think the only reason I was drawn to Chase in the first place was because the power in my blood recognized the power in his. He was like me. That didn't mean I liked him. And maybe he didn't even really like me. Maybe he was only drawn to my power.

I got out of bed with a smile on my face. Things were starting to make sense again, starting to look better. Maybe Chase and I would be able to figure out how to combine our powers and get the other Ophi to join us. Be a real family. And more importantly, keep off Hades' radar.

Alex was waiting for me by the stairs. I ran up to him and threw my arms around his neck.

"I guess you're feeling better this morning," he said.

"Good as new, and I think I've figured things out. I've got an idea. One that might convince a few more Ophi to come here and join us."

Over breakfast I told Alex and the others all about my plan. "So, here's what I'm thinking. Chase seems to have different powers than other Ophi. Stronger powers. Kind of like me. That's good news for us."

Leticia and Randy turned to Chase, looking him over with jealousy in their eyes. They were both still struggling with their powers, and now here was another Ophi with more abilities than them.

"What did you have in mind, Jodi?" Tony sipped his coffee.

Even Arianna had stopped fussing over the food and sat down. "Have you seen evidence of these powers Chase has?"

"Yes. Last night, something terrible happened." I looked at Leticia. She'd begged us not to tell Tony and Arianna what had happened, and since I hadn't wanted to deal with any more drama either, I had made the others agree. "I think an attack was made on Leticia."

"An attack?" Leticia looked horrified. Clearly, she hadn't considered this was a possibility.

I nodded. "I hate to admit this, but I think Hades is purposely trying to make me screw up. Do something he can deem as a deal breaker so he can come after me."

"You think Hades did that to me?" Leticia's voice cracked.

"I don't know how else to explain it. You just started choking. On nothing."

Leticia shook her head, still not believing this. "I thought it was the popcorn or something."

"You really think a popcorn kernel could take down an Ophi?" Alex asked.

I knew Alex was trying to help, but Leticia was sensitive. She wasn't going to respond to jokes. "Leticia, I think Hades came after you to get to me." I looked around the table. "I'm afraid he might come after all of you." My eyes lingered on Alex.

"So, we need to be ready," Alex said.

"Yes, and here's how." I got up and walked over to Chase. I took a deep breath and reached my hand out to him.

Chase looked at Alex and smiled before taking my hand.

"Don't get too excited," Alex said. "She's only demonstrating a point."

I closed my eyes and felt the surge of power between us. My hair danced like a gentle breeze was blowing it. Even without seeing him, I knew Chase felt it, too. I didn't want it to go too far, not with Alex and the others staring at us. Last night the connection between us had been… well, more than PG rated. I wasn't ready for the others to witness that. I let go of Chase's hand.

"When we form a connection, I can feel Chase's power. Like it's communicating with my blood."

Tony wrinkled his forehead. "I've heard of this, but it's very rare. It's almost like when you connect with the Medusa statue." He said it more as a statement than a question.

"You could say that, and that's exactly why I think we can use this combination of power. When I connect with Medusa, I get an energy boost. I'm stronger. It's what allowed me to bring Abby back before I even really knew how." I remembered the day Abby tried to prove she was as strong as me. She'd held both of Medusa's hands and died for it. Even though she was the last person I'd wanted to help, I couldn't let her die because of me. I had asked Medusa to help me bring her back. Which only made Abby hate me more.

"Whoa," Chase said. "I knew you could bring Ophi back and all, but you did it without any training?"

I shook my head. "Having Medusa help me was better than any training."

"Yeah, you brought Alex back no problem after Troy—" Leticia's eyes widened when she saw the look on Alex's face. She shoved a piece of toast in her mouth and looked away.

"You were dead?" Chase asked. "And wait, isn't Troy your father? Uncle Mason told me you're Victoria and Troy's kid, only they don't openly admit it."

Alex gripped the edge of the table, and for a second I thought he was going to lose it. How could Chase say those things? I was about to defend Alex when he stood up.

"You know what, Chase? I think you're jealous because Jodi cared enough to save me. She gave her blood to bring me back." He pulled up his sleeve and leaned across the table to shove his forearm in Chase's face. "Her blood is in my veins."

Chase swatted Alex's arm away and stood up.

"Enough!" Tony yelled. "Don't you two understand we may be at war soon? A war against Hades? How do you expect us to defeat a god when you two can't even be civil around one another?"

I walked around the table and stood at Alex's side. "Please. This isn't helping." I rubbed his arm, trying to calm him.

His expression softened at my touch. He leaned down and lightly kissed me. "I'll be fine. Morning training will burn off some energy, and I'll be good to go."

I didn't feel like eating anymore, so Alex and I headed to the cemetery. Leticia and Randy followed, which left Chase alone with Tony and Arianna. I knew they'd have a few things to say to Chase about the comments he'd made. The topic of Victoria and Troy was pretty much off-limits. It was an unspoken rule around here, and I knew Tony would make sure Chase was aware of it.

The air was crisp, and I filled my lungs with it. Since I had come into my powers, I was usually hot, thanks to my blood boiling in my veins to mix both sides of my powers. I welcomed the cool air on my skin.

Alex draped his arm around my shoulders. "What should we start with today?"

"Well, Randy is pretty good with raising one soul at a time, but he really needs more practice with raising multiple souls. I was thinking I could work with him, and you could help Leticia maintain her focus so she stops losing control over her corpses."

"You got it."

"Hey! Wait up!" Chase ran after us.

Alex rolled his eyes. "I was hoping Tony was really going to ream into him for a while. Maybe long enough for him to miss morning training."

"Alex, we need him. You don't have to like him, but you have to get along with him."

He pouted.

"For me?"

He sighed, and I knew I'd won.

Chase slowed down when he reached us. "So, I was thinking I could give Uncle Mason a call. Tell him about the power connection between you and me," he began, as if Alex wasn't even there. "I think together we could convince him and the others to join us."

"Really?" I was more than a little excited.

"Really." Chase smirked. "Let's show everyone what a great team we make." He stopped and reached his hand out to me.

He wanted to shake hands? Without thinking, I took his hand. But Chase's fingers squeezed mine, transferring power up my arms. Instantly my body tingled, overcome with power.

I pulled away, feeling completely self-conscious. "You want to take Leticia over there?" I asked Alex, pretending nothing had happened.

"Sure." He gave Chase one last glare and walked off.

Chase leaned in close to me and whispered, "How long are you going to try to deny what you feel for me? You can pretend Alex is the one you want, but when I touch you, I know it's me your blood craves."

I stepped back from Chase. "I don't know what you're talking about." Randy awkwardly moved past us. I was sure he'd overheard everything. The question was, how long would he wait before he told Alex?

Chapter 7

I followed Randy, yelling back over my shoulder at Chase, "Go work with Leticia and Alex. Until I know how much control you have over your powers, you'll start with the basics."

I didn't have to turn around to know Chase was fuming mad at that comment. I already knew he was powerful, but I'd demoted him to square one as if he were a beginner. I wasn't sure how training with Alex would go, but I couldn't handle working with Chase right now. Not until I got my emotions in check.

That's how it went for the next two days. Me training with Randy and avoiding Chase at all costs. I knew it couldn't go on like this forever, but I was willing to stick it out for as long as I could. Luckily, Randy never said anything to me or Alex about Chase's comment. Maybe he assumed Chase was just full of himself. By Saturday, Chase found a way to corner me.

"Hey, did you forget we have a phone call to make?"

"A what?"

"We were going to call Mason and see if we could convince him to get everyone out here. Now that we have our combined powers backing us up, I think we could persuade him."

"Right." In trying to dodge Chase, I'd forgotten all about that plan. "But we haven't trained together yet. I need you to master all the beginner skills before we can move forward." As much as I wanted the other Ophi here, I couldn't train with Chase. I couldn't be alone with him. It was too dangerous. Too dangerous for my relationship with Alex.

"You've had me in the baby group for days. I've raised souls and released them. What more do I need to prove to you?"

"You haven't raised multiple souls yet."

"Okay, then from now on I'll train with you and Randy."

What could I say to that? I'd set myself up.

"But I don't think we should wait to make this call. So what if we let Mason think we've already mastered our combined power? If it gets the others here, then it's worth a little white lie."

"All right," I said.

"Good, let's do it now." He tugged my arm, pulling me toward my office. Randy shrugged and headed over to Alex and Leticia to finish training.

"I told Alex I'd meet him before dinner." I tried to get Chase to at least slow down, but he was already pushing me through the door.

"I think lover boy can find the dining room on his own."

I sighed and walked into my office, taking a seat at the desk. I had Mason's number memorized. I'd called it about a thousand times before he'd called me back. I dialed and switched the phone to speaker.

"Hello?" Mason answered.

"Guess you forgot to check your caller ID," Chase said.

"What? Who is this?"

I heard Mason fumble with the phone. "Jodi?"

"Does my voice really sound that deep?" I asked.

"No, no. Who's with you?"

"It's Chase, Uncle Mason."

"Oh, Chase. It must be a bad connection. I didn't recognize your voice."

"No problem. Listen, we've got exciting news."

"Don't tell me you two hit it off and got engaged or something."

"No!" I yelled.

Chase laughed. "Not yet." He raised an eyebrow at me. "But Jodi and I do have a special connection. A power connection."

"What do you mean?" Mason asked.

"We can combine our powers. Turns out I have more power than the average Ophi, too. Like Jodi. Together we're unstoppable."

Mason was quiet on the other line, like he was thinking.

"You need to get everyone out here, Uncle Mason. Jodi and I have so much to show you."

"Chase, you know I can't. If you and Jodi are really as strong as you say, I'll send a small group, but I need to keep enough here to keep Serpentarius up and running. That's my best offer."

"Thanks, Mason. We'll take it." I tried not to sound disappointed, but I needed Mason. He would make a great teacher, and he could easily replace Troy. Arianna and Tony were great, but they always defaulted to me because I was the Chosen One. I needed an adult who took charge.

"I know it's not what you were hoping for, Jodi."

"That's okay. I appreciate whatever you can do."

"Take care." Mason hung up.

"Well, I guess it's a start." I stood up.

"You're not happy," Chase said. "I can tell."

"We need everyone. Otherwise we aren't strong enough to stand up to Hades." Even with everyone, I wasn't sure we'd be strong enough.

"Then I'll get you everyone."

"What?"

"I'll see you at dinner."

Before I could say another word, Chase was dialing the phone again. I gave him one last glance before going to the dining room.

"Hey, where have you been?" Alex slid a bowl of mac and cheese in front of me. I hated to admit it, but I was kind of getting used to the stuff, even if it was made with powered cheese.

"I called Mason. He's going to send a small group here."

"That's great."

I shrugged. "Yeah, but we need everyone."

"Give it time." He nudged me with his elbow and took another heaping forkful.

I picked at my food, mostly moving it around to make it look like I was eating. I'd barely eaten two real bites when Chase came into the room with a huge smile. "All taken care of. They'll be here on Monday."

"Who?" Leticia asked.

"Everyone," he said the word slowly, "from Serpentarius."

"Everyone?" I asked.

"Yup!"

Leticia squealed and threw her arms around Chase. "Oh, you're the best! You've saved us all!" She turned to me. "Don't you think so, Jodi?"

I nodded and went back to pushing my food around with my fork. The rest of the meal was filled with happy faces and people patting Chase on the back. I should've been happy, but something was off.

"We should celebrate," Leticia said. "Do something fun for once. No lessons or talk about training for one full night."

I didn't feel like celebrating. I felt like getting answers, but I was outvoted. Everyone was shouting out ideas. After what had happened during the last movie night, we skipped that idea. Randy suggested we play charades, but no one else went for it. Arianna said she'd found some board games in one of the hall closets, but that suggestion got groans from all the guys.

"I know." Tony got up from the table and left the room without another word.

"Are we supposed to follow him?" I asked.

Alex shrugged. "Why not?"

We got up and scanned the halls for Tony.

"Tony?" I called. "Where are you?"

No answer. We peeked in all the rooms and even closets downstairs. Nothing.

"Did he go to his room?" Leticia asked.

"Nope," Tony called from the stairs. "I went to the library."

"What for?" Alex asked.

"This." Tony held up what looked like a severed hand.

"Ugh! Where did you get that?" Leticia turned away, gagging.

He reached the bottom landing and turned the hand over in his palm. "I know it's a little…"

"Gross," I said.

Tony shrugged. "It has sentimental value to the school."

I crossed my arms, thinking he must be joking. "How can a severed hand have sentimental value?"

"This is the hand of the very first corpse raised by someone at this school. It was preserved to remind us that our power is our greatest gift."

"I don't want gifts like *that*." Leticia pointed to the severed hand.

"I don't expect you all to understand it now, but one day you will. When you understand how important this school is." Tony loved this school. It was all he had. He was thirty-eight and had never had a wife. I'd heard a rumor that he'd fallen for an Ophi who was already engaged to someone else. He never got over her. That meant he never had had a child either. Being Ophi and not being able to have a child was ten times worse than it was for a human. Tony hadn't been able to contribute to the Ophi line, so he'd dedicated himself to teaching Ophi kids.

"Why did you want to get the hand?" I asked. "I thought you had an idea for what we could do this evening."

"Maybe he wants us to raise a few corpses and chop off some hands of our own," Randy said.

We all turned and stared at him.

Randy shrugged. "What? Tony's the one who brought that thing down here."

Tony laughed. "I brought it because I had an idea for a game. A game that will let us get to know each other a little better."

"And it involves a severed hand?" I asked.

Tony shrugged. "I needed a spinner."

The guys burst out laughing. I had to admit it was kind of funny. I mean, a bunch of necromancers playing with a severed hand? But poor Leticia looked horrified.

"I'm not touching that thing," she said.

"You won't have to. I'm not actually playing, so I'll be in charge of spinning." Tony nodded toward the living room. "Come on. Let's learn a little more about each other."

"So, it's a get to know you kind of game?" I flopped down on the couch.

"Exactly. If we are going to be like family, then we should know a few secrets about each other." Tony dragged over the coffee table and another couch, so we were sitting in a rectangle. He placed the hand in the middle of the coffee table.

Maybe this game wasn't such a bad idea. I could get some answers out of Chase.

"Sounds interesting," Chase said. "I can't wait to hear everyone's darkest secrets." His gaze fell on me.

"Shall we begin?" Tony was already spinning the hand. It stopped with its fingers facing Leticia.

"Ugh, why did that creepy thing have to point to me?"

"All right, Leticia," Tony said, "tell us something we don't know about you."

"Okay." She paused, thinking of what to share. "Oh, I know. Once when Abby borrowed my shampoo and didn't return it, I snuck into her bathroom and dripped toilet water into her toothpaste."

"You mean you put perfume in her toothpaste?" Arianna asked.

"No." Leticia shook her head. "I used a cup to get water from the toilet, and I dripped it into her tube of toothpaste."

"Why didn't you just dunk her toothbrush in the toilet instead?" Randy asked.

Leticia's face turned red. "I didn't think of it," she said in a small voice.

We all started laughing. Poor Leticia. She really was kind of helpless—for someone who could raise the dead.

Tony spun the hand again. This time it landed on Randy.

"Um, I don't have any secrets like Leticia's, but I did steal a bag of Troy's favorite chips once. Man, he went crazy looking for it. He even blamed the servants. Like a bunch of living dead would eat potato chips."

"Boring." Chase dragged out the word. "At least Leticia's story was funny. You've got to have a better secret than that."

Randy fidgeted with his hands in his lap. "I do have one secret, but it's not something I want to share."

"Come on. That's the whole point of this game, isn't it?" Chase was pushing awfully hard. I hoped that meant he'd be more than willing to share when it was his turn.

"Yeah, Randy, you can tell us." Leticia put her hand on his arm.

Randy squeezed his fists. "All right, but before I tell you all this, I want to say that I know I was overreacting at the time. I don't feel this way now."

We all nodded.

Randy inhaled loudly. "When I first saw my dad after Victoria brought him back, I wanted to...I wanted to kill her. I wanted to make her pay for the way she'd mangled his body."

I remembered all too well how wrong Victoria had been to try raising the Ophi. It was a power reserved for me, but she wouldn't listen. She insisted on using my locket, the one Medusa had given me with her blood infused in the bloodstone, to raise those poor people. All she'd succeeded in doing was creating an army of living dead Ophi. I reached my hand up and touched my bare neck. The locket lay broken in my dresser drawer now. I hadn't been able to part with it. It didn't hold Medusa's blood anymore, but it still had special meaning to me.

No one had said a word for several minutes. We all waited to see how Alex would react to this. Finally Randy said, "I'm sorry, man."

Alex shook his head. "I don't blame you. Victoria was a monster. She acted without thinking about any consequences. I'm sorry for what she did to your dad, and to Leticia's parents." Alex was talking about her in the past tense. He'd already written her off as dead, and even though she was really serving Hades, I guessed she was as good as dead.

Randy leaned forward. "But she was only trying to help. I realize that now."

"You're saying you don't blame Victoria anymore? You're not upset that your father's soul was ripped from wherever it was and forced back into a body that was so mangled you barely recognized it?" I was on my feet now and practically yelling.

"Jodi," Tony said. "Please." He nodded slightly toward Alex.

"I'm sorry. Alex, I know they were your parents, but Victoria and Troy were awful."

Tony put a hand up to stop me. "Jodi, it's still Randy's turn, so why don't we—"

"I don't care about the hand or whose turn it is right now. You wanted us to share and get to know each other better, so I'm sharing." Tony nodded, and Alex looked up at me with pain in his eyes.

"I watched you eat mac and cheese at every meal, trying to get her attention, but she wouldn't give you the time of day. And when it came down to choosing sides in the end, your own father put a knife in your chest."

"Is this supposed to make me feel better?" Alex asked.

"I'm sorry. I'm trying to tell you you didn't deserve that. You didn't deserve any of it."

"So your big secret is that you feel sorry for Alex?" Chase asked.

"No!" That was the last thing I wanted Alex to think. That I was with him out of pity. "My big secret shouldn't be a secret at all. My big secret is that I think Alex is the greatest Ophi I've ever met, and I wish his own parents could've seen him for who he really is."

I sat back down, worried that my outburst had only hurt Alex. I hadn't meant to go off like that, but I couldn't handle listening to Randy forgive Victoria for what she'd done.

Alex stood up. "I'm going to call it a night. See you all in the morning."

"Alex," I said.

"In the morning, Jodi." He walked away, leaving me staring after him.

Chase got up and sighed. "Well, if Alex gets out of sharing, I'm going to bed, too."

"I think it's best if we all turn in for the night," Tony said.

I turned to him. "Sorry. It was a nice idea to get to know each other better."

He nodded and picked up the severed hand. I followed him up the stairs and said goodnight when I reached my floor. I saw Chase walking down the hall to his room, and I ran after him. It wasn't too late to get the answers I was looking for.

"How did you do it?" I called after him.

Chase stopped and turned around. "Do what?"

"Mason was dead set against coming. How did you change his mind in a matter of minutes?" I stopped dangerously close to him. Something told me Chase wouldn't be willing to shout the answer or risk anyone overhearing us. I had to be close enough for him to whisper.

He leaned into me. "Chase Baxter charm, I guess. You know all about that." He inched closer until our faces were almost touching. I tried to turn away, but I couldn't. Being this close to Chase was making my blood go crazy. My arms tingled with the desire to touch him. My brain told me to stop him, but I stayed frozen as he leaned in to kiss me.

Alex's bedroom door swung open. "What's going on?"

Chapter 8

"Alex!" I jumped, breaking free from my trance. "What are you doing?"

"I was coming to talk to you." He looked back and forth between Chase and me. "The question is what are *you* doing? Because it sure looked like you were going to let this creep kiss you."

I backed away from Chase and shook my head. "No! I wasn't. I mean, *he* wasn't."

"Oh, I was." Chase smiled at me.

"Jodi, go to your room. I don't think you're going to want to see this."

"Go to my room?" I shook my head. "Alex, you can't send me to my room."

"Fine. *Please,* go to your room. I'd rather you didn't see me kick this guy's ass."

Chase laughed. "Jodi, stay. This should be funny to watch."

Alex lunged at Chase, but I stepped between them, putting my hands on Alex's chest. "Enough." I leaned into Alex, hoping my touch would have some sort of calming effect on him. "He didn't do anything. He only made a stupid comment to get a reaction from you. Let it go. You're better than that."

Alex backed off slightly, but not much.

I reached up and kissed him softly on his lips. "Let it go."

Alex wrapped his arms around me, kissing me harder. He pulled me through the open door and into his bedroom. The second we were both inside, he slammed the door on Chase, locking it tight.

"What are you doing?" I asked, breathing heavily.

He shrugged. "Nothing."

"Nothing? Oh, really? So, you didn't pull me in here because you wanted Chase to think we're…" I couldn't say the words. I really liked Alex—loved him—but well, our relationship hadn't exactly reached the level of spending the night in each other's rooms.

"Let him think what he wants." Alex moved closer and kissed me again. The kiss was so passionate, my head spun. My body tingled. No wait. Not my body. My blood. My blood was mixing. Why was kissing Alex making me use my powers? I tried to control it, tried to calm my blood, but something was wrong. I pushed my hands against Alex's chest and forced my way out of his arms. Out of the kiss.

"What's wrong?" He looked hurt.

"I don't know." I stared at my hands and arms. "My blood is mixing, but I'm not doing it on purpose. It just happened when you kissed me."

Alex raised an eyebrow and smiled. "I knew I was a good kisser, but man."

If I hadn't been so freaked out, I would've rolled my eyes. "I don't think it was you." I couldn't tell him this happened every time I was near Chase. The power was overwhelming me, bringing me to my knees.

"Jodi!" Alex helped me up, supporting most of my weight. "What's happening? Can't you stop it?"

"No. It's like I have no control over it." Mumbled voices filled my head, like screams of agony. I pressed my hands to my ears to drown it out, but the sound wasn't coming from outside my body. It was literally in me. My mind was tuned into something. What was it? "Medusa," I called out with my thoughts. "Can you hear me?" Sometimes she popped into my mind. I couldn't make her do it, but if she wanted to communicate with me, she could. Was this her?

"Jodi, let's get you over to the bed so you can lie down." Alex was practically dragging me now. The second I felt the bed, I fell forward onto it. I couldn't support my own weight. I couldn't do anything.

I watched my veins ripple under my skin, looking like a bunch of snakes slithering down my body. Then, it stopped. All of it. My blood calmed. The voices hushed. I was me again.

I sat up slowly, expecting to feel dizzy or drained of energy, but I didn't. I felt normal.

"Take it easy." Alex put his hands on my shoulders and looked into my eyes. "Are you sure it's over?"

I nodded. "Whatever it was, it stopped."

Someone pounded on the door. My immediate thought was that it was Chase, looking for a fight, but Leticia shrieked, "Jodi! Are you in there?"

She sounded scared. I got up, but Alex held me back. "I don't think you should be moving around yet. Not until we figure out what happened to you."

"I'm okay. Really. Leticia sounds totally freaked." I rushed to the door and turned the knob. Leticia's face was white. "What is it? What's wrong?"

"The cemetery. You have to come see." She grabbed my arm and pulled me down the hall. I nearly fell down the stairs because she wouldn't ease off the pace or let go.

"Leticia!" I complained.

Alex ran after us, staying close to me. Obviously, he wasn't convinced I was okay. We hurried past the Medusa statue and out the front door. I didn't have to go much farther before I saw the problem. *All* the bodies in the cemetery had crawled from their graves. At once. And I knew I was the one who had raised them.

Alex looked at me, obviously thinking the same thing. My powers were out of control. The only thing I could think of was that it must have happened when I was kissing Alex. My blood had boiled, and I'd heard screams in my head because I was summoning all these souls.

"How did this happen?" Leticia struggled to catch her breath.

"I—"

"We'll figure that out later," Alex said. "Right now we need to put these souls back, and fast. Before Hades thinks we've summoned an army."

He was right. Hades would view a raising of this size as a personal attack. It didn't matter how quickly I released the souls. Something this big was going to get Hades' attention. I was sure it already had. Still, I didn't want to have all these zombies hanging around if Hades decided to show up in person.

"Jodi." Leticia tugged on my sleeve.

The zombies had seen me and were coming straight for me. I wasn't sure if I could command them all at once. It would require too much power, and even though I felt okay after raising all of them, I'd still used a bunch of my energy to do it.

"I can't do this by myself." I whipped my head around. "Leticia, go get Arianna and Tony. I need them to help me control the bodies while I work on releasing them."

She nodded.

"And hurry. These guys are angry, and I can't hold them all off."

Leticia took off. I glanced at Alex, but his eyes were already shut. He was calling on his own powers to help me. Unfortunately, Alex wasn't nearly as good at controlling souls other people had summoned. He wouldn't completely master the ability until he was an adult Ophi.

I willed my blood to mix and started commanding the souls closest to us. Some listened, and some didn't. It was too much. Alex grunted as a zombie slammed into him to get to me. Distracted, I got hit from the side. I fell to the ground with the zombie on top of me. I commanded the soul to release, and it slumped forward on me, but another zombie was already there to take his place.

I could hear Alex struggling. Something silver flickered to my right. Alex's knife. Bodies fell to the ground next to me. All it took was one drop of Alex's blood. The zombie on me opened his mouth, ready to take a chunk out of me. I lashed my forearm across his teeth, slicing my skin open. The second my blood touched him, he fell over. Someone pulled me to my feet. I turned to see Chase. He took my hand in his, squeezing it tight.

The zombies were still all over Alex, but Chase had managed to fend off the ones near me. Together we combined our powers. My body trembled as Chase's power flowed through me. I wasn't sure how long I could take this, so I sent out commands in waves, releasing soul after soul, hoping I'd get to them all before I collapsed under the power. I stayed focused on the zombies, but it got harder and harder to release them. The power was too much, and I couldn't control it anymore. My body shook, and my eyes rolled back. Warm blood ran down my face. It was like last time in my room, only this was worse. I could barely stand.

"Stop!" Alex yelled. "You're hurting her!"

Chase let go of me, and I fell into Alex's arms. My vision was blurred, but I could see there were only a few zombies left. I heard Arianna and Tony. They were here now, taking care of the rest. I could relax.

Alex sat down on the grass with me in his lap. "Jodi, can you hear me?"

I tried to nod, but couldn't tell if my head was actually moving. My veins throbbed, still feeling the effects of the power. My eyes weren't bleeding anymore, and the crisp air was drying the blood on my cheeks. Alex stroked my hair, and I tried to concentrate on his touch, letting it soothe me.

"Why doesn't it affect you when you two combine powers?" By the tone in Alex's voice, I knew he was talking to Chase.

"Because we're not truly combining our powers. I'm giving Jodi my power. Transferring it to her so she gets an extra boost."

"Why didn't you say that before?" Tony asked. He lifted each of my eyelids. I didn't know what he was looking for. Signs of life, maybe. I still couldn't form words or even move.

"I didn't want you guys to think I wasn't powerful." Chase's voice was small. "It was nice having everyone suddenly interested in me. I didn't mean to hurt her, though. She's so strong. I thought she could handle it."

"It took a lot of power to release all these souls," Tony said. "More power than any one Ophi should have."

"I can work on holding back. Not transferring so much at once." Chase sounded desperate. "I only let her take that much because there were so many zombies. I thought I had to. I had no idea it would do this to her."

My vision was getting better…clearer, and I could finally swallow.

"What do you mean, you had no idea?" Alex's voice was full of venom. "It happened when you did it last time, too. You knew exactly what would happen."

Tony held his hand up to silence Alex and Chase. "We'll talk about it later. Right now, I want to get Jodi inside. I think she needs another visit with Medusa."

Alex carried me inside. I had just enough energy to hold onto the statue's hands. Medusa's image came rushing to me as soon as I made the connection.

"Dear child, what happened?"

"Medusa, I need your help. I can't control my powers. I accidentally raised the entire cemetery. I didn't really know I was doing it, either. I felt my blood mixing, and I heard screams, but I wasn't trying to summon anyone." The words rushed out of me in a panic.

Medusa nodded. "What were you doing when it happened?"

My cheeks must have been the color of a fire truck. "Kissing Alex."

"Is that all?"

"What? Medusa, yes! We were only kissing. I swear."

"No, child. What I mean is, did anything else happen? Maybe right before you kissed Alex."

Chase. Chase had almost kissed me. He'd made me feel the blood in my veins, too.

"So, that's it." I hadn't said a word, only thought it, but Medusa could access my thoughts, too. "You have feelings for Chase."

"No, I like Alex. I love Alex. Not Chase."

"Your blood is telling you otherwise. Your emotions are extremely conflicted. You have feelings for both these boys. You know your power is tied to your emotions. You need to figure out how you feel about Chase or this won't stop happening, and we both know what that will lead to."

"Hades coming for me." I was kind of surprised he wasn't already here.

"You are one of mine, Jodi. I don't want to lose you to Hades."

"I don't want to be conflicted. I don't want to like Chase."

"The heart doesn't always listen to reason."

"What do I do?"

"Explore those feelings. See if they are really there. It may be the only way to get past this. And, Jodi, do it quickly. You don't have much time." Medusa vanished without another word, leaving me to wonder if she knew more than she was saying.

I had enough energy to make it until bedtime, so I let go of the statue. I still had to get my arm bandaged and clean up my face.

"Any better?" Alex asked.

"Yeah, a lot."

He hugged me tightly before letting me stand on my own. "Arianna said she'll meet you in your room to bandage your arm."

Normally, connecting with Medusa healed any cuts I had, but apparently the power overload had taken all of that healing power, because my arm was still a mess. "Okay. I want to get this blood off my face first."

"I'll help you."

We walked up the stairs, slowly. It was the only speed I could handle right now. Alex got me into bed, carefully positioning my cut arm so I didn't bleed all over my covers. Then, he went into the bathroom for water and washcloths. I closed my eyes and thought about what Medusa had said. I couldn't get past one thing. How could I explore my feelings for Chase without losing Alex? I knew he wouldn't let me date Chase while I was still his girlfriend. What guy would?

Alex came back and sat down next to me. He had a bowl of warm water in his hands.

"Is that the bowl from the hallway? The one that always has potpourri in it?"

Alex shrugged. "I couldn't find anything in the bathroom, so I had to improvise. I'm sure Arianna will understand."

I managed a weak smile.

Alex started washing the blood from my face. "You know your power overdoses give new meaning to putting a little color in your cheeks."

I knew he was trying to act normal, make me smile the way he usually did, but I was spent. I was scared I was losing control. Scared I was losing him. Scared I was losing this war with Hades. Because I *was* at war. I understood that now. The deal I'd made with him wasn't fair, and he knew it. Hell, it's why he'd gone along with it. He knew I'd screw up. He knew he'd ultimately get what he wanted...all the Ophi in the underworld, dead or alive.

"Hey." Alex dabbed more water on my face. "What did Medusa say?"

My breath caught in my throat. What was I supposed to say? If I told the truth, it would crush him. He'd get angry and dump me. With everything else going wrong right now, I needed Alex. I had to lie. I remembered what Tony had told Chase about giving me too much of his power.

"She said I couldn't handle that much power all at once. I have to ease into this."

"Makes sense. You know, Chase told us he doesn't really have this big power. He's just giving you his power on top of yours."

"His power is different. I can feel it. I know when we join powers, it's more of me taking from him, but his abilities are greater than an average Ophi's. I'm sure of it. "

"If you say so." Alex shrugged, dismissing the thought. It wasn't easy for him to sit back and watch Chase work with me in a way he couldn't. He was taking it as a major blow to his ego.

"I wish it were you." I verbalized what I knew he felt.

He gave me a small smile. "While you were connected to the statue, Tony said he wants you and Chase to start training together, learning to transfer power little by little."

Train with Chase? Not at all what I wanted to do. "I'm scared of trying this again."

Alex put the bowl of water on my nightstand and placed his hand on top of mine. "I know. I promise I'll be right there with you when you train. I won't let you out of my sight."

I shivered at the thought. How could I hide my feelings for Chase and the way his touch affected me with Alex watching us so closely?

Chapter 9

I had to find a way to tell Alex that he didn't need to watch Chase and me, but was there any way to do that without looking suspicious? I was mentally preparing some lame excuse about Alex missing out on his own training to babysit me, but before I could even attempt to get the words out Arianna walked into the room. She didn't even knock, but then again she'd said she'd meet me here and my door hadn't exactly been closed.

"Off with you, Alex." Arianna shooed him away with her free hand. In the other, she held a medical kit. "As soon as I get Jodi's arm cleaned and bandaged, she's going right to sleep. There's nothing more you can do for her tonight, so say your goodbyes and get moving."

I smiled, grateful for Arianna's mothering. Not only was she taking care of me, but she was also saving me from a very awkward conversation with Alex. One I didn't have the strength for right now.

Alex kissed me lightly on the lips. "Get some rest."

"I will." I squeezed his hand quickly and watched him walk out of the room. He paused at the door, but Arianna followed him and pushed him into the hallway.

"Goodnight, Alex," she said.

I gave a weak laugh as she closed the door. "Thanks. I know he's trying to help, but I'm exhausted."

"Of course you are." She sat down on my bed and rummaged through the medical kit. "Okay, let's see that arm." She wiped off the blood around the cut and put some ointment on the wound. "Not bad at all. Just a scratch. You'll be fine in no time."

She was right. The cut on my arm was the least of my worries.

"Now, tell me how you're really doing." Arianna put the medical kit aside and placed her hands in her lap. "You and Chase—what's going on there?" My eyes must have widened because Arianna continued, "Oh, don't go looking surprised. I worked at Serpentarius, remember? I saw young people catching each other's eyes across the club every night. I know what attraction looks like, and you and Chase are attracted to each other."

I tried to sit up more. "It's not like that, Arianna. I swear. It's not him. I mean, it's more like his blood, or at least the power in it." Here I was again, sounding like some blood-crazed vampire.

"Oh, so you haven't noticed how handsome Chase is? I heard Leticia say he's the hottest Ophi she's ever seen." Arianna waved her hand, dismissing the thought. "But you didn't notice that because you were too busy being attracted to his power." Her sarcasm wasn't lost on me.

"Fine. He's good-looking. But seriously, I'm not like Leticia. I'm not drooling over him. In fact, I don't even want to be around him. He scares me. The way he looks at me. The way his touch—" Oh, God, what was I saying? Why was I telling Arianna about Chase's touch?

She raised an eyebrow. "It's worse than I thought."

"No." I shook my head. "You're misunderstanding me. I only meant when he transfers his power to me…I don't like it. It freaks me out, and now I have to train with him, according to Tony."

"You don't think that's a good idea?"

"No. You see what combining powers with Chase does to me."

"Yes, I've seen the physical effects, but what I'm more interested in right now are the emotional effects." She lowered her voice even though we were the only people in the room. "Are you afraid to be close to Chase because his touch does more than transfer power to you?"

Yes, but I couldn't say that. It was bad enough Medusa could read my thoughts. I couldn't have Arianna figuring out what a terrible person I was for feeling this way about Chase.

"I'm going to take your silence to mean I'm on to something." She stood up. "Well, I've kept you up long enough. Get some rest. Sometimes a good night's sleep helps you see things more clearly in the morning."

I nodded, even though I didn't really believe that was true. I shut off the lamp on my nightstand and curled up under the covers. The last thing on my mind before I fell asleep was that I had to find a way out of training with Chase.

The dream hit me sometime near morning. I was walking down the stairs, heading to breakfast, but I stopped when I saw Chase leaning against the Medusa statue. He smiled at me and held his hand out. Without a word, I went to him, feeling the pull of his power in my blood. My body tingled at the sight of him; as I got closer, my blood bubbled uncontrollably.

"I knew you would come," Chase said.

"I'm supposed to meet—"

"Me," he said. "I called you here."

"But—"

"Shh. You'll understand soon." He pulled me closer and placed both his hands on my face. Blood rushed to my head, making me dizzy. Chase lowered his face to mine and kissed me. Softly at first. My lips tingled in response. His kiss got hungrier. My body felt like it was on fire, but I kept kissing him, unable to stop. I lost myself in the power. In Chase.

"Jodi?" Alex's voice was small and full of hurt. I pulled away from Chase and turned to see Alex staring at me. His face twisted in pain and confusion. "Why? How could you do this to me? To us?"

"Because this is her true nature." Chase wrapped his arm around me. "She belongs with me." His touch sent waves of power through me, making me hungry for more. I reached for his arm, wanting to pull him closer, but all the time my eyes were locked on Alex. While I relished in Chase's power, Alex was falling apart.

I shot up in bed, breathing heavily. For a moment the dream lingered in my mind, and instead of seeing my room, I still saw Alex's face filled with pain. Slowly, the dream vanished, and I was facing a room full of zombies.

"Ah!" I screamed, not because I was afraid of the zombies— although I knew I couldn't take them all on alone—but because I'd used my powers while I was sleeping again. In less than twenty-four hours, I'd raised the entire graveyard twice.

Leticia ran into my room. I could barely see her over all the zombies, but her scream rang through the room.

"Leticia, run!" She couldn't release souls yet. If she stayed here, she'd get attacked. I couldn't save her and myself at the same time. I heard her footsteps pounding down the hall, and I hoped she was going for help. If fear sent her running straight out the door of the mansion, I was screwed.

My blood was still boiling in my veins. The effects of the dream hadn't worn off. I started giving commands, releasing some and telling others not to move. Releasing took more time than a simple command of "Stay." I kept my focus and worked through the group. I wasn't sure I was strong enough for this yet, but what choice did I have?

Alex ran into the room, followed by the others. "What happened?" He looked around, and I couldn't help wondering if he was searching for Chase.

"I was asleep, and when I woke up, they were here."

"Did you have a dream? About me?" He obviously thought this was exactly like last night, after we'd kissed in his room.

"Yeah." Alex had been in my dream, so it wasn't a total lie. He stepped over the bodies of the souls I'd released and came to me. Arianna and Tony were already releasing the other souls.

"Jodi, you need to figure this out. Hades is going to come after you if you don't stop this."

"I know. I'll figure it out. Something is going on with my powers. Maybe they're increasing. I'll have to learn to control them better. I'll talk to Medusa some more about it."

The room shook with a loud rumbling. Sounds of glass shattering and wood splintering filled the air. The entire mansion was going to come down. The floor split open. Alex grabbed me and pulled me toward the bathroom and away from the crack. Bodies toppled into the darkness. Arianna and Tony huddled in the doorway. I couldn't see Randy or Leticia in the hallway, but I hoped they were safe.

Black smoke swirled out of the crack in the floor. This was it. Hades was coming for me. I'd broken our agreement, and he was coming to collect my soul.

Hades emerged from the smoke and stared directly at me. "I think it's about time we had a talk, Jodi Marshall."

He was every bit as gorgeous as I remembered. Gorgeous in a completely terrifying way. After my first meeting with Hades, I'd discovered where the term "tall, dark, and handsome" came from. Why he chose to appear to me in this form, I didn't know, but he certainly knew what my type was. Physically at least. His personality was horrifying.

"Hades, please, let me explain." I put my hands up in surrender. "I didn't know I was raising those souls." I pointed to the bed. "I was asleep. Something is going on with my powers. I don't know how to control them. But I released the souls. We worked together to get them back to you as soon as possible." I had to get it all out before he interrupted. Before I lost my nerve.

"It's not her fault." Alex came to my rescue. "She's trying to figure out what's going wrong with her powers."

Hades narrowed his eyes, and I felt them burning into me. Literally. My entire body felt like it was on fire, and I knew it would be that easy for him to kill me. I tried to cry out, but the pain in my throat wouldn't allow it. I crumpled in Alex's arms.

"Stop!" Alex yelled. "You're killing her!"

Chase ran into the room, pushing past Tony and Arianna. My eyes burned, and I actually saw flames. I was looking at Hell, but I could sense Chase's blood. He came closer, and the fire went away. Hades stared at Chase, no longer interested in burning my soul. Chase didn't say a word, and neither did Hades. They just stared at each other. Finally, Hades turned back to me. I cringed, afraid he'd pick up where he'd left off, but he only spoke.

"Figure out what's happening, and learn to control it. Soon. I won't tolerate much more of this." He waved his arm around the room, and a whirlwind of black smoke swept most of the bodies into the crack in the floor. He glared at me one last time before disappearing into the ground. The floor sealed up behind him, but my room was still a mess.

"Well, he's pleasant," Chase said.

"Thank you," I said. "If you hadn't come in here and broken Hades' stare…"

"Any time. I won't let anyone hurt you, Jodi." Chase gave Alex a look before he turned and left the room.

I shivered even though I was still burning up from Hades' stare. Chase had declared war on Alex. He'd openly shown his feelings for me in front of everyone. Alex was shaking with rage. I buried my face in his chest, squeezing him tight. I wanted to show him that I'd chosen him, regardless of how Chase felt.

Randy finally stepped into my room. "Hey, where was Chase during all that?"

Leticia let go of his arm. "What do you mean?"

"When we heard you scream, we all came running. Everyone but Chase."

We all looked back and forth between each other. No one had an answer.

Alex pulled away from me. "I'm going to find out."

"No, please. Let it go. Maybe he didn't hear Leticia. Maybe he was in the shower."

"His hair wasn't wet," Leticia said.

Randy smirked. "And if you hadn't already raised them, the dead bodies in the cemetery would've heard Leticia, too."

Alex stared at me. "Why are you defending him, Jodi?"

"I'm not. I just don't think we should all go storming his room, making accusations. We'll never get an answer out of him that way."

"He does like to avoid answering questions," Randy said.

"What do you mean?" I'd experienced this about Chase, but I wasn't aware he was keeping things from the others. I mean, what would Randy ask him that Chase wouldn't want to answer?

"The other day I asked him about his parents. I was curious if either of them had more powers than other Ophi, because Chase had to get it from somewhere, right? But he wouldn't answer. He changed the subject, and when I tried to bring it up again, he made up an excuse and left."

"He's hiding something," Alex said. "More reason to make him talk. He's got a lot of things to explain."

I looked to Arianna for help, but she shrugged. Tony saw us exchange a glance and said, "Let me talk to Chase. He'll only feel threatened if we all go asking questions."

I mouthed a "Thank you" and he nodded.

Alex noticed, and he gave me a questioning look, so I changed the topic. "We'll have to rebury these bodies right away. Hades took several bodies with him, which means we have fewer corpses to train with. We can't afford to lose any more."

"I'll get started on it now," Tony said. "You all can help me after breakfast."

We nodded.

"Oh, and, Jodi, if you don't mind, I'm going to leave the bodies here until we get the graves dug, okay?"

"Sure." Unfortunately, I was getting used to having corpses in my bedroom.

Everyone left, going back to their own rooms to finish getting ready for the day, but Alex stayed behind with me. I hugged him, loving how safe I felt in his arms. I wanted to only want Alex, but something inside me was screaming for Chase, and I didn't know how to make it stop.

Alex pulled away. "I saw that little exchange between you and Tony. What was that about?"

I sighed and sat down on the bed. "Listen, I know you hate Chase, and I know he gives you a hard time, but we're short on numbers. Hades was in my bedroom threatening me. He could've killed me, Alex. If Chase hadn't—"

"No! Chase did *not* save you from Hades. He showed up late because he was doing God knows what." Alex was yelling now. "He's not the good guy. I mean, did you see the way Hades looked at him? It was like he recognized evil."

That was crazy. Hades and Chase had locked eyes, but I figured it was only because Hades hadn't seen Chase before. He wasn't here at the school when I'd made the deal with Hades two months ago. "I'm sure Hades was surprised to see a new face around here. That's all, and really—whatever it was, I don't care. All I know is I'm alive right now. Can't we take two minutes to be thankful for that?"

Alex pulled me to him and kissed me lightly on the lips. "You know I'm thankful you're alive. I watched you die once, remember? After you drank Medusa's blood."

"I didn't die."

"The human part of you did."

Sometimes, I forgot there was a difference between being human and being Gorgon. But Medusa's blood had transformed me, made me fully Gorgon. Hades hated me for that. I'd killed the human in me, and there was no soul to show for it. As far as Hades was concerned, I owed him my soul.

"I think you should leave the school," Alex said.

"What?" I nearly stumbled back in surprise.

"I'll go with you. We'll go somewhere Hades can't find you. Just until you get your powers under control."

"I can't leave. I have a job to do. The Ophi from Serpentarius will be here tomorrow. It took months to get them here. How would it look if they came and I'd taken off?"

Alex started pacing. He was determined to find a way to save me. I didn't say a word. Just let him think. Finally, he stopped. "Did you ever consider that Hades might want you to get all the Ophi under one roof so he can take us out in one shot?"

I was starting to wonder about that. We were sitting ducks here. Hades could kill us all in our sleep if he wanted to. But I had a feeling Hades was a god of his word. We'd made a deal. Sure, he was hoping I'd screw it up so he could kill me. But if I didn't, we'd be okay. Hades would honor our deal—I hoped.

Except I was screwing up, and Chase was a big part of that.

Chapter 10

Breakfast was quick. We had bodies to bury, and I couldn't exactly sit and enjoy my pancakes knowing Tony was digging graves on his own. I hurried the group along, giving Randy a long hard stare when he reached for a second helping of pancakes.

"I'll take a few to go." Grabbing a handful, he got up from the table.

"Fine. Everyone else good?"

Leticia stood up. "I'm ready. I can't eat a thing after seeing Hades. He scared the appetite right out of me." I was with her there.

Arianna shooed us out the door. "You all go help Tony. I can handle clean-up on my own today."

"Ari, you're a life saver." I gave her a quick hug and followed the others out to the cemetery. Tony was dirty, sweaty, and dead tired. He'd managed to dig up seven graves already. I wasn't sure how he'd done that many so quickly, but then again, he'd had a lot of practice.

"Take a break," I told him. "Go shower, get something to eat, and put your feet up. We'll take over from here." Thanks to Hades, there weren't that many bodies left. Most had fallen into the earth when he came out of it. And since we didn't know which body belonged in which grave, we could simply dig them all up in a straight line. We'd be finished by lunchtime.

Tony stuck his shovel in the fresh dirt and wiped his brow. "Sounds good to me. Any of Arianna's pancakes left?"

"Yeah, I stopped Randy from polishing them all off."

"Thanks."

"No, thank you. It was my mess, and you've been—" I didn't know what to say. How did you apologize for raising an entire cemetery of corpses, drawing Hades' attention, and nearly killing every Ophi in existence?

Tony put his hand on my shoulder. "No one blames you, Jodi. Whatever is going on here isn't your fault."

"Of course it is. It's my powers that are screwing things up, and I have no idea how to fix it."

"We'll figure it out. I'm going to cancel lessons this afternoon. I want to do some research and make a few phone calls. Someone has to have some idea what's happening to you. I can't believe you're the first Ophi this sort of thing has happened to."

Why not? I was the only Ophi who was part human—or at least I used to be. The only Ophi who could raise our own kind without turning them into zombies. The only Ophi who was answering to Hades. Being the only anything was nothing new to me.

Tony must have taken my silence as a protest. "I mean, if that's okay with you. You're in charge, and if you don't want me cancelling lessons, I can do my research this evening after dinner."

"No. Cancelling lessons is a good idea. We'll be digging graves and burying corpses all morning. I could use the afternoon to train these guys some more."

Tony nodded. "We'll figure this out. I promise."

"Thanks, Tony."

He gave me a small smile before walking away. Everyone else was busy digging already, so I grabbed a shovel and got to work helping Alex.

"He's right, you know." Alex didn't look at me. He was focused on shoveling, and his tone was completely serious. "You have to stop blaming yourself. It's not like you know what's wrong with your powers."

Sure. Except I *did* know what was wrong with them. I was conflicted. I liked Chase. As much as I wished I didn't, I liked Chase. I didn't know how long I could keep lying, especially to Alex.

He stopped digging and looked at me. "Hey, you don't think it's us, do you?"

"What do you mean?" Did he know something?

"Well," he stepped closer and lowered his voice, "your powers keep going all crazy when we're together or you're thinking about me."

I smiled at him. "No, I don't think we're the problem. You're the only thing in my life that's right."

He wrapped one arm around my waist and pulled me to him. He kissed me as if we were the only two people in the cemetery, and in that moment, we were. I forgot about the others. This was how I wanted things to be. Why couldn't it be this simple?

"Seriously you two." Randy flung dirt at us.

"Hey!" I jumped back, trying to avoid the dirt.

"Hey, yourself. If you two don't stop making out in front of me, I'm going to throw myself in this open grave just so I don't have to see it anymore."

"Funny." I rolled my eyes.

Leticia leaned on her shovel and stared at Chase. "I think it's romantic the way they can't keep their hands off each other, don't you?" But Chase wasn't paying any attention to Leticia. His eyes were fixed on me.

Alex glared at him. "You got a problem, Chase?"

"I was just thinking."

"About what?" Leticia was drooling a little.

"About how every time I see these two it's something different. One minute they're kissing, and the next minute they're fighting. I'm waiting for their relationship to implode."

"That's it!" Alex lunged at Chase, and the two fell backward into an open grave.

"Alex!" I yelled.

"Chase, are you okay?" Leticia called down into the grave.

Luckily, it wasn't deep, so they didn't fall far. But there wasn't a lot of wiggle room, and since they were intent on beating on each other, dirt was spilling from the sides of the grave right on top of them.

"Stop!" My blood was going crazy. My skin rippled, and my heart raced. Sweat poured down my face. I wanted it to stop. I begged my blood to stop mixing, but it wouldn't.

Leticia screamed. "Guys! Stop! It's Jodi. Something's happening to her!"

Alex and Chase climbed out of the grave, clawing at each other in the process. Chase reached me first, and he placed his hand in mine.

"Don't touch her!" Alex yelled, ripping Chase's hand away from me. "Every time you touch her, you almost kill her."

Randy grabbed Chase's arm before he could take a swing at Alex. "He's right, man. The last thing Jodi needs is an extra power boost from you right now."

"Jodi, look at me." Alex was holding my face in his hands. "Focus on me. Don't worry about him or anyone else. Look at me."

My body was on fire, and my blood wouldn't stop bubbling. If I didn't stop this soon, the power was going to consume me.

"Oh, God!" Leticia yelled. She pointed toward the school.

Alex let go of my face, and we both turned to see what had Leticia so scared. The corpses from my room were walking toward us. My blood had called them to me.

"Well, at least we don't have to carry them all out here," Chase said.

Alex squeezed his fists and turned toward Chase. "Alex." I reached for him, but he wasn't going to listen to reason. He was determined to pound on Chase. I did the only thing I knew would make him stop. I pretended to faint. I let myself collapse on the ground, which, considering how much energy my body was using to summon all those corpses, was more than easy to do.

In seconds, Alex was at my side, cradling my head in his lap. I opened my eyes and tried to look as helpless as I could. I needed him to feel bad enough for me that he'd forget about Chase. "I need your help," I said in a soft voice.

"Anything."

"Lure the corpses into the graves. I'll release them after they're in the ground."

"Are you strong enough? I could have Leticia get Tony and Arianna."

Damn. Playing the damsel in distress wasn't the easiest thing to do. Yes, I was tired, but I was still strong enough to release the souls. Hell, I was silently commanding them all to obey the others right now, knowing the others couldn't control them on their own.

I nodded. "I think I can do it."

Alex stood up and motioned to Randy. "Come on. We have to get them in the graves."

Randy stepped back. "Me? You want me to control them? I didn't summon them. You know I can't do that."

"I can." Chase walked past Alex and closer to the zombies. They were almost to us now. He stopped for a moment and stood absolutely still, tapping into his power. "Get in an open grave." He repeated the instructions several times. I was right. Chase did have more power than the average underage Ophi.

Alex followed Chase's lead. Well, almost. When he got to the last zombie, he stepped close and whispered something the rest of us couldn't hear. I watched in horror as the zombie approached Chase from the side and swung at his head. Chase turned as the zombie's fist connected with his cheek. He went down hard.

"Chase!" This time Leticia wasn't the only one worried about Chase. I was at his side, too. Alex stared at me, no doubt wondering where my sudden burst of energy had come from. He knew I'd been faking. He knew I'd tricked him. Worse, he knew that I definitely did have some sort of feelings for Chase. Alex grabbed the zombie by the arm and flung him into the last open grave.

"Make sure Chase is okay," I told Leticia, but she was practically cowering behind Chase now.

Everyone stared at Alex. His jaw was clenched, and his nostrils flared. He didn't look like the same guy who'd had my back since I came here.

"Alex, you need to get a hold of yourself."

"Don't tell me what I need, Jodi. What I need is—" He stopped, meeting each pair of eyes on him. "Screw this." He headed for the house.

"Um, Jodi," Randy said. "The zombies aren't exactly staying in their graves."

I wanted to go after Alex, but I couldn't leave the others to deal with the zombies. I watched Alex for another second before I turned to the graves and started commanding my blood to mix. I was instantly lightheaded. I'd spent most of my energy already. Chase came up next to me and started releasing the souls, too. I was thankful for that, and I was especially thankful that he was doing it on his own instead of trying to transfer his power to me.

Once all the souls were back where they were supposed to be, I headed inside for a much needed visit to Medusa, but when I opened the front door, I saw Alex was already holding Medusa's right hand. His brow was furrowed, and he looked like he was concentrating on something. Normally holding Medusa's right hand was a power rush, almost euphoric. So, why did Alex look so strained?

I waited for him to release her hand before I spoke. "Alex." My voice was soft and almost pleading.

He met my eyes without saying a word.

"I'm sorry I tricked you out there. I didn't know what else to do to make you stop attacking Chase."

"Do you really want a boyfriend you have to protect?" His words were filled with anger.

"What are you talking about? *You're* my boyfriend."

"Are you sure about that?"

"Are you breaking up with me?" The words came out slowly and painfully.

"Do you want to break up?"

"Alex, I don't want to play games. Please, just give me a straight answer." I stepped toward him, wanting to be as close as possible.

"Then stop playing games, Jodi. You're the one who's doing this. Not me. You've changed since Chase got here. You're different, and I'm not sure I like it."

I felt like someone was squeezing my insides. Alex didn't like me? Was that what he was saying? "Alex, I love you."

"What about Chase?"

"What about him?"

"Do you love him?"

"No!" I didn't. I barely knew him.

"Then what is it? Why does he make you act so differently? Why do you stick up for him?"

"I—" How could I explain what was happening to me without destroying my relationship with Alex?

"You like him." Alex turned away.

I couldn't let him leave like this. It would be the end of us. "Wait! Please, let me explain. It's not what you think."

He stopped but didn't turn toward me, so I went to him. I was going to have to be the one to hold onto what we had. "Alex, ever since Chase contacted me and said he was coming, something changed in me. In my blood. It's like my blood recognized the power in his blood. But that's it. I don't like him. I promise. To be honest, he scares me a little. The power he has—that he transfers to me—scares me. But I know I have to figure out how to use it if I'm going to save the Ophi."

Alex stared at me with his arms crossed, guarding his emotions. "So, you aren't attracted to him? You don't think he's hot, like Leticia does?"

I felt the blood rush to my cheeks, and I knew I was turning red. Not good. I couldn't lie my way out of this. "He's not ugly." It was the closest to the truth I could get. "But that doesn't matter. I'm sure you find other girls attractive. It doesn't mean anything." I stepped closer and put my hands on his forearms, uncrossing his arms. "It doesn't change how we feel about each other."

"Are you sure about that?"

I stepped into him, resting my face on his chest. "Yes. You are the only Ophi I want."

He wrapped his arms around me and squeezed tight. "You have to set Chase straight. I'm not putting up with his comments. I don't like the way he looks at you or the way he openly shows his feelings for you. You can't expect me to sit back and take that."

I leaned my head back so I could look at him. "I know. I'll talk to him. Tell him that I'm not interested and he needs to stop or—"

"Or what?"

"I'll ask him to leave." Why was that so hard for me to say? I had Alex. He was perfect for me. Yet, I didn't want Chase to leave. As much as he scared me and caused trouble for me and Alex, there was a part of me that wanted Chase here. God, what was wrong with me?

Alex smiled. "That's what I was hoping you'd say." He leaned down and kissed me. The kiss was so passionate I felt my legs shake. Good thing Alex was still holding me tight. We only stopped when the front door swung opened and Leticia rushed in, bumping right into us.

"Sorry," she said.

Alex looked annoyed by the interruption, but I said, "It's okay. Is something wrong? You look like you're in a hurry."

"Jodi." Leticia's voice shook. "We finished burying the bodies, but there's something you should know."

"What is it?" I wasn't sure I could take any more bad news right now.

Leticia lowered her head and stared at her feet. "We lost a lot of corpses to Hades."

"Yes, I know." Why wouldn't she spit it out already? How bad was the news?

"Well, we think one of the bodies he took was…" She stopped and looked at me.

"Leticia, you're killing me here."

"Your dad."

I tried to swallow, but there was a lump in my throat the size of a baseball. How hadn't I noticed my dad's body was gone? I'd seen his corpse before, and I'd never forget it. Even though I'd only met him that one time in the cemetery, when Victoria raised him to torture me, I'd recognize him anywhere. I'd been too preoccupied with all the drama of Chase and Alex, and now my dad's body was in the underworld with Hades. Who knew what torture Hades was putting his soul through? And now that Hades had his body too, I couldn't raise him. I'd never see him again.

Chapter 11

Since I'd come to the school, I'd had almost no contact with my mom. I'd emailed her once to tell her I wasn't coming home but that I was okay. I deleted the email account immediately after I sent the message, because I knew if I got any emails back from her—which I definitely would have—I would've broken down and called her. I couldn't let myself do that. This whole situation was too crazy to ask her to understand. She thought my dad had been some teenage jerk who didn't want to take responsibility for getting his girlfriend pregnant. That was awful, but the truth would've been more painful to hear. How did you tell your mom that the guy she loved and had a child with wasn't really human? That he was a Gorgon necromancer who was killed by his own kind barely a month after their baby was born?

Except now, my mom was the woman whose boyfriend and daughter walked out on her. I'd destroyed her life and mine. I had no parents left. At least knowing my dad's body was nearby had given me a false sense of comfort. I'd never planned on raising him again, but I marked his grave and kept flowers on it. It was my way of letting him know I didn't blame him for what had happened. Now, he was lost to me too. Hades had taken the one last piece of family I had.

I crumbled to the floor, sobbing uncontrollably. Alex bent down and wrapped his arms around me. He rocked me like a baby and whispered in my ear, but nothing registered. I was tuned out. All I could do was cry because the emotions inside of me were spilling over. Finally, the tears stopped coming. Alex took my head in his hands and raised it so I was looking at him.

"Hey, we'll find a way to get him back, okay? I'll strike a deal with Hades myself if I have to. I won't let him take your dad away from you."

"He already has, and it's my fault. Everything is my fault."

He shook his head. "No. Don't say that. You never asked for this to happen."

"I might not have asked for any of this to happen, but I gave in to it. No, I didn't just give in to it. I became the freaking leader of the Ophi. I ruined my mom's life, and I sentenced my father to be Hades' slave in the underworld." Somehow, I managed to find more tears, and they spilled over my cheeks.

"Jodi, I'm so sorry. I'm the one who came to get you. I'm the one who brought you here."

I wiped my face and looked at him. "If you hadn't come for me, my mother would be dead. Don't you dare blame yourself. I killed her. You saved her. I owe you everything for that."

He kissed my cheek and picked me up off the floor. Leticia stood there, trying not to stare at us. "Um, I'm going to wash up before lunch. I'm sorry, Jodi. About everything."

I nodded. "Thanks, Leticia."

The front door opened, and Chase and Randy walked in.

"Jodi, are you okay?" Chase asked.

Alex put his arm around me and started walking me toward the stairs. "She'll be fine. I'll take care of her."

I didn't even fight him. I couldn't handle Chase right now. I didn't have the energy. Alex waited in my room while I washed my face and tried to make myself look somewhat normal. The puffiness under my eyes wouldn't go away, but at least I'd stopped crying. I took two aspirin for my headache, and several deep breaths, before I walked back to my room.

"All set?" Alex asked, getting up from the bed.

"I guess. Thanks for taking care of me."

He reached for my hand. "Always."

Everyone was already eating when we got to the dining room. I stopped in the doorway. I wasn't the least bit hungry, and I didn't feel like sitting through a meal with everyone talking about Hades, my dad, and my out-of-control powers.

"What is it?" Alex asked.

"You know, I think I need some fresh air," I said. "I'm not really in the mood to eat. I'd rather go for a walk."

"I'll go with you." His stomach growled in protest.

I smiled and patted his stomach. "No, go eat. I'll be fine. I can use the time alone to clear my head."

"Are you sure? I could grab a sandwich to bring with me."

"I'm sure. Sit and relax. We have a long afternoon of training ahead of us. I want to look like we actually know what we're doing when the others arrive tomorrow. The last thing I need is for them to turn right around and go back to Serpentarius."

"Okay." He lightly kissed my lips. "I have my cell, so call me if you get lonely or if you just can't stand being away from me anymore."

I smiled. That was my Alex, cocky in a cute way.

"See you later." Chase caught my eye before I left, but I quickly turned away. No need to invite trouble. I walked down the hall and past the Medusa statue. Part of me wanted to stop and talk to her. Get her advice about my dad and Hades, but I really did want to clear my head and forget about everything for a while. I decided I'd talk to her later.

The air had a slight chill to it, the way I liked it. I didn't want to go anywhere near the cemetery or my dad's empty grave, so I headed around back and went into the woods. When I was younger, I loved walking in the woods, but I hadn't really done it since I came into my powers. I hadn't done a lot of things I loved to do before I stopped being human. When I'd drunk Medusa's blood, I thought I was doing the right thing. Saving the Ophi and becoming what I was meant to be. Now… well, I wasn't so sure.

I missed being human. I missed my best friend Melodie, my mom, Matt. I tried not to think about Matt. Poor Matt, who died for kissing me. Poor Matt, who I brought back as a zombie. He was my biggest regret. Alex had been able to save my mom. He'd gotten to her before I could bring her back wrong. But Matt—Alex hadn't been in time to save him from me.

Sometimes, I wondered what my life would have been like if I hadn't come into my powers. If I'd stayed human. I'd probably be in the cafeteria with Matt and Melodie complaining about how boring life was. There was nothing I wouldn't do for a little boring in my life now.

I completely lost track of time, and before I knew it I was out of the woods and on a road. I had no idea how far I'd walked or how long I'd been out here. I reached for the cell in my back pocket. 1:10. I'd walked for over an hour. Everyone was probably wondering where I was. I saw I had a missed call from Alex. I forgot I'd silenced my phone. I dialed him back as a car came down the road. A car I'd know anywhere. Melodie's car!

Without even thinking, I waved my arms in the air. The car went past me, but the brake lights came on and it slowed to a stop.

I heard a faint voice and remembered I'd called Alex. I put the phone up to my ear. "Jodi? Are you there? Where are you?"

"I have to call you back." I ended the call as Melodie stepped out of the car. I smiled. Seeing her was like seeing a room full of presents on Christmas morning. I wanted to rush up to her and give her the biggest hug, but I felt the wetness on my cheeks and stopped.

"Oh, my God! Jodi! It *is* you!" Melodie's shrieky voice sounded amazing. Like home. She rushed over to me, but I backed away. I couldn't let her touch me, not while I was crying.

"Stay back, Mel. Please." I held my hands in front of me to stop her.

"What? Why? Jodi, what's wrong? Are you hurt? Where have you been? Your mom's been worried sick. We all have."

"I know. I'm sorry."

"You just left. You didn't say a word to anyone. Your mom said you emailed her, but when she tried to email you back, she got a message saying the account had been deleted."

I nodded and continued to back up. Melodie wouldn't stop coming toward me. "Please, Mel. You have to stay away from me. Don't come any closer, okay? Please. If anything happened to you, I'd—"

"What are you talking about? You're acting crazy."

"Look, can we go somewhere and talk? Your car, maybe?"

"Do you need a ride home?"

Home. There was nowhere I'd rather go, but I couldn't. If I went back, I wouldn't be able to leave again.

"No. I want to park somewhere and talk. Can we do that?"

Melodie laughed, breaking the tension. "I don't usually park with girls, but hey, why not?"

I laughed. Good old Melodie. I hadn't realized how much I'd missed her. We walked to the car, and I got in the back passenger seat, as far from Melodie as possible.

"What do I look like, a cab driver? Get in the front."

"No, I can't. Mel, trust me, okay?"

"Trust you? You haven't explained a single thing to me, and you're asking me to trust you?"

"I know, but you're my best friend."

"Am I? 'Cause last time I checked, you skipped town without telling me, your best friend."

I didn't have a response to that. I wasn't even sure why I was in the car with her or why I'd flagged her down. This was all so stupid of me.

Melodie drove down the road and turned into a park. I looked out the window and did a double take. "This is Emory Park."

"Yeah." Melodie cut the engine and turned to look at me. She wrinkled her forehead. "What's with you? You're acting like you don't know where you are."

I thought I didn't. When Alex had taken me to the school, we'd driven for hours. He'd encouraged me to take a nap because the drive was going to take so long and it was late. Yet here I was, only a little over an hour's walk from the school, and I was in my hometown. How was this possible?

"He lied to me." I got out of the car and looked around.

Melodie got out and walked over to me. "Jodi, what's going on? Please, talk to me. Or at least let me take you home."

"No. I can't go home."

"Why not? Where have you been, anyway?"

I shook my head. This was all so unbelievable. Alex had lied. He'd tricked me. I could understand not telling me in the beginning, when it was the hardest to be away from home and before he really got to know me. But why hadn't he told me the truth after we got together?

"I can't believe he did this to me!" I was angry. Really angry. I'd been feeling so bad about the whole Chase situation, which I didn't really have much control over. Now that I knew Alex had lied to me, that he was still lying to me, I was furious.

"Who?" Melodie's eyes widened. "Oh, my God! You ran away with him, didn't you?" She grabbed my arm, but I yanked it away. "The strange guy from school? The one who was stalking you?"

I shook my head. I couldn't let her know the truth, or anything close to it. It was too dangerous. Especially now that I knew the school was so close to home. "No." I wracked my brain for a believable excuse. "It's my dad. I found my dad." Technically it wasn't a lie.

"Your dad? I didn't even think you knew who your dad was."

"I didn't, but I found him. It was something I had to do. I'm staying with him." The lies rolled off my tongue a little too easily. I hated this. I hated not being able to tell my best friend the truth about who I really was.

"I don't get it. Why would you just leave your mom?"

"Believe me, I didn't want to. I miss her so much. It's killing me that I'm not with her." My eyes burned with the threat of more tears. I had to keep them in. I breathed deeply and squeezed my eyes shut until I felt the tears subside.

"Do you know Mr. Quimby went to see her?" Melodie sat down on a bench. "He told her you were mentally unstable. I heard him. I went to your house and saw his car in the driveway. Your mom and Mr. Quimby were talking in the kitchen. I heard your name and had to know what they were saying, so I listened in through the back window."

"What else did he say?" I sat down at a wooden table, no longer able to stand.

"He said he'd been teaching for a while and had seen this sort of thing before. Kids taking off because they weren't thinking clearly. He said that's what probably happened with you."

"I'm not crazy. Please, tell my mom I'm not crazy." I reached for her hand but stopped myself. Physical contact was too risky.

"Tell her yourself. She's really hurting right now. Let her know you found your dad. Even if you want to live with him—though I don't know why you'd do that—you have to at least tell her. She deserves that."

"I can't. I can't see her. It's too hard. Please, Mel, just tell her I'm staying with my dad because I need to get to know him. Tell her I'm okay and that I love her." I stood up. I couldn't stay any longer. This had been a mistake. A huge mistake. I ran.

"Jodi!" Melodie's footsteps pounded the ground behind me.

She wasn't going to let me go, and I'd never outrun her if she got in her car. I made a split-second decision. I ran around the car and got in the driver's seat, locking the doors so she couldn't jump in. I turned the key, which was still in the ignition, and floored the gas. The tires screeched as I pulled a U-turn in the middle of the road. Melodie ran after me, screaming my name. I rolled down the window just enough to yell out, "I'm sorry, Mel!"

I sped away, unable to believe what I'd done. I stole my best friend's car. I left her stranded. Her cell and purse were lying on the passenger seat. Crap! She couldn't even call someone to pick her up. She was going to have to walk home. Some best friend I was. Now she was definitely going to think I'd lost my mind. Like it wasn't bad enough I'd killed the one guy she had feelings for. Sure, Matt had been my almost boyfriend, but Melodie was the one in love with him. I'd broken her heart and stolen her car. Yeah, I was best friend of the year.

I thought about turning around and throwing her purse and cell out the window. It was the least I could do for her now, but at this point did it really matter? She was going to hate me either way, and I deserved it. No, I couldn't turn back. Seeing Mel had been a mistake, and I wasn't going to make that mistake twice. I kept driving.

I didn't really know the way back to the school. I'd walked through the woods, not taken the roads. I did my best to keep heading in the direction I thought the school was in. Turns out none of the roads actually led to the school. That was when I remembered the road to the school wasn't really a road. It was a beat-up old driveway that looked more like an overgrown trail. I slowed down and scanned the woods for any clearings big enough to fit a car through. Nothing. Why was this place so difficult to find? Maybe because all the residents were deadly to humans? That was a pretty good reason.

I spotted an area barely big enough for a car and pulled off the road. The car bounced and jostled more than a car should. I felt like I was rocketing off the ground every few feet. This couldn't be right. The road Alex had taken was bumpy, but it wasn't this bad. I didn't have my seatbelt on. I'd been in too much of a hurry to get out of there before Melodie could stop me, and now I was being thrown around the front seat like a bag of groceries. I tried to hit the brakes, but with all the bouncing around, I wound up slamming on the accelerator instead. I turned the steering wheel hard to the left, trying to follow what I thought was a path, but a huge tree blocked my way. I slammed on the brakes, making the tires skid on the dirt and grass. I screamed as the car slammed into the tree. I lurched forward, and the last thing I felt was my forehead smack against the steering wheel.

Chapter 12

The sound of a voice made my eyelids flutter opened. My head rested on the steering wheel. I raised it slightly, afraid to move too much before I knew how badly I was hurt. Blood was smeared across the steering wheel and dashboard. My blood. I wasn't dead, but I was definitely banged up.

"Are you all right?"

I looked to my left. A man, a hiker judging by his clothes and walking stick, was leaning in the broken window. He reached for me.

"Stay back!" I yelled. He was human, and my poisonous Gorgon blood was everywhere.

"I'm here to help you. Try to relax. I promise I won't hurt you."

That wasn't what I was afraid of. He had no idea how dangerous I was to him.

"Please." I held a bloody hand up to keep him back. I quickly lowered it before I came in contact with him. "You don't understand. You can't touch me. It isn't safe."

"I know you're not supposed to move an unconscious person in case they injured their neck or spine, but you seem like you're moving okay, so why don't you let me help you out of the car?" He pointed to the front end. "I don't like the way the hood is smoking. I don't know much about cars, but I'm not willing to risk this thing catching fire with you inside it."

My eyes shot to the smoke pouring out of the hood. It didn't look good. I had to move. Fast. Still, I couldn't let this guy touch me.

"Okay, I'm going to get out, but you have to back up. I mean it. Don't touch me. No matter what." I stared him in the eyes, keeping my face serious. He had to listen to me.

"Whatever you say, but I promise I won't hurt you. I only want to help."

I believed him. He seemed nice enough, and I wasn't really scared for my safety. If he turned out to be a serial killer on the run, I'd just bleed on him. I waited for him to step away from the car, and I reached for the door. I pulled on the handle, but it was jammed.

"It won't open." I tugged harder.

"Here, let me try." I backed up in the seat as he reached for the door. "It's locked. I have to reach in and open it from the inside."

"No!" I leaned farther toward the passenger seat as his arm came into the car. "Stop! Please, stop!"

"Listen, I'm only opening the door. I won't touch you." He fumbled with the door handle. "Is there a trick to this? Has it ever gotten stuck like this before?"

How would I know? I'd been in the car numerous times, but that was months ago. Melodie could've been having problems with it.

I shook my head. A sizzling sound came from the hood of the car and a puff of smoke burst into the air. "Ah!" I couldn't help screaming. The car was going to go up in flames, and I was locked inside it.

"Try the passenger door." His voice was steady, but the terror in his eyes showed his true feelings.

I reached over and opened the door—right into a tree. "There's not enough room to squeeze out."

"Then, you're going to have to come out through the window. I'll help you."

"No! I mean, I can do it myself."

"Do you have any idea how banged up you are? You might get dizzy the second you lean out this window, and you're running out of time."

Something crackled under the hood. He was right. I couldn't stay here any longer.

"Back up again. I'm doing this on my own."

He started to protest, but I cut him off. "Look, if you don't back up, this car is going to explode with me inside it. Do you really want that on your conscience?"

He backed up.

I twisted, bringing my legs up onto the seat. I pulled my sleeves down over my hands to protect myself from the jagged glass that was still attached to the bottom of the window. I went out headfirst. It was a dumb idea since it meant I was definitely going to fall on the ground, but the thought of keeping my head inside a car that was about to go up in flames was too much to handle. The crackling got louder. I leaned forward, committing to face-planting, but my jeans got caught on the broken window.

"Ah!" I yelled as the glass tore into my skin.

The guy rushed forward and lifted my torso. I felt the glass come out of my leg and the warm blood pour onto his hands.

"No!" I cried.

His eyes rolled back in his head as my blood poisoned him. Choking, he fell to the ground. I went with him, landing half on top of his lifeless body.

"Jodi!" Alex's voice shot through the air. He ran to me as I lifted myself off the hiker's body. "Oh, my God, Jodi!" Alex took one look at the car and scooped me into his arms. "We have to get out of here." He went as fast as he could, carrying my weight, but we were barely twenty feet away when the car burst into flames. We dropped to the ground, and Alex shielded me from the car parts that flew through the air.

I peeked around his arms and found the hiker on the ground. His clothes were on fire. I turned away, as bile rose up from my stomach. He'd only wanted to help me, and now he was dead. Dead because of me and my blood. I'd poisoned him, and the fire from the car I'd stolen and crashed into a tree was burning his body so I couldn't even raise him. I couldn't fight it. I threw up until my stomach and chest ached. Alex held my hair and rubbed my back. When I was finished, I sat up and wiped my mouth on my sleeve. There was a time when I would've worried about looking unladylike, but I wasn't a lady. I was a monster. A poisonous monster who had killed again.

Alex stood up. "Someone's going to see the smoke and call the cops. We have to get out of here."

Cops. Maybe I needed to be locked up. I was a killer. I should've been put away where I couldn't hurt anyone. It's not like I was helping the Ophi anymore either, so what good was I to anybody?

"Let them come. Let them take me away."

Alex grabbed both of my arms and yanked me to my feet. I winced from all the cuts and bruises I'd gotten in the accident. "Great idea. Let the cops touch you while you're covered in your own blood. How many more do you want to die?"

He was the other Alex again. The one who could turn off his emotions and act stone cold. The one that reminded me so much of his parents. Still, what he said was true. I'd kill every human who came near me right now. I couldn't stay. I had to go back to the school.

"Let's go." I shook his hands from my arms and walked off in the direction Alex had come from.

"It's this way." He pointed to the right. "I've been out here for hours searching for you. I wasn't coming from the school when I found you."

I walked past him, glaring at the face I thought I knew so well. "Funny thing about the school," I said. "It's not far from my home."

"The school is your home."

He was avoiding the real issue here.

"You lied to me. You completely took me for a fool. You drove me around for hours, in the dark, when I was too tired to stay awake and see where we really were. You encouraged me to go to sleep." I stopped walking and turned around to face him. "How far did you drive in the wrong direction just to throw me off?"

"I did what I had to do."

"No. You did what you were *told* to do."

He stepped past me, continuing to walk back to the school. "You're right. I did what I was told to do. For your own good. I had to get you here. To convince you to give up your old life." He stopped when he realized I wasn't following him. He stormed back over to me. "How hard would it have been for you to stay away from your mom if you knew she wasn't far away?" His face was bright red, and his voice was shaking with anger. "It took killing her to get you to come with me. Tell me you wouldn't have checked on her. Tell me you wouldn't have made contact with her. Spied on her. Something! Until you did something stupid again and killed her for the second time!"

"You don't get to be angry!" I shouted back at him. "You don't get to decide what's best for me. You lied to me. Even after everything we've been through together, you kept this from me. What does that say about us, Alex?"

"It says that I'm willing to do anything to protect you."

I didn't know how to respond to that. I believed he thought that was true and that made it okay in his mind, but it wasn't okay with me. I couldn't be okay with this. With him. Not right now.

"Take me back to the school. I don't want to talk about this anymore. I don't want think about what happened today."

"Jodi." His voice softened, but there was still anger in his eyes.

"No." I shook my head. "I'm done for now."

He looked at me, but I turned away. I was hurt. Betrayed. Even if he didn't see it that way, it was how I felt. He led us back to the school, and without a word I went up to my room and locked the door behind me. I heard Leticia in the hallway. She knocked and called my name, but I didn't answer. I buried my head in my pillow and cried. I didn't even care that I was bleeding all over the covers. I cried for the hiker who hadn't deserved to die for trying to help a girl in trouble. Even if the girl was Gorgon. I cried for Melodie who was carless, best-friendless, and stranded at the park. I cried for my mom, who was undoubtedly going out of her mind, not knowing her lost daughter was only one town over. And I cried for Alex and me. Our relationship was deteriorating faster than it had begun.

I skipped dinner to change the sheets on my bed and take a long hot shower. So long, I ran out of hot water. Even the warm water felt good on my aching body. I washed out all my cuts, noticing they weren't as bad as I'd thought. I wrapped a towel around me and sat on the edge of the tub, letting the steam wash over me. I couldn't help thinking my life had become a living hell. I had dead bodies stalking me in my sleep. Death was everywhere I turned, mostly because I was causing it. I thought about turning myself over to Hades. I didn't have any fight left in me. At least in the underworld, I wouldn't be able to hurt the living anymore.

Finally, the steam evaporated, and I started to shiver in my towel. I got up and went to my room, eager to get dressed and warm up, but the second I stepped into my room, I jumped back in shock. Chase was standing next to my dresser, holding Medusa's locket, which had been buried in my top drawer since I'd drunk the blood inside the bloodstone.

"What the hell are you doing here?" I stormed over to him, holding my towel up in one hand and reaching for the locket with the other. "And what are you doing going through my stuff?"

He wrapped his fingers around the locket before I could grab it.

"Do you mind? That belongs to me. Medusa made it appear to me when I came to this school."

"I know. I heard the story. Uncle Mason kept up with everything that went on here. He still does."

I narrowed my eyes at him. "You mean, *you're* keeping him informed."

"You should be happy I am. If it wasn't for me, he and the others from Serpentarius wouldn't be coming in the morning."

I held my hand out. "My locket."

"Turn around." He held the locket up by the chain. "I'll put it on you."

"It's broken. I broke the clasp when I yanked the locket from Victoria's neck. That's why it's been sitting in my dresser drawer. That, and the locket doesn't hold Medusa's blood anymore."

"No, it doesn't. You do." He eyed me like I was the last piece of devil's food cake in a room of starving people. I had no doubt he wanted my blood. He held the locket out to me, showing me the clasp. "I fixed it."

"Oh. Well, thanks, I guess."

"Turn around."

I didn't want to let him put the locket on me. I didn't want him touching me at all. Things always got complicated when Chase touched me. But, he obviously wasn't going to leave until I let him put the locket on me, so I turned around.

He slipped it over my head and fastened the clasp. "There. I know it doesn't have Medusa's blood anymore, but it seems to me you should still wear it."

I faced him, reaching my fingers up to touch the empty bloodstone. "I guess you're right."

"In fact, you should consider putting some of your blood in the stone."

"What? Why? I'm not Medusa."

"I know, but you are the most powerful Gorgon, like she once was."

"Yeah, and then I'd have to worry about some power-crazed Ophi, like Victoria, stealing the locket to tap into my powers. No, thank you. I'll keep my blood in my veins."

He shrugged. "That's fine. It was just a thought."

"Don't think I've forgotten you somehow broke into my room and went through my stuff. Care to explain?"

"I came looking for you. Leticia said she saw you come home but you wouldn't let her in here. She said you were pretty banged up. I wanted to make sure you weren't going to bleed to death."

"How did you get in? I locked the door."

He smiled. "I found a set of keys in the bedroom across the hall from yours."

"Why were you in Abby's old room?" I knew she had keys to my room. Unfortunately, she'd used them after I moved in.

"I was exploring. Call it boredom. Things weren't exactly exciting without you around." He looked down at me, and I realized I was still only in a towel.

I opened a dresser drawer and pulled out a pair of yoga pants and a tank top. "I'll be right back. Then, you can tell me what made you think you had the right to use those keys to get into my locked room."

Someone knocked on the door.

"I'll get that."

"It's probably Leticia." I headed back to the bathroom.

"What the hell?" Alex said when Chase opened the door.

I turned as Alex pushed his way into the room. Chase smirked when Alex's eyes fell on me.

I looked down at my towel and the clothes in my hand. This didn't look good at all. Especially after the fight we'd had in the woods.

"Alex, it's not what you think. I came out of the shower and Chase was in my room. I didn't know he was here."

Alex narrowed his eyes, his gaze falling on my neck. "You just got out of the shower wearing Medusa's locket?"

"No, I—I mean, Chase—"

"Yeah, I think I can piece this together myself." He turned toward the door.

"Alex, wait."

He paused, and for a split second I thought he was actually going to hear me out. But he pulled his arm back and punched Chase square in the face. Chase stumbled backward. Alex looked at me. There was nothing soft or caring in his expression. He looked like a younger version of Troy. Then he stormed out of the room, slamming the door behind him.

Chapter 13

Chase rubbed his jaw. "I've got to hand it to him, I wasn't expecting that. I mean, I should've been, considering I'm in his girlfriend's bedroom and she's wearing nothing more than a towel." He eyed me and raised his eyebrows.

"Get out." I'd had enough of Chase. I'd had enough of this entire day.

"Until tomorrow then," he said before he left.

I sighed, long and hard. I dropped my towel and got dressed. I barely had my clothes on when someone knocked on the door.

Ugh! I stormed over to the door. "Seriously, Chase, leave me alone. I'm not in the mood to—" I flung the door open. Leticia was standing there looking confused.

"Not in the mood to what?"

"Sorry, I thought you were—never mind. What's up?"

"I wanted to check on you. I was in the hall when Alex went storming out and then Chase came out. Is everything okay?"

"Come in." I didn't really want to talk, but I needed some girl time. I'd had enough of the guys for one day.

Leticia came in and went right to my bed, plopping down like she was in her own room.

"Make yourself comfortable."

"Thanks." She'd totally missed my sarcasm. "So, I was wondering what you know about the others coming tomorrow. Are any of the guys our age? Are they cute? We need some cute guys around here who aren't totally obsessed with you."

"Excuse me?"

"Come on." Leticia picked up my pillow and hugged it to her chest. "You've got Alex, who is majorly hot, and then Chase shows up and he wants you too."

I wasn't exactly sure I had Alex anymore. After finding out he'd been keeping this huge secret from me, whether he'd had good intentions or not, I wasn't sure I could trust him. "It's a little more complicated than that."

"Yeah, well I wish my life was complicated by two guys fighting over me." She put the pillow down and started picking at a loose thread on my bedspread.

"No, you don't. Trust me. When two guys are fighting over you, you don't have either of them. They spend all their time competing with each other, and you're left out in the cold."

Leticia shrugged. "I don't know. I'd take just one guy looking at me the way either Alex or Chase looks at you. I mean, Alex is totally in love with you. That's obvious. And Chase couldn't be more attracted to you. The guy looks like he wants to devour you."

I knew Chase's stare all too well. It made me feel drawn to him, and completely scared at the same time. "You think that's a good thing?"

"Yeah. Have you seen any guy look at me that way?"

"What about Randy? I always kind of thought you two were—"

"God, no! He's like a brother, or cousin even. Definitely not the dating type. Besides, he doesn't seem all that interested in girls."

I sat down on the bed. "You mean he likes guys?"

She shrugged. "I don't know. He doesn't show any interest in anyone. He just wants to train and learn about being Ophi. When we both first got here, he talked to me all the time, but now, not so much. He probably thinks I'm a hopeless case. I can't seem to get control of my powers."

"You're not the only one." I tucked my leg up under me.

"Yeah, but your powers are awesome. Right from the start you could do stuff I still can't do. I'm starting to wonder if I'm even really Ophi.

I mean, I should be able to control the souls I raise by now. Maybe Randy's right. Maybe I am hopeless."

"No, you're not, and you don't know if he even thinks that." I wasn't sure how to tell her what I thought was really going on. I didn't want to bring up memories she might not be able to handle, but it was obvious her lack of control over her own blood was killing her. "Listen, Leticia, our powers are tied to our emotions."

"Yeah, I know. I take notes during Tony's lectures."

I nodded. Leticia was the perfect student when she was in a classroom. She had the theory part of being an Ophi down pat. But out in the cemetery, she couldn't figure out how to put all that knowledge to use.

"Think back to before Victoria raised the Ophi in Washington."

Her body instantly tensed, like I knew it would. I didn't back off. She needed to understand what was going on with her. I wasn't going to keep this from her the way Alex had kept the truth about where we were from me.

"You changed after Victoria brought your parents back. You're not the same person anymore. That's understandable, but it's also what's holding you back."

"You think I fell apart at the sight of my mangled parents." Her voice couldn't have been more shaky.

"I think you acted the way anyone would have in your situation."

"Oh, really?" She stood up. "Victoria brought Randy's father back. He was worse than my parents, and Randy's fine. A little angrier than he used to be, but his powers still work. And you. You saw your dead father for the first time ever. And—"

"My powers are messed up royally." I stood up so we were facing each other again. "I know how you feel, Leticia. I'm going through the same thing." Actually I was going through worse, but that wasn't going to get me anywhere with Leticia. "My powers are screwing up big time, and in ways that could hurt all of us. I'd rather not be able to use my powers than do what I'm doing."

"That's not true."

"No?" My voice was getting loud. I was starting to lose it. "I killed a man today. A human. He was trying to help me, and I killed him. And what's worse is, I couldn't even bring him back because the car I'd just stolen from my human former best friend burst into flames and took his body with it."

"Jodi." Leticia was staring at my hands. They were shaking in response to my blood, which was bubbling so much you could see it through my skin.

I shook my arms out and took several deep breaths. I couldn't do this again. I couldn't let my emotions cause someone else to get hurt, or raise another soul.

"I'm sorry. I had no idea." Leticia put her hand on my shoulder. "Can you stop it?" She was looking at my hands again.

"I'm trying. I'm really trying."

"Think good thoughts."

Good thoughts? I didn't even know what they were anymore. Nothing in my life was going right.

"I'm going to get Arianna," Leticia said. "She's good at calming people down. I'll be right back. Just try to make it stop, okay?"

I nodded, continuing to breathe deeply. Leticia ran from the room. There was only one way I knew how to calm down. A hot shower. Yes, I'd already taken one, but I didn't care. I went right to the bathroom and got in the shower, fully clothed. No time to undress. I could've raised half the graveyard by then. I let the water wash over me, and I felt my blood simmer and then return to normal.

"Jodi?" Arianna called from my room.

"In here." I poked my head out from behind the curtain.

"Leticia said you need some help."

"I'm okay now." I turned the water off and opened the curtain.

Arianna stared at me, soaking wet in my tank top and yoga pants. "Are you sure?"

"I know it looks strange, but really I'm fine. I promise. I'm going to put on dry clothes and go to sleep."

"Would you like some hot tea before bed? I boiled a pot of water. You could join me."

"Thanks, but no. I want to go to bed."

"Alex told me what happened."

I wrapped a towel around me before my wet clothes made me freeze. "Did you know? Did you know I was so close to my home? To my mom?"

She shook her head. "I didn't know where you were from. I knew we were close to Serpentarius, of course, but not that that meant anything to you in particular."

I believed her. Arianna was trustworthy.

"Don't be too hard on him. Alex did what he thought was best for you."

"It's not up to him to decide what's best for me."

"I know that, but put yourself in his shoes. What would you have done if the situation were reversed?"

"I would've told him."

"Are you sure? Or are you letting your emotions control you?"

My emotions. I wished I could turn them off completely. They were ruining everything. "He didn't think I could handle it. He thought I'd go back to my old life."

"Didn't you?" She stepped closer. "When you found out where you were, what did you do?"

I looked down at my feet. "I flagged down Melodie's car."

"Alex knows you pretty well." She put up her hands in surrender. "I'm not taking sides, but it seems like what you did was exactly what Alex was trying to protect you from." She walked over to me and kissed the top of my head. "You can't blame him for wanting to protect you from what happened this evening."

No, I couldn't. "Thanks, Arianna."

"Anytime, hon. Goodnight."

"Goodnight."

She left, and I stood there shivering in my wet clothes. I had to fix things with Alex. I couldn't let this destroy us. I put on pajamas and ran to his room without even combing my hair. I must've looked like a drowned rat, but I didn't care. I had to see him.

I knocked on his door, but there was no answer. "Alex?" Still nothing. I tried the knob. Locked. Where else would he be? I went to Randy's room and knocked.

"Hey, Jodi." He looked me over.

"Hey, I know I'm a mess. I'm looking for Alex. Do you know where he is?"

"He was heading out to the cemetery the last time I saw him."

"Why would he go there?" We'd already reburied all the bodies. Was he training on his own?

Randy shrugged.

"Thanks. See you in the morning." I turned and ran downstairs, heading right past the Medusa statue and out the front door. The cool air slammed into me. I was only in pajamas and my hair was soaking wet. My teeth chattered, and I shook from head to toe, but I kept going. The lights were on in the cemetery, and I saw Alex sitting up against the mausoleum. I jogged over to him.

He looked up at me and wrinkled his brow. "You're going to get sick coming out here like that."

"I don't care." I stood in front of him, shaking uncontrollably. "I understand why you didn't tell me where we were. You know me too well. You knew I'd go back home, that I'd find some way to at least glimpse my old life. You were right. What I did today was stupid. I hurt Melodie, and I killed an innocent man."

"Is that all you did wrong?" His stone cold eyes bored into me. He was angry, which meant he was still thinking something had happened between me and Chase.

"I didn't cheat on you, if that's what you're thinking. Chase was in my room when I got out of the shower. He had my locket in his hands. He had gone through my stuff. I was furious."

"So furious you let him stay and hang out." He pointed to the locket on my neck. "Did he put that on you?"

I lowered my eyes. "Yes, but it's not what you're thinking."

Alex stood up, chucking the rock he'd been holding. "I think you can't stay away from him. I think you give him certain liberties the rest of us don't have."

"What?" I couldn't believe this. Was he implying I let Chase—no, I couldn't even think it. "You can't be serious." I'd come here to make up, and Alex was accusing me of screwing around behind his back.

He stared at me and finally his expression softened. "Why do you let him in? Why can't you tell him to leave you alone? That you're with me? You said you were going to get him to back off."

"I'm trying, but he won't take the hint."

"He can't take a hint if you don't drop a hint."

"You're saying I'm leading him on?"

He didn't deny it.

Suddenly I wasn't freezing anymore. I was warm. No, I was hot. My blood was going crazy again. I had to stop this. I couldn't live in the shower. Alex moved closer to me and rubbed my arms. The blood in my veins rippled in waves.

"Jodi." He was scared for me. He wrapped his arms around me. "Am I doing this to you?"

"My emotions are doing it."

"But it's because of me, isn't it?"

Now it was my turn to not deny something. He pulled away and looked into my eyes. He was searching for something. An answer to fixing what was wrong with me. He pressed his lips to mine. I wasn't expecting it. We were in the middle of a fight, but here he was, kissing me. It took me a few seconds to respond, to wrap my arms around him and kiss him back. I felt my blood cooling. Alex was calming me. I continued to kiss him, long after I was back to normal. I was afraid to let go. Afraid we'd go back to arguing. All I wanted was to be in his arms.

Finally, he pulled away. "Are you better now?" He held onto my arms, feeling to make sure my blood wasn't surging through my veins anymore.

I nodded. "Thank you." Who knew what Alex had stopped me from doing this time? I was just grateful he had.

"I wasn't sure that was going to work. Lately, it's me kissing you that gets your blood all riled up. Why did it have the opposite effect now?"

Was he viewing this as a bad thing? "I don't want kissing you to make me lose control of my powers. It would mean I couldn't kiss you anymore." I hoped that would be enough to convince him this was a good sign.

"So, you still want to be able to kiss me? Only me?"

"Alex, I never kissed Chase. I swear."

"I want to believe you, but I've seen the way you get around him."

I took his hands in mine. "I came here because I wanted to tell you that I believe you. You were only trying to protect me by keeping the truth from me. It wasn't easy for me to accept. I still don't think it was your choice to make, but I know you wouldn't intentionally hurt me. I need you to do the same for me. To believe me and know I wouldn't hurt you like that."

"The question is, would you keep the truth from me to avoid hurting me?" He didn't take his hands away, but he wasn't giving in to me yet either.

I shook my head. "No. That's not what I'm doing. I'm telling you the truth."

He let go of my hands, and my heart sank, but then he reached for my face and pulled me to him. He kissed me hard, spinning me around so I was backed up against the mausoleum. He kissed me until I was completely breathless. When he pulled away, I noticed a light flashing on and off in one of the bedroom windows. Alex couldn't see it because he was only looking at me. I tried to keep my focus on him, but I couldn't. It was Chase's room. He was trying to get my attention. The light stayed on, and his silhouette was in the window. He was watching me. My body tensed.

Alex leaned into me and kissed me again. I kissed him back, but my eyes stayed glued to the window. Glued to Chase.

Chapter 14

Who was I? I didn't want to be the girl who thought about another guy while kissing her boyfriend. I forced my eyes away from Chase, which, surprisingly, was harder to do than pulling away from Alex.

"Sorry, I'm freezing." I wrapped my arms around myself.

"No problem. Let's get you inside." He put his arm over my shoulder and kept me close as we walked inside.

My eyes rose to Chase's window. His light was off, but I could sense he was still watching us. I laced my fingers through Alex's. He walked me to my room and kissed me goodnight.

"I'll come get you before breakfast." He gently kissed me again.

I smiled and nodded before going in my room and shutting the door. I leaned my back against it and slid to the ground. I was out of control. I shouldn't want anything more than Alex. He should've been enough. My teeth chattered again, so I got up and took my third hot shower of the day. Then I crawled into bed and pleaded with myself to only dream of Alex, but the second I closed my eyes, it was Chase's face I saw.

I tossed and turned all night, afraid to let myself sleep long enough to dream. I actually set my alarm and repeatedly hit snooze so I would keep waking up. It was pure torture, but it was better than waking up to a room full of corpses. Or should I say half-full. We were running low on corpses these days.

Alex met me before breakfast, like we'd planned.

"Hey, did you have trouble sleeping? You look beat."

"Thanks, that's just what a girl wants to hear from the guy she's dating."

He laughed and kissed my cheek. "You look beautiful, but I can tell you didn't sleep well."

"I appreciate the little white lie. I woke up a lot. My alarm kept going off." There, that wasn't a lie.

"Is it broken? I could look at it for you."

"No, that's okay. I think I fixed it." Yeah, I fixed it, when I finally shut it off.

We passed Chase in the hallway. "Sleep well?" he asked.

I wondered if he had any trouble sleeping. Probably not. "Fine." I looped my arm through Alex's as we walked past Chase.

Breakfast was louder than ever. No one could stop talking about the Ophi from Serpentarius coming today.

"What time are they getting here?"

"Are any of the guys cute?"

"Should I set some extra plates?"

"Whoa," I said. I didn't really know the details. Chase was the one who had convinced Mason and the others to come. I turned to Chase. "Tell us what you know."

He downed his orange juice and leaned back in his chair. "Okay, Uncle Mason said they'd be here some time today. He had to close things up there. I'm sure he worked late last night, so I'm guessing they won't be here before noon."

Arianna nodded and got up from the table. "I'll plan for a big lunch then. What are we taking about, number wise? I've made up all the beds to be on the safe side, but I need to know how much food to make and how many plates to set."

Chase counted on his fingers. "There's Uncle Mason, Aunt Carol, Thayer, Jared—"

"Jared?" I jumped at the name. I knew him. He was Matt's cousin.

"Yeah, he's a bouncer there."

"I know. I used to date his cousin."

Alex put his hand on my leg. He'd known Matt. They hadn't gotten along, and Alex had ended up having to kill Matt after I turned him into a bunny-eating zombie, but he knew I had cared about him. He knew it wasn't easy for me to talk about him. "You going to be okay with having him here?"

I nodded. "But I'm confused. How were they cousins? Matt is—was—human."

"They weren't really cousins." Chase surprised me. I didn't know he knew who Matt was.

"You knew Matt?"

"Yeah. I told you I used to hang out with humans a lot." The way he said it made it sound like he and I had had some big heart to heart. I knew it was intended to make Alex suspicious. "Jared introduced us. Their parents were good friends, and Matt always called Jared's father Uncle Thayer, so Matt assumed Jared was his cousin. They weren't really related."

I couldn't help feeling jealous that Chase and so many other Ophi could be around humans and keep their powers under control. I wanted to change the subject. "So who else is coming?"

Chase eyed me for a second before rattling off five more names.

"All nine of them." Arianna looked stressed. Sometimes I forgot that she used to work there and knew all of them. "I've got a lot of work to do this morning."

"We'll clean up after breakfast, and we can help with lunch, too," I said.

"Oh, no you won't. You all have more important things to be doing." She turned and winked at Randy. "I heard someone has almost gotten the hang of summoning multiple souls. Wouldn't it be impressive to show the other Ophi from Serpentarius when they arrive?"

Randy smiled and took another bite of his pancake. "That's why I'm eating a little extra this morning. I want to have enough energy to get it right this time."

I didn't have the heart to tell him summoning the dead had nothing to do with food. He was so excited.

"I'm ready to get out there when you are, Randy." I finished my coffee. I usually tried not to drink caffeine, but with the little sleep I got it was a necessity this morning.

"Just let me finish these first," he said with his mouth full.

"Are you two training alone?" Alex asked, keeping his voice low.

"I think that would be best. Randy is really close to getting this right. I want to help him as much as possible."

Alex nodded. "I'll take Leticia and work on controlling souls after they've been raised. She's getting better. I think in a few more days she'll have it."

"Take her to connect with Medusa before you go out. I think that will give her the confidence boost she needs."

"Good idea."

"Does this mean you and I aren't going to work on joining our powers?" Chase was standing right behind me. I hadn't even noticed he'd gotten up from his seat.

"Oh, um, yeah. Not today. Helping Randy is more important right now."

Chase shook his head. "I doubt that. Uncle Mason is going to be pissed if he gets here and finds out we lied about our combined powers."

I looked at Alex. He was trying to stay calm, I could tell. I also knew him well enough to know it was a struggle for him.

"We'll tell Mason that it's a power drain on me, and we had to slow down our training until my blood gets used to the connection." I pulled that out of nowhere, but I thought it sounded pretty good.

Chase glared at me for a second before walking out of the dining room.

"Guess that means I'm stuck with him this morning," Alex said.

"Sorry."

"No, it's fine. I'd rather have him where I can see him. I don't trust him, and I don't want him near you."

Randy shoved his last pancake into his mouth. "Ready."

I laughed. "Me, too."

Alex smiled at me. "See you out there in a few."

I nodded. "Good luck today, Leticia. I have a good feeling about this morning."

She smiled, but it was a timid smile. "Thanks. I'll do my best."

I took Randy out to the row of graves that still had bodies in them. I picked two at the end of the row. I sort of remembered them being a man and a woman, possibly a couple at one time.

"This will work," I said.

Randy took a deep breath and pulled a pocketknife out of his jeans. "Wish me luck."

"You don't need luck. You've got this." I was trying to be more encouraging, like a good teacher.

Chase came out of the school and watched us. Or should I say watched me? Randy was the picture of concentration. He cut the tip of his right index finger and dripped blood on each grave. I tried to focus on Randy, on helping him tune in to his own blood and raise both bodies in front of him, but it was hard to do with Chase staring at me. I hoped Alex and Leticia would get out here soon. As the corpses climbed to the surface, I saw Randy shake.

"Relax. Remain in control. You need to give two separate commands now. At the same time. One aloud and one in your mind. Your blood will carry the silent message to the soul. Got it?"

He nodded, but he swallowed hard, showing his fear.

"I'm right here if you get into trouble, but I know you can do this."

Before the bodies were fully out of the ground, Randy started spouting orders. "Stop! Don't come any closer. Stay where you are. Don't move until I tell you to." He got quiet, and I knew he was repeating the orders in his head, but the one corpse, the male, wasn't listening.

"Jodi!" Randy yelled.

"Stop him, Randy." I didn't want to take over. I didn't want another incident like with Leticia. If Randy thought I didn't have confidence in him, he might never master his powers. "You can do this. Concentrate."

He stumbled backward, falling over a headstone. He toppled to the ground, cringing like a baby. I'd never seen him so scared. It wasn't like him at all. The zombie stalked over to him.

"Stop him!" I yelled again. "You have the power, not him. Use it!"

But Randy didn't even try. He cowered on the ground while the zombie jumped on top of him. Randy's scream pierced the air as the zombie bit into his shoulder.

"Randy!" Leticia yelled, running toward us. Alex was right with her.

I was frozen, unable to believe what was happening a few feet in front of me. The zombie collapsed on Randy's chest. Alex rushed over and pulled the corpse off. I saw Randy's blood dripping down the side of the man's mouth. The poisoned blood had killed him instantly.

"It's okay," Alex said, leaning over Randy. "It's not that bad. Really."

But it *was* that bad. The zombie had bitten a chunk of flesh from Randy's shoulder. Randy was bleeding all over the ground. Alex pulled his shirt over his head and applied pressure to Randy's neck.

"He needs a doctor."

Chase stepped forward so he was next to me. "One of the Ophi who's coming here from Serpentarius used to be a doctor. An Ophi doctor. His name's Carson. He can help."

"What if Randy doesn't make it until then?" Leticia panicked. "He needs help now."

"Bring him to Medusa," I said. "She'll give him enough power to keep him alive. Then we'll bandage him up as best we can until help gets here."

"Arianna should be able to bandage him up," Alex said. "But we have to get him inside first."

Chase walked over and grabbed Randy's legs. "You got his upper body?"

Alex nodded.

Leticia and I walked with them, making sure they weren't going to accidentally bump Randy into anything on the way inside. Arianna was dusting the Medusa statue when we came in.

She gasped. "What happened?"

"He was bitten by a zombie," Alex said. "He needs a doctor, but in the meantime we have to stop the bleeding."

Randy fell in and out of consciousness.

"Bring him to the couch." Arianna waved the guys toward the living room.

"No," I said. "He needs to connect with Medusa. His power is draining out of him. He won't make it if we don't do something fast."

Arianna nodded. "Okay, but be careful not to overload him. He can't handle that in his weakened state."

Alex and Chase carried Randy to the statue, and I took his right hand, connecting it to Medusa's. Since I had to hold Randy's hand in place, it meant I was in on the connection, too.

Medusa appeared to me. "His injuries are too severe. My power cannot sustain him, my child. It is not enough."

"I know. Help is on the way, but I didn't know what else to do."

"I'll do what I can."

"Thank you, Medusa." Tears trickled down my cheeks. I couldn't let Randy die. I could bring him back, but he'd come back exactly the way he was when he died. I'd be raising him just so he could die all over again. There had to be something I could do. I felt fingers lightly graze the back of my hand. By the tingling sensation that followed, I knew it was Chase. What was he doing? Alex was right there. He was bound to notice.

Then I got an idea. "Medusa, can I transfer some of my power to Randy? Would that help?"

"Transferring that much power would severely weaken you. I am the only one who can give my power without being affected. I don't advise you doing this, Jodi. Let Randy take what he needs from me."

I hated feeling helpless. This was my fault. If I had stepped in and stopped the zombie, Randy would be okay.

"I feel a surge in your power, my child," Medusa said.

Oh, God, Chase was still rubbing my hand. Medusa could tell something was affecting me. Did she know it was Chase?

"My emotions are running on high. It's my fault this happened."

"Whether or not you could have prevented this, you can't let your emotions consume you. It is affecting your power."

"I know."

"That's enough for now. Any more of my energy, and Randy will not be able to handle it. His system will crash."

"Thank you again, Medusa."

I took Randy's hand away from Medusa, and mine away from Chase. "Let's get him bandaged up now."

Arianna had a medical kit waiting, and she cleaned the area before applying gauze and medical tape. It seemed like every time she got everything in place, she had to change the gauze because it was soaked with blood.

"There's no need for you all to stand around like this. You've got more time to train before the others arrive. Standing around here isn't helping Randy. Now go." She shooed us from the room.

We were all in a daze, but we walked back outside. I hoped the fresh air would make me feel a little better, but it didn't. I could see the corpse of the woman still sticking halfway out of the grave, waiting for Randy's next command.

"I need to release her soul," I said.

Alex put his hand on my shoulder. "I'll come with you."

Leticia and Chase followed too, not saying a word. I stood facing the woman and willed my blood to mix. Once the tingling sensation spread throughout my body, I said, "I command you to return to where you came from. I release your soul." She fell forward, her face in the dirt.

"So, I guess we spend the rest of the morning digging graves?" Chase said. "Sounds fun."

Leticia moaned. "I spend half my life digging graves."

Chase turned to me. "Well, I bet Jodi and I could get the bodies to crawl right back into the ground. No digging required."

"I wish you'd crawl into the ground," Alex said.

"What's the matter, bro? Worried your girl and I will make too good a team?"

Before Alex could answer, two cars pulled up. The Serpentarius Ophi were here. Mason got out of the first car and came right over to Chase.

"Hey, Uncle Mason."

"No time for small talk," I said. "Where's Carson? Randy's been hurt, and he needs a doctor."

"I'm Carson," said a short blond guy with glasses.

"Great. He's right inside. In the living room. Arianna's taking care of him."

"I'm on it." He headed inside, but the others stayed.

"So," Mason said, "before we get settled here, I want to see this amazing power you and my nephew have perfected."

I looked at Chase, my eyes the size of golf balls.

"Sure thing, Uncle Mason." Chase took my hand before I could stop him, and the second our skin made contact, I felt the rush of power go through me. More power than any person, Ophi or not, should have.

Chapter 15

"What are you doing?" My voice was barely a whisper.

Relax. Chase's voice ran through me. He wasn't speaking out loud. He was speaking through our connection. Through our blood. If I wasn't already so freaked out, this would've totally thrown me. He rubbed the back on my hand with his thumb. *Give in to me, Jodi. It's that easy. Our connections have only failed because you've fought them.*

Could that be true? Had I been the problem all along? Mason and the others were watching, expecting to see something truly phenomenal. If I didn't make this work, they'd get right back in their cars and go home. I couldn't screw this up. I had to listen to Chase and figure this out quickly.

Okay, what should we try to do? I asked, speaking through the connection like Chase had.

Let's get Mr. and Mrs. Nasty Corpse back in the ground.

Normally, I didn't approve of treating the corpses or the souls we raised like they were beneath us, but this guy had taken a chunk out of Randy.

Let's start with him.

You got it.

I took a deep breath and let go of my anxiety. I let the walls come down and allowed Chase's power to flow into mine. Chase was right. When I stopped fighting it, the power was incredible. My body tingled like an electric current was running through me. I'd never felt so alive—so good.

Go ahead, Chase said. *Raise him again and give him a command.*

I focused my attention on the corpse. The one who'd attacked Randy. I let my power reach out to his soul. I felt it, heard it crying in agony as I ripped it from Hell. I stuffed him back in his rotting body. "Get up!" I was talking aloud now, so the others could hear. I had to make them see and hear what I was doing. Show them how Chase and I were working together.

The corpse rose and stood before me. Even though I was using Chase's power, too, the corpse only acknowledged me.

"Grab a shovel and return your body to the earth you dug out of. Once you're buried, you may release your soul back to where it came from."

I heard gasps from some of the new Ophi and Leticia. Then Alex's voice cut through all of them. "That's torture, Jodi. You can't make him do that. What's gotten into you?"

I ignored him. I tuned into my power and reached out for the woman's soul. Her screams were ear-splitting. She tried to resist me, to fight, but she was no match for Chase and me. I wrenched her soul back into her body, still half-stuck in the ground.

"Dig your way back into your grave. When you get there, you may return your soul to Hell." My voice didn't sound like my own. It was deeper and filled with hatred.

Chase squeezed my hand and our connection intensified. I had a feeling the more we connected physically, the stronger our powers would be. I turned toward him and reached for his other hand. Instantly my hair whipped behind me, even though there was no wind. I wasn't aware of anything but Chase. I stared into his eyes, and he smiled at me.

"You and me. This is how it's supposed to be."

"This is amazing." The power was intense, but in a good way. I wasn't afraid of it anymore. It felt right being with Chase like this. I wanted more. More of the power. More of Chase. I squeezed Chase's hands tighter. "Hold me closer."

"Anything you say, Jodi." Chase stepped toward me so we were toe to toe, and there was barely any space between us.

I could smell him and almost taste his minty breath. I breathed him in, and my eyes closed in response. The connection between us was intoxicating.

The souls releasing broke my trance. I looked down at the ground. The corpses were buried and the shovels lay next to the graves again.

"Well done," Mason said. The smile on his face was wide with satisfaction. "I've never seen anything like that."

"Hey, you can let go of my girlfriend now," Alex said.

I looked down, realizing I hadn't let go of Chase. I avoided Alex's eyes as I tried to slip my hands from Chase's, but Chase smiled and squeezed my hands, sending tingling sensations through my body. I closed my eyes in response.

"I don't think she wants me to let go," Chase said.

Chase's hands were ripped from mine. I opened my eyes to see Alex shoving Chase in the chest.

"Stop!" I yelled, not sure who I was trying to protect.

"Well, well," said a red-haired girl with long legs. "Looks like they'll be plenty of entertainment around here."

"Lexi, why don't you and the others go see if Carson needs any help with the injured boy." Mason nodded toward the school.

"Sure." Lexi smiled at me, but it was the most unfriendly smile I'd ever seen. As she walked past me, she said, "I think I'll take my sister's room. I believe it's right across the hall from yours."

No way! Lexi was Abby's sister? Ophi could only be born between the dates of November 29 and December 17, under the sign of Ophiuchus, and the child's parents had to be 25. It was this strange way that the gods controlled how many Ophi there were in the world. Since Abby and Lexi's parents were only 25 once, that meant Abby and Lexi had to be unidentical twins. This was not good news for me. Lexi must have hated me for sending her twin to the underworld as Hades' slave.

I stood there speechless.

Chase smoothed out his shirt and stepped away from Alex. "I'll show you guys to your rooms." He winked at me before heading toward the house. The others followed. All but Alex. He stayed behind with me. I could barely look at him.

"I tried to tell myself this was all one-sided. That it was just Chase being a dick. But after seeing you touch him like that—"

"We were only connecting our powers. That's all."

"No, that's not all. You couldn't get close enough to him. You were clinging to him. And the look on your face." He ran his fingers through his hair. "You loved every second of that. Whatever it was."

I shook my head and reached for him. "It was the power, not Chase."

"Wrong again, Jodi. It was all about Chase. The things he said to you…and you didn't even disagree with him."

Oh, no! I'd thought Chase and I were using our connection to speak privately, but we must have started talking out loud. Alex had heard Chase say we were supposed to be together. He'd heard me practically agree.

"Alex, I was—"

"Don't." He turned away like it was too painful to even look at me.

"Alex?" I didn't know what to say, how to make this better.

"I should've known." He smacked the side of his leg with his fist. "Damn it, I think I did know, but I wouldn't admit it to myself."

"What are you talking about?"

"Chase. He's what's messing up your powers." He spun around. His face was bright red, and his breathing was heavy. "Ever since you started emailing him, you've been different. And to think I thought your emotions were throwing off your powers because you were falling in love with me."

"I am in love with you!" I reached for him, but he put his hands out to stop me.

"No, Jodi. You can't love me when you obviously feel this way about him." He said "him" like it was the most vile word in the English language.

"I do love you, Alex. I'm sure of that. It's the only thing I know for certain. I don't have a clue what's going on with my powers or why Chase affects them the way he does. But I know how I feel about you, and none of this stuff with Chase changes that."

He shook his head. "It does change it, Jodi. You didn't see yourself when you connected with him. You didn't hear yourself. You made those souls do unbelievable things. The Jodi I fell in love with couldn't have done that. You've changed."

"No." My voice was weak. Was he right? I had made those souls suffer. I'd tortured them just to give Mason and the others a reason to stay here. "Mason—"

"Don't use him as an excuse. You changed. You're different. You're mean. Mason had nothing to do with that."

I squeezed my fists. Ugh! Why wouldn't he listen to me? "What can I say to make you believe me? Tell me, please."

"I don't want you to tell me what I want to hear. That's useless, meaningless." He started toward the school.

"Where are you going?" I practically had to run to keep up with him.

"I can't stay here."

"Fine. Let's go to my room and talk."

"No." He took the front stairs two at a time.

"Alex, wait up."

He threw open the door and stormed past the Medusa statue. He went straight up the stairs and to his room.

"Okay, we'll talk in your room," I said, but Alex shut the door in my face. This wasn't like him at all. I pounded on the door. "Alex, let me in. We need to talk about this."

"I'm tired of talking," he yelled through the door.

I tried the doorknob. Of course it was locked. I thought about going to my room, letting him cool off. But I was afraid to. Alex had never been this angry with me. What if he didn't cool off? What if he ended things instead? I couldn't give up. I had to make him listen to me. I leaned my back against the wall next to his door, determined to stay here until he came out. I wouldn't let him leave his room without talking to me.

Lexi walked out of Abby's room—her room now. She saw me and flashed her wicked smile. Just great. I wasn't up for another round with her right now. She headed toward me, stopping about five feet away and crossing her arms.

"Don't tell me your boyfriend's locked you out." Her voice was laced with mock sympathy. "I bet he'd let *me* in his room." She stepped toward his door, but I blocked her path.

"Lexi, I'm not in the mood for games."

"Who's playing games?" She stepped closer, challenging me.

"Alex has good taste. He'd never go for a girl like you, so you might as well turn around and go back to your room."

She looked me up and down. "Good taste, huh? I kind of doubt that if he's stooped so low as to date you. But maybe since my sister is no longer here, he didn't have a lot of choices. You or that cowardly girl—what's her name? Morticia?"

"Leticia. And for your information, Alex never dated Abby. He couldn't stand her. Like I said, he has good taste."

Lexi started laughing. "At least you have some fight in you. Abby led me to believe you were a sniveling little girl."

I crossed my arms, mimicking Lexi's former stance. "That's funny, considering I sent Abby straight to the underworld on Hades' coattails."

Lexi narrowed her eyes at me. I'd struck a nerve. She leaned closer, and I struggled not to back away. I didn't want to look weak or easily intimidated. Good thing there was a wall behind me to keep me from cowering.

"Abby was a pussy cat compared to me." She winked. "I'm the real bitch in the family."

Somehow, I believed that. "Is that why you and your family tossed Abby out? Sent her here and didn't talk to her again?"

"Oh, we talked. Maybe my mom disowned her, but I never did. We texted—kept each other informed."

Alex's door opened, and both Lexi and I turned to him. He was carrying a duffel bag, the same one he'd had when he brought me here over two months ago.

"Where are you going?" I asked.

Lexi stepped toward him, dragging one finger down the front of his shirt. "Don't tell me you're leaving. I was hoping we could get to know each other better. A lot better."

I smacked her hand away. "Don't touch him!"

Alex rolled his eyes at Lexi and pushed past her. "Jodi, I'm going away for a while. I'll see you when I get back. If I come back."

"What? Alex, you can't leave. I need you." I raced down the stairs after him.

He opened the front door and stopped in the doorway. He sighed and finally turned to me. He looked as awful as I felt. It was my fault he was hurting. I reached for him again, but he stepped back. "I need time away from all this. From us."

Wide-eyed, I shook my head. "No, we need to be together."

"I'm sorry, but I can't stick around while you try to figure out what's going on with you and Chase. It's not fair to me."

"I don't want Chase! I want *you*. I love you!" Tears streamed down my face. Things couldn't end this way.

Alex's eyes jerked to his right at something behind me. I assumed it was Lexi, tagging along to watch the show. Alex looked at me one last time before turning and walking away.

"Alex!" I yelled, going after him, but someone grabbed my arm and spun me around. Chase. Before I could react, he pulled me to him, pressing his lips firmly against mine. My body responded to him as if this was normal. As if this was what my body had wanted for days. My lips tingled, and the sensation traveled through me. There was nothing I could do to fight it. The power took over. I gave in. My blood surged in my veins. I felt every drop of blood, and it gave me more pleasure than I ever could have imagined. I kissed Chase back, weaving my fingers in his hair. He lifted me off the ground, and our bodies pressed against each other.

I felt like I was spinning. Or maybe the room was spinning. It was freeing and completely amazing. Then my body temperature rose. I was hot all over, and it wasn't showing any signs of stopping. I was burning from the inside out. I thought of the pain I had felt when Hades' eyes burned into me. This heat was similar, but I wasn't in pain. The heat was rising, and I was aware of it, but it didn't hurt me. Like I was the fire, not the thing being burned by it.

An electric current rushed through me as Chase kissed me with even more intensity. I couldn't breathe. My head felt disconnected, and my legs shook. My arms dropped down to my sides. I couldn't hold them up anymore. I was weak. I hung limp in Chase's arms, yet he was still kissing me. I tried to say his name, but the word wouldn't come out.

I heard screams and repeated thumping like things were toppling over. Finally, I turned my head to the side, breaking free from the kiss. Chase raised his head and looked at me. He lowered me to the ground, and we turned toward the screams.

Lexi and Leticia cried out in pain. Leticia had blood running from her eyes and nose. Lexi was choking up blood. It was horrible to watch, yet I was frozen in place, unable to move or look away. They collapsed on the living room floor. Randy was lying lifeless on the couch above them. The toppling noise continued, and my eyes flew to the stairs. Tony was tumbling down them. I gasped as his body reached the bottom, and his head slammed onto the floor.

Tony was dead. And I had a feeling all the other Ophi I'd brought here were dead, too.

Chapter 16

Chase looked like he was completely drained and in shock. He wasn't going to be of any help to me right now. I was weak too, but I forced myself to reach for Medusa. She was my only hope in saving the Ophi. I'd never raised more than one Ophi at a time before. Technically, I'd only raised a total of three since I'd become Ophi. I wasn't sure this was possible, even without needing to spill my blood to raise them, but I was certain I needed Medusa's help.

The second my hands met hers, I called out, "Medusa, please! I need you. They're all dead. All of them. You have to help me bring them back." I was hysterical. My sobs were uncontrollable, and if I hadn't been communicating in my mind, I was sure Medusa wouldn't have understood me. I doubted I could form audible words right now.

"I know, my child. I sensed the shift in energy." She was in front of me, holding my hands in hers. "Concentrate, Jodi. Reach out with your powers. Feel for their souls. We must trap them before they release. If Hades gets hold of them, he will stop us."

"But how? Isn't that against the rules?"

"Hades isn't playing by the rules anymore."

"What do you mean?" She knew something. I knew she did. Why was she being so cryptic?

"There's no time to explain. Close your eyes and reach for their souls."

I didn't argue. It wasn't the time. I had to save the others. I wouldn't be the girl who led an entire race to its extinction. I mixed my powers with Medusa's. It was an incredible feeling. Not like the way it felt when Chase and I combined powers, though. That was an entirely different kind of rush. I saw Tony's soul leaving his body, but I forced it back inside. I didn't have time to be nice about it. I had to move on to the next one. I could feel Medusa's power reaching out farther in the house. Most of the new Ophi were in the conference room. I could sense them as Medusa restored life to their bodies. Leticia was next on my list. I pushed her soul back inside of her and commanded her to come back to life. To breathe. On her first inhale, I turned my attention to Randy. His soul was harder to convince. His body was in bad shape still. Every time I put his soul back inside him, it seeped out again.

Medusa finished with the others, including Lexi, who I'd conveniently skipped over. I continued to struggle with Randy. Why wouldn't he listen to me? Medusa reached her powers out to him, but she didn't have any better luck.

"He's too weak, Jodi. His body was already dying when this happened. Every time we put his soul back, he dies all over again."

"Are you saying we're torturing him?" I fought the soul as it found another way out of Randy.

"Yes, my child. I'm afraid so. There's nothing we can do for him." She squeezed my hands, trying to console me.

"Keep trying. Don't let go of his soul. I'll get Carson. He'll heal Randy, and then his soul will stay inside him."

"Jodi, I understand you don't want to let him go, but Carson has already done all he could for Randy."

"How do you know that?" I was screaming now. No longer speaking only through my mind. "I can't let him die. Hades will take him and keep him from me."

"It's not Hades keeping him from you, Jodi. It's his body. You know the rules. When you raise someone, they return exactly as they were before they died. Randy was dying. He can't be saved." I felt her ease her powers. She wasn't helping me anymore.

"No!" I struggled, squeezing her hands, trying to take her powers whether she wanted me to or not. But it didn't work. I fell to my knees.

"I'm sorry, my child," Medusa said, as my hands slipped from hers.

Leticia screamed, and I scrambled to my feet. I rushed to Randy, examining him. His shoulder was still bleeding. The couch was soaked with his blood. That's how the soul kept escaping, through the gaping hole where his shoulder used to be. I pressed my hand to his blood-soaked bandages, applying pressure. Then I willed my blood to mix. I didn't have much energy left, but I had to try.

"Get Carson!" I yelled to anyone who would listen. Chase finally snapped out of his trance and went for Carson. I tuned out the room and focused on Randy's soul. I reached out for it. But this time, instead of forcing it back inside Randy's dying body, I faced it head on and pleaded. "Don't go, Randy. Please. I'm getting help. Stay with me while Carson finds a way to stop the bleeding. Please!" I felt warm blood drip from my nose and ears. Holding Randy's soul was killing me.

Hands were on my shoulders, pulling me away from Randy. I figured it was Carson, trying to move me so he could save Randy. I reached for Randy's hands, not wanting to break the connection and lose his soul, but the person holding my shoulders continued to pull me back. Randy's soul slipped away from me. I couldn't hold on, not with someone tugging me away from him.

"Stop!" I yelled, commanding both the soul and the person pulling me away. Neither listened. Blood spilled down my cheeks as I fought against them, and then I felt an arm around my neck. Someone yanked me back, and Randy's hands were torn from mine. His soul drifted away from me. He was gone. Dead. And I couldn't bring him back.

Leticia was crying next to me. I couldn't see her through all the blood blurring my vision, but I recognized her sobs. Arianna was shushing her, saying, "He's at peace now, honey. He's at peace."

But he wasn't. He was with Hades. I knew it. Hades didn't let Ophi souls rest in peace. They had too much power. Power he wanted. I sat myself up, wobbling in the process.

"Take it easy," Chase said. I was in his lap. He was the one who'd pulled me away from Randy.

"You? You stopped me?" I blinked the blood from my eyes and turned to face him. He looked horrified, and I realized it was because I was bleeding from all parts of my face.

"You need to lie down." He reached out like he was going to carry me to my room.

"No!" I swatted at him and stumbled backward into the couch. I used it to help me to my feet.

"Jodi," Arianna said. "Chase is only trying to help you."

"Is everyone okay in here?" Tony came toward us, rubbing his head. No doubt because he had a massive headache from his tumble.

"Are you okay?" I asked. "I saw you fall down the stairs."

"I'm not exactly up for a few rounds in the ring, but I'll live. Thanks to you and Medusa."

I swallowed hard. How did I tell him—and everyone else—I thought it was my powers that had killed them in the first place? I couldn't. They'd hate me. They'd turn me over to Hades before I could wash the blood from my face.

"Randy," I choked out, changing the subject. "I couldn't—his soul wouldn't hold on."

Arianna let go of Leticia and came to me. "Carson did everything he could, but the corpse...his bite was too big to repair."

Carson stepped closer to me. "One of Randy's smaller arteries was severed. I didn't have the medical equipment needed to save him."

"Then get it!" Leticia yelled.

"It wouldn't matter now," Chase said, and it was the first time I saw him look sympathetic toward anyone here besides me.

"Why not? We can get the equipment Carson needs and bring Randy back," Leticia said. "Jodi can do it, can't she?" She sobbed when Carson shook his head.

I didn't want to break down and cry like a baby in front of everyone. I was supposed to be the leader. The strong one. But the look on Leticia's face when she realized I couldn't help Randy was too much.

"Leticia, I—"

She turned and ran upstairs. I knew in that moment she hated me. I was the one who had gotten Randy hurt. If I had stopped that zombie, Randy wouldn't have been bitten. This was all my fault.

Tony went over to the couch. "Chase, will you help me move Randy? We can bury him in the mausoleum. There are some empty caskets in there."

"Sure, but can I help Jodi first? I'd like to take her to her room and help her get cleaned up."

"No," I said. "Randy should be our top priority. I'll help you both."

"No way, Jodi." Chase grabbed me by my shoulders. "You need rest. You drained a lot of your powers."

"Chase is right," Arianna said. "Why don't you go upstairs and take a nice warm bath? We can take care of Randy."

"A warm bath sounds like Heaven right about now," Lexi said. I'd forgotten she was even here.

"Your bathroom doesn't have a tub," I said to her.

"Yours does, and I'm sure my fearless leader would be more than happy to accommodate me." She gave me a wicked smile and started to walk away, but Arianna grabbed her roughly by the arm.

"Lexi, you're fine. Jodi is the one who needs the hot bath, so I suggest you go to your own room for the time being. I'll be up to check on Jodi shortly, and if I find you anywhere near her bathroom, taking what she needs, I'll have you back at Serpentarius before sundown."

Lexi glared at Arianna and shook her arm free. "Whatever you say, Mother."

My heart stopped. Mother? No way. Lexi couldn't be Arianna's daughter. That would mean Abby was Arianna's daughter, too.

Lexi stomped upstairs as I stared at Arianna, waiting for her to tell me it wasn't true. She looked at me and sighed.

"Not all Ophi are good, Jodi. Sometime we fall for the wrong ones."

So Arianna had fallen for a bad Ophi? An evil guy who passed his evil qualities down to their twin daughters? I grabbed my head, putting my hands over my ears. My palms stuck to the partially dried blood trailing down the sides of my face. "You sent Abby away. It nearly killed her—made her evil."

Arianna sighed. "She was obsessed with power and proving herself. I thought sending her to Troy and Victoria might scare her out of it. But when her letters arrived and all she talked about was how great it was not to hold back her power, I knew I'd lost her."

"So, you stopped reading the letters and returned them unopened." I remembered the drawer full of letters Abby had kept.

"I thought if she knew how upset I was…maybe she'd come home." Arianna nodded to Chase, unable to continue talking about Abby. "On second thought, you take Jodi upstairs. Run her a bath and then wait for her in her room. Keep Lexi away from her."

"Sure thing." Chase took my arm, but this time my blood didn't react. I stared at his hand on me, wondering why his touch was different now. He leaned down and whispered, "Don't worry. I'm not using my powers."

He'd been doing that on purpose?! I thought it was the way our blood naturally reacted to each other, but it had been Chase doing it all along.

Arianna put her hand on my shoulder as I walked by. "I'll be up to check on you soon, and then we can talk."

I knew she wanted to explain about Abby and Lexi. I had a lot of questions for her. Like why she never told me, and why she didn't hate me for sending Abby to the underworld. I wasn't sure I could handle that today, though. So much had already happened.

"Maybe our talk can wait until tomorrow? I think I could sleep until morning at this point."

She nodded and gave me a weak smile.

Chase walked me upstairs. He kept his arm around my back and was being a gentleman for once. Not forcing his power on me or trying to bully me into choosing him. Now that Alex was gone, he didn't feel the need to compete anymore. It was the first time I had thought about Alex since he left. Since he walked out on me and my world came crumbling down. This was more proof of how much I needed him. But what was I going to do about Chase?

We'd combined powers twice today, and both times, it had made me feel better than I'd ever felt in my life. My blood craved Chase, but look what I had done when I gave in to that craving. I'd taken out every Ophi under this roof. I knew I was responsible for their deaths. I'd felt my blood doing things it had never done before. It was like the night Leticia was choking in my room. The night she'd died. Chase had been touching me, combining our powers, and Leticia died because of it. I was convinced Chase and I could do both amazing and devastating things together. We were that powerful, and it scared the hell out of me.

Inside my room, Chase left me sitting on the bed while he drew me a bath. I reached up and took the locket from my neck. Nothing good had happened since I'd put it on, and now I wanted it off. I wished I'd never drunk the blood from the bloodstone. I wished I'd never killed the human in me. That I'd never become the leader of the Ophi. I didn't want any of this anymore. None of it seemed worth it. Not without Alex.

I put the locket back in my dresser drawer before slumping on my bed and crying. My tears washed most of the blood from my face and I wiped the rest away with my sleeves. Chase came back into the room and sat down next to me.

"Oh, Jodi." He leaned over me and kissed me. I stopped crying, taken aback by his action. He wasn't my boyfriend. He wasn't Alex. We'd only kissed once, and that had had terrible consequences. I pulled away.

"Don't worry. Nothing bad will happen. I promise. I'll keep my powers under control, and you will too." He leaned forward and kissed me again. He didn't let me go, and finally, I gave in, kissing him back. He brushed the hair from my wet cheeks and looked at me.

"What are we doing?" I asked. This was all so confusing. It wasn't what I wanted, not really. So, why wasn't I stopping him?

"What we're supposed to be doing." He kissed me again, more passionately this time, and he let a tiny bit of his power find its way to me. The tingling spread through my lips and into my chest, filling me with energy. I felt better, more alive. He was on top of me now, and still I was trying to pull him closer.

"Jodi, are you—"

I pulled away from Chase to see Arianna standing in the doorway. Embarrassed, I scrambled out from under Chase and stood up. He leaned back on the bed as if he'd done nothing wrong.

"I came to see if you were finished with your bath," Arianna said. "But I see you haven't even started."

"That reminds me," Chase said, "I left the water running." He ran to the bathroom, hopefully before the tub overflowed.

"Um, I was waiting for it to fill?" It came out more like a question than a statement.

Arianna walked over to me and kept her voice low. "Jodi, do you know what you're doing? Alex left today, and already you're with Chase?"

"No." I shook my head. "I'm not with him. He kissed me. I was caught off guard. That's all. With everything that's happened, I was upset and I guess I wasn't thinking clearly."

She sighed. "Honey, that boy is pouncing when he should be giving you time. I don't like it at all. You be careful around him."

I nodded, but she didn't look convinced.

"What if Alex had come back and seen what I saw?"

"Alex doesn't want to be with me." The words stung my chest.

"No, what Alex doesn't want is Chase's hands all over you." She shook her head like she was trying to get the image out of her mind. "I'm not telling you what to do, but if I were you, I'd be focusing on trying to get Alex back here. Not trying to replace him."

Replace Alex? I couldn't. I was about to tell her that, but Chase came back into the room. "It's all set."

"Good," Arianna said. "Then you can come downstairs and help me with dinner while Jodi takes her bath."

Chase looked annoyed, but he followed Arianna. He brushed his hand along my arm on his way out, and the tingling sensation of his touch rippled through me. God, how did he do that? It made my common sense go out the window.

I got into the bathtub and lowered myself so that only my head was above the water. The warmth felt incredible, but it was powerless against the events of the day. Seeing Alex walk out of my life, Tony fall to his death, Randy's soul float away, lost forever—it was all stuck in my mind. But as huge as those things were, they took a back seat to Chase. He was becoming more and more of a mystery to me. Why could one touch from him make me lose control? Why was he so different from all the other Ophi? Then, the biggest question of all popped into my head. Something I should've asked myself right away, but I'd been too caught up in the moment to notice.

Why hadn't Chase died with all the others?

Chapter 17

That was all I thought about for the rest of the night, long after the water in the tub turned cold. Long after Arianna brought me dinner on a tray because I never came downstairs. Long after Chase knocked on my door and I pretended to be asleep. When I woke up in the morning, the only explanation I could come up with was that Chase had survived because our powers had been connected. I had kept him alive.

Then, another thought struck me. How far had my powers reached? Had Alex been far enough away that he wasn't affected? I had to ask Medusa. She would know. She had a way of sensing all of us, of knowing what was going on.

I threw the covers off and ran downstairs. All I was wearing was the long-sleeved shirt Alex had given me my first night here. It was like a dress on me. Well, more like a mini, but I didn't care. I needed answers now. I reached the statue and grabbed Medusa's hands.

"Medusa?" I called with my mind. "I need you."

Her face appeared to me. "Yes, my child?"

"Alex—where was he when I killed everyone? Was he affected by my power?"

"I reached out to every Ophi who was affected. He was not among them. He was safe."

I breathed a long sigh of relief. I hadn't harmed Alex. He was okay. He was still gone, but at least he was alive.

"Thank you, Medusa."

"Jodi?" Chase pulled my hand from Medusa's.

I looked at him. "Why did you do that?"

"I wanted to make sure you were okay. You looked upset."

"I'm fine. I needed to talk to Medusa."

"You should be careful how much time you spend connected to her. All that power could wear you out." He brushed his finger against my cheeks, making my face tingle from his touch.

"Please, don't do that."

"Sorry. I have to remember to hold back my power when I'm around you. Your blood screams to mine, and what can I say? I tend to give in to it."

I looked down at my bare legs. "I should go get dressed."

"Why? I like the look."

"It's Alex's shirt." I wasn't sure why I wanted Chase to know that.

His face went cold. "On second thought, take it off."

"I don't get it. Why do you hate him? I mean, he should hate you. You came here and openly tried to take me away from him."

"I didn't have to try very hard." He smiled and wrapped one arm around my waist.

"Stop it." I smacked his arm away and started for my room.

"I can make you forget about him, Jodi."

I stopped at the top of the stairs, but I didn't turn toward him. "No, you can't, and I don't want to anyway." I turned and ran to my room, locking the door behind me. I didn't want him following me. If he caught up to me, he could use his power on me. Make me give in to him. I leaned against the door and sank to the floor. I was losing control of everything. I'd been reduced to hiding in my room. Some leader I was.

It took me a minute to realize the shower was running in my bathroom. I got up and walked in there. Steam hit me in the face. Someone was using up all my hot water. A pair of leather knee-high boots rested on the bench outside the shower. I only knew one person who dressed in knee-high boots. Lexi.

My blood was boiling, but not in a Gorgon sort of way. I was mad. I marched over to the shower, reached my arm in, and turned the water to freezing cold. Lexi screamed and jumped back, bumping against the back of the shower by the sound of it.

"What the hell!" She shut off the water and peeked her head out.

"My thoughts exactly. How did you get into my bathroom?"

She reached for her towel and disappeared behind the curtain again. A moment later she came out wrapped like a burrito. "I have my ways."

"Found spare keys in Abby's room?"

She narrowed her eyes. "Think you know everything, don't you?"

"I know you're just as big a bitch as Abby was."

"What do you mean *was*?"

I shrugged. "Being trapped in the underworld as Hades' slave is as good as dead." I had no idea where this burst of self-confidence was coming from. It wasn't like me to act this way.

"You wish," Lexi said.

"I don't believe in wishing. I wished you to the underworld the second I found out you were Abby's sister, but that didn't do me any good."

"No, it didn't, but don't worry. You'll be wishing again soon." She grabbed her clothes and boots off the bench. "You'll be wishing you were dead."

I matched her glare. "Don't count on it."

"Abby will be kicking your sorry soul around the underworld soon enough. Just like that pathetic kid you killed earlier. What was his name, Ricky?"

"Randy. And believe me, she wouldn't dare."

Lexi laughed. "Honey, you obviously don't know my sister." She walked out, leaving me imagining all the awful things Abby was probably doing to Randy's soul right now.

Breakfast was quiet. Even though there were so many new faces at the table, I could only focus on the ones who weren't there—Randy and Alex. I'd trade all the Ophi from Serpentarius to have them both back. I couldn't even remember why I'd pushed so hard to get these guys here.

Arianna came up behind me with a tray of eggs. "I've arranged for a small ceremony tonight. We'll meet at the mausoleum at eight."

I felt my orange juice coming back up, but I fought it. The acidic taste burned the back of my throat. "Thanks," I choked out.

"Hi," said a brunette sitting next to me. "I'm McKenzie. We didn't really get a chance to meet yesterday."

"Hi." I put on the best fake smile I could manage. "Thanks for coming, McKenzie."

She smiled back. "That's Lucas across from us. He's the same age as me. We both just came into our powers."

I nodded, pretending to follow along.

"Have you met Mason's wife, Carol? She's a sweetheart. She sort of takes care of me since my mom and dad aren't around anymore."

"Oh," I said, suddenly being brought back to the conversation. "Do you mind me asking what happened?"

She pushed her eggs around on her plate. "They died. They were part of the group in Washington. Hades came after them."

My fork missed my eggs and screeched across the plate. Oh, God! Another person whose parents I'd sent to the underworld? I couldn't take much more of this.

"I know what happened," she said. "And just so you know, I don't blame you."

"Thanks." It was a stupid thing to say, but nothing else seemed right either.

"Where are your parents?" McKenzie asked.

"My mom's human, so I'm not allowed to see her anymore, and my dad is in the underworld like your parents. Hades took him from me a few days ago." It felt like a lifetime ago.

"Oh, sorry." She took a sip of juice and continued telling me who everyone was. "You know Lexi. She needs no introduction."

She could say that again.

"That guy with the goatee, he's Thayer. Jared, the dirty blond sitting next to him, is his son. They're both nice. You know Carson already," she said, moving right along. "Then there's Asher. He's one of my favorites. After Carol, of course. Asher is really strong, and he's not afraid of anything."

"What about Mason? What's he like?" I'd only talked to him a couple times on the phone. He seemed nice enough, but not overly helpful.

McKenzie shrugged. "He's cool. He's been weird lately, though. Not his usual self. I guess that's because he's away from home. You wouldn't believe how much he loves Serpentarius. I never thought he'd leave it to come here. Not even with all of us begging him."

"Well, I'm glad he changed his mind. We all need to stick together if we're going to stand up to Hades."

McKenzie dropped her fork and stared at me. "We're going to fight Hades?"

"Well, not 'fight him' fight him, but we are stronger in numbers. He won't come attack a group this big. It's too risky."

McKenzie nodded. "Oh, okay." She looked scared, and I couldn't help thinking I had a younger version of Leticia on my hands.

"Hey," McKenzie said, "where's Chase?"

I looked around the table. How hadn't I noticed he was missing? "I don't know. I saw him earlier."

"Weird. He never missed a meal back at Serpentarius. I forgot what a great cook Arianna is. The food's gone downhill since she left."

McKenzie kept talking, but I wasn't listening. I couldn't help wondering where Chase was. For some reason, I didn't like not knowing.

After breakfast, Mason, Carol, Thayer, Carson, and Asher said they wanted to meet with Tony and Arianna to discuss the situation some more, so they all headed to the conference room for some adult Ophi conversation, while the rest of us went outside. I split the group up into training teams as soon as we got to the row of graves that still had bodies in them.

"Okay, those of you with more experience will come with me. We'll work on commanding multiple souls at once. That will be Jared, Lexi—" I looked at the others, realizing I had more newbies than anything else. Plus, I really didn't want to spend the morning with Lexi. "On second thought. I'll take the less experienced ones, Leticia, McKenzie, and Lucas. We'll work on maintaining control over souls once they're raised."

"What about us?" Lexi said. "Do we watch the youngsters screw up, or do we actually get to have a little fun?"

"Raising souls isn't fun," I snapped.

"Then you're not doing it right." Lexi whipped a nail file out of her back pocket. I thought she was going to mock me further by giving herself a manicure in the middle of my lesson, but instead she pricked Jared's finger.

"Ow!" he said. "What was that for?"

"I can't wear a Band-Aid on my finger for the rest of the day," she said. "I just did my nails." She flicked his finger, getting drops of his blood on one of the graves.

"Lexi, how do you expect to control that soul if you didn't raise it?" I could do it, but I knew she couldn't. She wasn't that far along in her training.

"I don't. I want to see how Jared does." She smiled at him.

"Thanks a lot. I wasn't even ready for this." Jared looked about twenty-one, but like most Serpentarius Ophi he wasn't used to using his powers.

Lexi laughed and turned to me. "He gets stage fright sometimes."

"Shut up. I do not. I just need time to get my blood to do what I want it to."

"Well, then you better hurry." Lexi pointed to the hand coming up out of the grave. "Your zombie slave is here."

"Crap!" Jared closed his eyes and threw his head back. I wondered who'd taught him that technique. He looked possessed.

The zombie was almost completely out of the grave, and Jared still wasn't ready. Images of Randy getting bitten by the zombie flew into my head. That was not going to happen again.

"Stop!" I commanded the soul. "Turn to me. I'm in charge here."

The zombie turned and faced me.

"Hey," Jared complained. "I was almost ready."

Lexi laughed. "Ready to what? Run away when that thing attacked you?"

Jared looked at me. His eyes were full of hate. I didn't care if he was mad at me. I was doing what I had to.

"I lost a friend to a zombie because he wasn't ready. I'm not taking any chances."

"So, how exactly do you expect us to train?" Jared asked.

"When you're ready to take over, I'll be more than happy to hand this guy to you." I stared at Jared. "What do you say? Now that you're ready and not being ambushed by Lexi, do you want to give it a try?"

Jared nodded and closed his eyes again.

"Stop," I said. "Closing your eyes when a zombie is coming for you is a sure way to get yourself killed. Never take your eyes off them. Use your mind's eye to focus yourself and get control of your powers."

Jared shrugged. "Guess that makes sense."

"Good. Now focus on this guy and nothing else. Reach out to him with the power of your blood."

Jared fell silent, concentrating as hard as he could. "Got it."

"It's him you want," I said to the zombie, releasing him from my control. The corpse turned to Jared again and reached for him.

"Stay where you are." Jared's voice shook.

"You have the control, Jared. Don't let him think otherwise," I said.

Jared focused on the soul, staring him in the eyes. "Lower your arm."

The zombie lowered his arm but kept advancing.

"Stop!" Jared's voice was strong, confident.

The zombie stopped short.

"Great!" I said. Jared had real potential. He was already an adult Ophi, so he'd be a quick learner. "Think you can release him?"

Chase came up behind me. "Why not have a little fun first?"

"Where have you been?" I asked.

"Why? Did you miss me?" He brushed his hand against my back, and chills ran through me. "I bet these guys would love another demonstration of our combined powers."

Lexi's eyes widened. "See, now here's a guy who knows how to have fun." She batted her eyes at Chase, and I tensed up.

Chase leaned down and whispered in my ear, "Don't worry. She's not my type. No need to be jealous."

Oh, God. I *was* jealous. What was happening to me?

"So, what would you all like to see us do?" Chase sounded like the ringleader of a circus, only he and I were the main attraction.

"Can you really make them do anything you want?" Lucas asked.

"Let's find out," Chase said. "Think of something really tough."

"Chase, don't." I reached for his arm, but he put his hand over mine, letting his power flow to me. He was playing dirty. He knew I couldn't resist him when he did that.

"Can you make him stab himself?" Lexi suggested.

In my mind I was screaming "No!" Out loud, I made more of whimper. I was lost in the power. Chase was controlling me. He turned to me and smiled. "What do you say, Jodi? Should we give it a try?"

"No, no, no!" Why couldn't I say that out loud? I had to get through to him. I had to make him stop. He was squeezing my hand so tightly. It hurt and felt amazingly good at the same time. He turned toward me, taking both my hands. He was really going to do this. He was going to torture this corpse, and he was going to force me to help him. I had to snap him out of it. The power was going to his head. I didn't know what else to do to shock him, so I reached up on my toes and kissed him.

He kissed me back, and the power shot through us. This was a bad idea. I hadn't shocked him at all. All I'd managed to do was fuel his power. Intensify it. I tried to pull away, but I couldn't. My blood was responding to his against my will. I wasn't in control at all. I heard screams and finally Chase turned to see what we'd done. With the connection broken, I staggered back, my eyes falling on the body.

The corpse was lying in a heap on the ground. Lexi's nail file was jammed into his neck. Leticia and McKenzie stared at me in horror. Like they were looking at a monster. The monster I'd become.

Chapter 18

I couldn't take my eyes off the corpse. His soul was still inside him. I could feel it, and it was in agony. Leticia and McKenzie backed away in fear, and they had every right to. What I'd done was awful, unforgiveable. This wasn't what being Ophi was about. It couldn't be.

"Well, Jodi, I have to hand it to you," Lexi said. "You're darker than I thought. I didn't think you'd actually go through with it. Maybe there's hope for you yet."

Leticia glared at me with puffy, red eyes. "You're no better than they were." She didn't need to clarify who *they* were. I knew. She thought I was as bad as Victoria and Troy. Just as heartless. Maybe I was. Leticia grabbed McKenzie's arm, and they walked off toward the school. Lucas didn't say a word, but he followed them. I stared after them, realizing that, to everyone else, it looked that I had done all this. They had no idea that Chase could use his power to control me.

The soul was screaming to me. No one else could hear or feel the souls the way I could. If they could, they wouldn't do these awful things. I walked over to the body and mixed my blood. "Go back to where you came from. I release your soul." I felt the soul leave; as it did, it reached out toward me. I felt like a strong wind was blowing me back. That had never happened before. The souls weren't supposed to be able to touch us.

"What was that?" Chase asked, steadying me.

"He pushed me." I stared at the corpse. "When the soul released, it pushed me."

"Souls can do that?" Jared asked. He didn't look happy with me either, but at least he wasn't running away.

I nodded. "I didn't think they could, but it definitely happened."

"What, he was pissed off and decided to try to fight back?" Chase smirked. "I say we bring him back and teach him a thing or two."

I whipped around to face him. "What is wrong with you?" My blood started to boil. "I didn't want to hurt that guy. You made me do it."

"I should've known you were too weak to do it on your own." Lexi walked off.

"Hey, wait a minute," Chase said. "You kissed me, remember? You combined our powers. I have to say, I didn't hate your method. In fact, I'd like to try it again." He stepped toward me, but I backed up.

"Don't. Don't touch me." I waved him off. "Whatever this is between us, it's over. I'm done. I don't want your powers. I don't want your help. I don't want you."

He advanced on me, and I shivered. He was scaring me.

"I bet one little touch and you'd be saying different." He reached for my face.

"No!" I backed away farther. "I mean it. Stay away from me, Chase."

Jared put his hand on Chase's chest, holding him back. "That's enough, man."

Chase laughed, which only freaked me out more. This guy was seriously crazy. He was using me to get to my powers, and the truly frightening part was that, if he touched me again, I was going to give in. I couldn't fight him, couldn't resist his touch. I did the only thing I could. I ran. Ran from Chase. Ran from the school. I was hurting everyone. I wasn't a leader. I was a liability.

I sprinted behind the school, glancing back to see Chase following. His running was almost effortless. Nothing at all like mine. I struggled to breathe as I forced my legs to go so fast they were out of control. I ran into the woods and kept going, weaving in and out of the trees. There was nowhere to hide. I had to keep running. If I could reach the road, maybe I could flag down a car, the way I'd flagged down Melodie. Melodie. Her image invaded my mind. Could I really risk running into her after what I had done? She'd probably run me over if she saw me. Oh wait—she didn't have a car anymore, thanks to me.

"Come on, Jodi, you can't outrun me." Chase was closing in on me. I had to do something.

I cut off to the right, remembering the road was closer to the school on that side. As much as I didn't want to remember what had happened to Melodie's car or the hiker who'd tried to save me, I wished I'd come across the remains of the fire soon. At least then I'd know I was close to the road. Close to help.

"Why are you resisting me, Jodi?" Chase yelled. "You know you want me as much as I want you. Give in to it. Stop fighting. It's not like Alex is here to get in the way anymore."

I was struggling to breathe, yet Chase was having no trouble at all yelling to me while he ran. He was in much better shape than I was, which meant this wasn't going to end well for me. I knew he'd use his powers on me the second he reached me, and then it would be all over. I'd give in, and he'd have control.

I pushed my legs off the ground as hard as I could, forcing myself to go faster. I wasn't giving up. No matter how much it hurt. I saw something big and black out of the corner of my eye. Melodie's car! I headed toward it, squinting through the trees, trying to make out the road. I was still too far away.

"Does it really have to go down like this?" Chase yelled. I turned slightly and saw he was making a beeline for the car. He thought that was what I was running toward. He was going to cut me off. I quickly changed directions, knowing it would take me longer to reach the road this way.

"Clever!" Chase laughed. "Hey, did I mention I'm a runner? I could compete professionally if it weren't for the whole sweating thing." He laughed. "I'd kill my competition in more ways than one."

Crap, crap, crap! I turned to see how much ground he'd gained on me when I saw him hurdle a fallen tree. He cleared it with ease and even smiled at me as he landed. I couldn't look at him. He was psyching me out. I focused up ahead again and saw the road. I grunted and forced my body into a sprint. I poured everything into it. All my energy was focused on making it to the road. I heard a car coming. If I could get out of the woods, make myself visible, I'd have a chance. I'd throw myself onto the car's hood if I had to. Anything to get away from Chase.

I stepped out from the trees and waved my arms. The car was getting closer. One foot hit the asphalt, and then I was hit from behind. Chase was on top of me, pinning me to the shoulder of the road. The car drove past, not even noticing us. But I noticed it. The license plate read, MOM1208. Mom. My grandparents had gotten her the custom license plate after I was born. Even though she was only 16 at the time, she was so happy to be a mom. She never regretted having me, even after my dad left. She never regretted the life we had. No matter how much she had to work or how much she hated her boss.

"Mom," I cried.

"Hush," Chase said. "I'll make you feel all better." He brushed the tear from my cheek and transferred his power to me. My body tingled, making me forget the pain I was feeling. Making me want nothing more than to be with Chase, to feel this power we could create together.

After a few minutes, I felt the power subside. It slowly went away, leaving me feeling content. I knew I had run away, that I had wanted to get away from Chase, but now I had a hard time remembering why.

"Better?" He kissed me gently on the lips.

I nodded.

"Ready to go back now?" He stood up and extended his hand to me. I took it and let him help me up. He held onto me, and we started walking back toward the school. "That was your mom's car back there?"

"Yeah." I didn't want to talk about it. I wasn't sure if I was glad she hadn't seen me or if I wanted to be in the car with her right now.

"It wouldn't have ended well if she had stopped."

Was he threatening her? "Would you have hurt her?" I stopped walking and stared at him. I tried to take my hand back, but he squeezed it, sending a burst of power, getting me under his control again.

"You don't have to be afraid of me, Jodi. We were meant to be together. I won't hurt you. Why can't you see that?" He pulled me along, so we were walking again.

"If you hurt my mom, it would destroy me."

He didn't respond.

"And you made Alex leave. That hurt me. You made me torture that corpse, and that hurt me, too. If you really don't want to hurt me, you wouldn't try to control me like this. Using your power to get what you want is cruel." I should've been yelling at him, but with him still sending little surges of power my way, a gentle voice whispering the truth was the best I could do.

"I didn't make Alex leave. He left because he wasn't really in love with you. You weren't in love with him either."

I stopped. "Yes, I was." I tried to take my hand away again, but Chase hit me with another dose of his power, but this time it was the poison. I crumbled to the ground, and he caught me before my head hit a fallen tree branch.

"Please," I whispered. "You have to stop. I can't handle much more. You're going to kill me."

He looked down at me like he was considering what I said. "I won't let you die, Jodi."

"Stop controlling me. Please."

"I will once you admit the truth to yourself." He leaned down and kissed me again. "You love me. You've loved me since before me met. You felt it, too. The attraction between us. Alex left because of you, Jodi. Because you love me."

No. I wanted to yell, scream, and spit in his face. He was doing this to me. He was controlling me like a puppet. But I knew if I said what I really felt, he'd just dose me with poison again. It really was killing me, whether he wanted to admit it or not. If I was going to survive, I was going to have to play along. Pretend what he'd said was true.

"Say it, Jodi. Say you love me."

He stroked my face, sending just the slightest bit of poison through his touch. He had no idea how much he was hurting me. I had to make it stop.

"I love you." I didn't say his name, and I pictured Alex's face in my mind while I said it.

Chase wrapped me into a hug and kissed me. It physically pained me to kiss him back. I hated him. I wanted to claw his eyes out. But I had to play along or he'd kill me and leave me for the wild animals. Chase's hands were all over me, and I instinctively pushed him away.

"Need a little more?" I knew he was talking about his power.

"No! Please, Chase. I'm really in bad shape. I need to lie down. I don't even know if I'm strong enough to make it back to the school." A plan was forming in my mind. "Do you think you could go get your car and come back for me?" I laced my fingers through his, trying to play the part of the loving girlfriend.

"No need," he said. "I'll carry you."

"Don't be silly. It's way too far for you to carry me."

"Jodi, sweetie." He kissed my cheek. "How dumb do you think I am?"

My eyes widened. My acting skills weren't cutting it.

"I know, if I leave you here, the second I'm gone you'll run for the road again."

Maybe not run. My energy level was seriously depleted.

"I won't. I'm not strong enough to anyway."

"Alex may have been an idiot, but I'm not." He scooped me into his arms and started walking. "Hmm, you may be right about one thing. It's definitely too far to carry you like this." Chase stopped and looked around. His gaze fell on Melodie's car, and he walked over to it.

"It's totaled," I said.

"A little burned, but not totaled."

"The whole thing was up in flames. You can't drive it."

He smiled, and I followed his eyes. He wasn't looking at the car. He was looking at the body next to it.

"No! You can't be thinking of raising him. Chase, that's going too far."

"Don't worry, sweetie. I wouldn't think of raising him without your help. In fact, I'd prefer if you did it. You know, as a way to show me you're going to be on my side from now on." He put me down right next to the corpse.

"I can't. I won't do that. He was only trying to help me. I would've died if he hadn't freed me from the car."

"Well, then you wouldn't want his death to be in vain."

I narrowed my eyes at him. "What are you talking about?"

"You're either with me or against me, Jodi. Believe me, you don't want to be against me." His expression softened, and he cupped my face in his hands. "I really don't want to hurt you. We'd make such a great team." He lowered his hands to right above my heart. "But I will hurt you if I have to."

I looked at his hands, poised and ready to send a burst of poison straight to my heart. A burst I was sure would kill me.

"Why are you doing this?" I asked.

"Because I need you to see that you and I aren't like the others. We're better. I deserve the best, and that's you. If I can't have you, I *will* kill you. So, you better start proving that you want to be with me."

My eyes stung with the realization that I was defenseless against him. Part of me wanted to let him kill me, to end it so I didn't have to become the monster he wanted me to be. But if I died, that would be the end of the Ophi. I was sure of it. My death would mark the end of my deal with Hades. He'd go after the others, until there were no Ophi left.

I stared Chase in the eyes. "If you want me to love you, then you need to be someone I could love. Not a monster."

"I'm powerful. That doesn't make me a monster. You fighting me is making me a monster. If you would've just come back with me, none of this would've happened."

"Fine," I said. "I'll go back with you."

"No." He crossed his arms like a bratty child. "Now you need to prove yourself to me." He nodded at the corpse. "Raise that soul and make him carry you back to the school."

He was crazy, and I was crazy for not fighting him.

"Jodi, you have five seconds before I dose you with more poison than you can stand."

I squeezed my fists, feeling my blood already mixing in response to my emotions. I glared at Chase. "Fine, but understand I will hate you for making me do this."

"No, you won't. You will love me, Jodi, or I will kill you." He motioned to the body.

I stepped around him, careful not to make contact. I didn't need any of his power. I reached out for the soul, muttering an apology at the same time. He recognized me instantly, and when he realized I was forcing him back into his charred body, he screamed in agony. I cried, but I continued to control him, to hurt him more than he'd ever been hurt. I watched the corpse rise and come toward me.

"Good girl," Chase said. "Now, make him carry you."

My mouth didn't want to move. It killed me to say the words. "Carry me to my home. Follow Chase."

Chase smiled as the corpse reached for me and picked me up. His burned body was wet and bloody in some places where his flesh had melted away. I struggled to keep from throwing up. Chase laughed.

"See, it would be so much easier if you decide to love me." He walked with a smile the entire way back.

The corpse struggled under my weight, but no matter how much he hurt, he couldn't stop. He was powerless against me. We reached the school grounds, and I saw Tony was in the cemetery teaching the others. He'd taken over the lesson for me, but he stopped the second he saw us. His eyes went back and forth between me and the corpse. "My God, Jodi. What on earth have you done?"

"She's a ruthless one," Chase said. "But man are her powers awesome." He looked at me and smiled. "Come on, sweetie, don't you think the poor guy's had enough? You can walk the rest of the way, can't you?"

He was pinning this all on me. Making me look like the bad guy. I wanted to punch him in the face. To tell everyone the truth about what had happened. Instead, I commanded the soul to put me down. His flesh stuck to me in several places, and the tearing sound it made was sickening. He stared down at his arms in obvious pain.

"I release you. Please, return to where you were. I'm so sorry," I choked out. Tears filled my eyes.

Chase came over and put his arm around me. He sent waves of power through me. Not enough to consume me. I was sure he didn't want anyone else to know what he was doing. "Aw, hon, I know you feel bad about making him do that." He took my face in his hands and said, "I forgive you." He kissed me, and I truly wanted to die.

When he pulled away, everyone stared at me in horror, and there was nothing I could do to convince them of the truth.

Chapter 19

I was in serious trouble. Suddenly everyone was looking at Chase like he was the good guy. I was the girl who was out of control with power. Only I didn't want the power. I wasn't trying to use it. It was all Chase, but no one else could see that. Even Jared, who I'd hoped had seen a glimpse of Chase's true colors, was looking at me like I was no better than him. I needed help. I needed Alex. But since Alex wasn't here, I had to hope Medusa would be enough.

"I'm really drained. I need to go visit Medusa before lunch." I tried not to sound as disgusted with Chase as I actually was.

"Sure, babe. No problem. I'll go with you." He didn't let go of me. He clearly didn't trust me and was only acting sweet to keep up appearances with the others.

"No, you missed training this morning. Stay. Finish up with the group. I'll be fine."

I looked to Tony for help, hoping he'd back me up the way he usually did. He clearly seemed upset and confused by my behavior, but he nodded. "I could use your help, Chase."

Chase wrapped me in a hug and whispered in my ear. "Don't do anything foolish, Jodi. I'll find out if you do. I promise you that." He kissed me, dosing me again with his power. He was seriously going to kill me.

I wobbled back, still feeling the effects of his touch. Why couldn't anyone else see what he was doing to me? If Alex were here, he'd notice it. He'd put an end to it. I swallowed hard, fighting back the tears that came with thinking about Alex. I turned toward the school and walked inside. I hurried to Medusa and squeezed her hands.

"My child, what's happened to you, now? Your power is all off balance." Her expression was one of worry. "You need to release my left hand. You have too much poison in your blood right now. You need the blood from my right side."

"But if I let go I won't be able to talk to you, and I need to talk to you."

"I can still appear to you. Go on and release my left hand."

I did as she said, and the life-restoring power flowed through me, replenishing my energy. I sighed, relief washing over me. "Thank you. I needed that."

"Now, tell me what's happened."

"Chase. He's evil, Medusa. He's trying to kill me. He keeps sending me waves of power, but somehow he's only sending me power from the left side of his body."

"I can tell. You are filled with it. Jodi, I must warn you that, if you allow this to continue, you will turn evil. You'll become like Victoria and Troy. Only worse."

"Worse?" I was practically screaming in my mind. "How is that possible? They were awful."

"You must stay away from Chase."

"How? He drove Alex away—or I did because my stupid blood was attracted to Chase's power." Attracted to his power. Did that mean I *was* evil? If I was craving the evil in Chase, that had to mean I was evil, too.

"No, Jodi," Medusa said, reading my mind. "There is more going on here."

Again she was keeping something from me. "What do you know? I keep getting the feeling that you're hiding something. What aren't you telling me, Medusa?"

She shook her head. "I see more than you think, but I'm bound to the deal the Ophi made with Hades when they rescued my spirit. I cannot reveal to you what's truly happening. If I do, the deal will be broken, and Hades will claim my soul once more."

I couldn't let that happen, but if she knew what was happening to me, there had to be a way for me to find out. "Can you give me a clue? Anything?"

"All I can say is this: *That which has the power to save, has the power to destroy.*" She shook her head again. "I've said too much already, and you've had enough of my power for one evening. Be careful, my child, and good luck." She vanished, and I let go of her hand.

That which has the power to save, has the power to destroy. What did that mean? All Ophi had the power to restore life or to kill. This wasn't anything new to me. Ugh! A hand pressed against my back, and I knew it was Chase before he even transferred his power. I whipped around.

"Don't. Please. I finally feel like myself again. Please, don't do this."

Chase grinned at me. "Don't you see? I'm trying to show you who you really are. Your true self is who you become with me." He pulled me to him, hitting me with his life-restoring power, making my body tingle and crave his blood. I couldn't fight it. I gave in, and before I knew what I was doing, I was kissing him.

The door opened behind us, and Lucas stumbled in. He was clutching his throat and choking. Not again!

I pulled away from Chase and reached Lucas as he fell to the floor. "Lucas?" I felt for a pulse, but there was none. He was dead.

"Chase, help me." I couldn't believe I was asking him for help, but no one else was around, and with the way my energy level had been roller coasting, I wasn't sure I could raise Lucas alone.

Chase bent down next to Lucas while I mixed my blood and focused my power on bringing Lucas back to life. I reached for his soul. It was still in his body, so it should've been easy for me to bring him back, but his soul wouldn't listen to me. Something must have happened when Chase and I connected. He'd affected my power somehow. I struggled, feeling my body shake. I reached out for Medusa's hand, but Chase grabbed me instead.

"Chase, what are you doing? I need help. He's fighting me. I can't bring him back alone."

Chase laced his fingers through mine, and I waited for the tingling feeling that came with Chase's power. I didn't feel it. He wasn't helping.

"Chase! Please!"

"I'm trying, Jodi. I'm giving you everything I have. Why isn't it working?" His voice was strange, as it had been in the cemetery when he was putting on a show for everyone.

"Oh, God!" McKenzie gasped.

My eyes were closed, focused on Lucas's soul, but I knew the others were here now. They were watching. Chase was determined to have them see me fail. He was pretending to help, but really he was letting me fail. Letting Lucas die. He couldn't get away with it.

"Chase, you jerk. You're not helping me! You're not giving me any of your power."

He squeezed my hand, sending his poisonous blood to me in such a concentrated form I instantly crumbled under the strength of it. I fell to my knees as it burned through me. He was going to kill us both. I had no choice. I stopped focusing on Lucas, letting his soul leave. I concentrated on pulling free from Chase. I jerked my hand from his and fell to the floor sobbing.

"No!" McKenzie screamed. "Lucas!" She threw herself on his body and wept.

I pounded my fist against the floor before glaring at Chase. "Why? Why did you do that? You poisoned me! You let Lucas die! We could've saved him."

Chase faked sadness. "Oh, Jodi. Don't do this. Don't look for someone to blame. We weren't strong enough. You couldn't save him. I don't know why, but you couldn't. No one blames you." He bent down and reached for me, but I backed away.

"Don't touch me!" Everyone was staring at me now. Looking at me like I'd lost my mind. Maybe I had. I'd lost Randy and Lucas. Alex had walked out on me. Chase was poisoning me, and no one would listen. It was driving me mad.

"Let me take you to your room." Chase was still pretending to be the perfect boyfriend.

"Jodi," Tony said, "maybe you should let Chase help you." Oh God, Chase even had Tony fooled.

"No." I turned to Arianna. She was my last hope. "Please, Arianna. Will you help me?"

She nodded and extended her hand to me, but Chase waved her off. "Lunch is ready, right? You all go eat. I'll take care of Jodi." Chase turned to Mason. "Uncle Mason, will you take care of Lucas' body?"

"Of course," Mason said. He looked at me and shook his head. "Jodi, I suggest you listen to Chase, before things get even more out of hand."

They were all turning on me. All but Arianna, and Chase wouldn't let her near me. How had this happened? Chase reached for me, giving me a small pleasurable dose of power. The one I couldn't fight. Instantly, I became a different person. I knew I was angry with Chase, yet when he touched me like that I wanted nothing more than to be with him. Yes, I was definitely crazy. Arianna gave me a puzzled look, no doubt completely baffled by the change in my reaction to Chase.

He took me up to my room, holding my hand to keep me passive and under his control. He brought me to my bed and tucked me in.

"See, Jodi. It could be like this all the time. I don't have to hurt you. I don't want to hurt you."

I nodded. After using my power to try to save Lucas and getting a dose of poison from Chase in the process, I needed Chase's life-restoring power. I didn't want him to leave. I willingly held his hand.

"You understand now, don't you?"

I did. He was stronger than me. If I didn't give in to him, he'd kill me and the others. He'd proven that with Lucas. "I understand."

"Good." He kissed me. "I'll go get you some food. We'll eat up here. Just the two of us."

I was torn. I wanted to get away from him, yet I didn't want him to go. My body, my blood, was at odds with itself. "Hurry back."

He smiled. "I knew you'd come around." He kissed the back of my hand. "I'll make you much happier than Alex did. I have so much more to offer you."

He left, leaving me to think about Alex. Now that Chase wasn't touching me, my head wasn't cloudy anymore. Alex was the one I loved, not Chase. What was I doing? I couldn't give in to him. I had to get out of here. Flinging the covers off me, I ran to the door, peeking out. The hallway was empty. Everyone was downstairs in the dining room. I doubted they were eating after what had happened to Lucas. They were probably discussing how to overthrow me. Maybe making plans to give me to Hades in exchange for their freedom.

I couldn't think about it now. I had to run while I had the chance. I didn't head toward the stairs. There was too much of a chance of running into Chase that way. Instead I turned right and went up to the third floor. I had to hide out. Make Chase think I'd run away from the school. Once he was out searching for me, I could come up with a plan. Lock him out or something until I could get help.

I went to the library, figuring it would be the last place Chase would look for me. Plus, no one ever came up here. Tony did on occasion, but maybe if I got him alone I could make him listen to reason. I went straight for the computers and logged in. I sent Alex an email, hoping he'd be online and respond. I needed to tell him what was going on. I didn't dare explain in the email though. I didn't want to leave anything Chase could trace. I simply told Alex I was in trouble. I waited ten minutes for a reply before logging out. Then, I logged in under Alex. I knew his password; I'd actually guessed it as a joke about a month back. "Macandcheese" was an obvious guess, so I never thought it would be right.

Alex had two recent emails, both opened and responded to. The first was from Arianna. She wanted to check up on him and make sure he was okay on his own. I checked his sent folder for his reply. He said he was fine, that he went to find Ethan and would be staying at Serpentarius. Not to worry.

Serpentarius wasn't that far away. If I really could escape and get there, Alex could help me stop Chase from whatever evil he had planned. But the more I thought about it, the farther away Serpentarius seemed.

I noticed another sent email, more recent. It was to someone named Ethan. I opened it. It said, "We need to talk about Chase. I'll be at your house tonight at nine." I went back to the inbox. There was a response from Ethan.

"I'm out of town. Need to reschedule." That was all it said.

Who was Ethan, and what did he know about Chase? I checked the sent messages one more time to see if Alex had responded to me. He hadn't. I logged off. I heard a commotion coming from the second floor. Chase must have figured out I was missing. I ran to the back room and locked myself in. Chase didn't have a key. Tony did, but I hoped Chase would assume the door was always locked and I couldn't have gotten in. I ducked under the desk and stayed absolutely still, listening.

"Jodi?" Leticia called into the library.

"Oh, please," Lexi said. "If she's hiding in here, do you really think she's going to answer you?"

"Ow!" Leticia said. Lexi must have pushed by her.

"Toughen up," Lexi said. "I've never seen such a weak Ophi before. You make McKenzie and Lucas look like gladiators, and they're pathetic."

"Don't talk about Lucas like that," Leticia said. "He just died. Show a little respect."

I smiled. Leticia was actually standing up to Lexi. Good for her.

"The weak *should* die." I got what Lexi was hinting at, and I was sure Leticia got it, too. Too bad Chase wasn't interested in Lexi. They seemed like the perfect match. Thinking that made me hate myself more for giving in to the power of his touch.

"Anything?" Tony asked. He must have just come into the room.

"No," Leticia said. She actually sounded happy. Did she not want to find me because she thought they were better off without me?

Tony cleared his throat. "All right. I'll tell the others. You two head to class."

"Class?" Lexi spoke as if Tony had cursed at her.

"Yes. I don't think we should let Jodi's disappearing act disrupt our training. I'm sure she'll show up soon." I was glad Tony was getting them out of here, but sending them to class meant they'd be directly across the hall from the library, and I'd be stuck under this desk until dinner.

I waited until the library door closed before I peeked out. The office had windows, so coming completely out of hiding wasn't an option. I doubted Chase would go to class. He was determined to find me. I made sure no one was in the hallway and reached for the laptop sitting on the desk. Pulling it into my lap, I logged in under Alex again. I figured the school might have some way to keep record of us logging in, and since it would be my name they'd search for, I wanted to avoid leaving a trail. I went to Alex's sent messages, and this time there was a reply to me.

I opened the message and two words stared back at me. "Got it." What did that mean? He understood I was in trouble? He got my message? What? I took a risk and sent him another message—from his own email account. I thought maybe seeing the desperate measures I was taking might make this all sink in and get a better response than "Got it." My fingers flew across the keys.

Alex, don't email me on my account. Reply to this message—if you are going to reply. I need help. You were right about Chase. He's evil, and he's hurting me. He's found a way to control me with his powers. I'm helpless against him. I need you, Alex. Please. I'm so sorry about what happened. I love you. ~J

I knew it was his personal email account, but I still couldn't convince myself to type my whole name. He'd know it was me. I didn't mention going into hiding. If Alex showed up, I'd come out. I'd risk everything to be with him.

I had hours to kill before dinner. I peeked out again and saw Tony had the lights off in his classroom. Must be another thrilling PowerPoint presentation on the history of the Ophi. I couldn't say I was sorry I was missing it. Still, I was bored out of my mind under this desk. I decided to do a little digging, see if there was anything on the Internet about Chase. I pulled up a search engine and typed his name. Nothing. Not a single match. Like he didn't exist. That was strange. I typed in Alex's name out of curiosity. Nothing. I tried mine. Nothing that actually pertained to me. There were other Jodi Marshalls, but all my old records and stuff were gone. Deleted.

The only conclusion I could come to was that the Ophi didn't want records on themselves. They'd practically deleted my identity. There was one problem with that plan. They couldn't erase my mom or my friends. They knew I existed, which meant there was still some imprint of me on the human world. I spent over an hour searching Melodie and my mom. I stared at their images on the screen and read Mel's blog. She raved about the Valentine's Day dance. The one I would've gone to with Matt if I hadn't come into my powers. She didn't mention her car being stolen by her former best friend, though. That was odd. Although, there was a picture of a different car in her profile picture. Nothing fancy, but definitely newer than the clunker I'd stolen. I was so wrapped up in Melodie's life without me that I barely heard the key turn in the lock.

"No, problem, Tony." Chase came into the room.

Oh, please no! If he walked around the desk, I was done for.

Chapter 20

I didn't move. The laptop was still in my lap, and my knees were sticking out from under the desk. Chase was going to find me and kill me. Or worse, he'd use his power on me to turn me into his slave again. If I'd had the choice, I'd pick death.

He moved to the bookshelf on the wall. I tensed up when his legs came into view. No way was I getting out of this. I thought about hitting him over the head with the laptop and making a run for it, but I figured he'd hear me and catch me before I could do any damage to him, so I stayed like a sitting duck.

"Did you find them?" Tony came into the office. He walked right over to the desk, and his eyes fell on me.

"No. Didn't you say they were on the shelf under the severed hand?" Chase laughed. "By the way, it's awesome that you use a severed hand for a paperweight."

Tony continued to stare at me. I mouthed the word "please," hoping he would understand. Chase's little charade had done a good job of fooling Tony, but maybe seeing how desperate I was now would make Tony understand that I wasn't losing my mind. That Chase was doing something horrible to me.

"You know, I just remembered I never made the copies," Tony said.

Chase turned around, and Tony stepped toward him, blocking me with his legs. "I'll make the copies," Chase said.

"No, that's okay. Why don't you go back to class and tell everyone to study the image on slide twenty-six? It's fascinating. I think you'll all get a kick out of it. I'll be back in a second."

Chase left, and I finally could breathe again.

"He's gone," Tony said. "Now, do you want to tell me why you're under the desk with my laptop?"

I handed him the computer. "Sorry. I needed to look up something."

"From under there?"

"I didn't want anyone to see me."

"By 'anyone,' are you referring to Chase?" Tony put the laptop back on his desk.

"Yes."

"Because…" His face softened. Maybe he did suspect Chase was up to something.

I wanted to blurt out everything. Tell him how awful Chase really was. That Chase was making me look like the bad guy to everyone else, but really he was to blame. So why wasn't I?

"Does this have anything to do with Alex?" He put his hands up in defense. "I don't like to pry, but you and Alex were awfully close, and now all of a sudden you and Chase are inseparable."

Yeah, because Chase wouldn't let me out of arm's reach. I looked down, avoiding Tony's eyes.

"You don't have to tell me," he said. "Maybe you should go for a walk to clear your head. I bet you'll feel better by dinnertime."

A walk. Like into town? I could go find Alex. I couldn't just let Tony go on believing Chase was the good guy, yet something was telling me this wasn't the time to tell Tony everything. Chase could walk back in.

"Thanks, Tony. I think I will, but please don't tell Chase you saw me. He's not what he seems to be. He knows his power is affecting me, hurting me—"

"Hurting you?" Worry spread across Tony's face. "Jodi, we have to do something if—"

"I'm not sure what to do about it yet. I have to think this through. I think Chase is up to something, but I don't know what it is. Please, just don't say or do anything yet. Let me figure it out first."

Tony nodded, but I could tell he didn't like this at all. "You're the boss, Jodi, but be careful. And might I suggest you take the back way out?"

"Back way?" I'd been sitting here this whole time when there was another way out?

"Right there." He pointed to a door next to the copier.

"I thought that was a closet."

"No. It leads to the storage room, which has another exit."

"The one in the hallway." Boy, did I feel like an idiot. "Thanks."

I made sure no one was watching before I ducked into the storage room. It was pitch black. I'd never come in here before. No one but the adults ever did. That kind of made it the perfect hiding place. I'd have to remember that for next time, although I hoped there wouldn't be a next time.

I felt my way along the walls to the other exit. It was in the same hall as the classrooms but farther down. As long as no one was in the hallway, I'd be able to get away unnoticed. I put my ear to the door, listening for footsteps or any other sounds. All quiet. I opened the door a crack. The hall was clear. I stepped out and ran for the stairs. I took the back way out of the school and headed straight for the woods. As long as Chase wasn't at the classroom window, I was sure I'd made it undetected. I had to stop a few times, too drained to run the whole way, but I made it to Melodie's car. The road wasn't much farther, and this time I was going to make it.

I was so close, and I wasn't going to let anything surprise me this time. I got to the road and ran into the center of the street. I'd make someone stop for me. Breaks squealed and a big gray car came skidding to a stop. My heart pounded, not because I'd almost been creamed, but because it was Alex.

I ran to the passenger side and got in. He pulled away quickly without saying a word. His tires screeched around the turn, and I struggled to get my seatbelt on before I was thrown through a window. I looked at him, but his eyes stayed focused on the road. I didn't know if I should say something or wait for him to talk, but I'm not that patient.

"How did you know I'd be here? I just emailed you about an hour ago." I held onto the door for support as Alex launched the car around another bend in the road.

"I answered your email from my phone. I knew if you tried to get away you'd head for home. You're really predictable, Jodi. You're lucky I got to you before he did."

I could tell he was avoiding Chase's name. "You're right. The first time I ran away, he caught me. That was this morning. This day has been one unending nightmare. He's pure evil, Alex. I should've listened to you."

He still didn't look at me. "You smell like his cologne. How do I know this isn't a trick? That you didn't lure me out here so he can come out of nowhere and—"

I reached for his hand on the steering wheel. "Because you know me." I smiled, trying to ease the tension. "And because we're in a car doing 85 on a windy road. He'd never catch us."

Alex slowed down, but he didn't face me. I let go of his hand.

"If you think he's evil, why are you getting close enough to him to smell like him?"

I had to tell him everything. The way Chase really made me feel. The way I was defenseless against the connection we had. I took his hand again, hoping that, by touching him, he'd know I how I felt about him. Know how difficult this was for me to say and how much I didn't want to hurt him.

"When Chase touches me, he transfers power to me. It's not like anything I've ever felt. It's—"

"You can tell me, Jodi. I can handle it. I need to know everything if we are going to fight him."

"Fight him? What do you mean? He's one of us." As I said it, I felt my blood mixing. The whole Alex/Chase situation was screwing me up again. Making me unsure of everything.

"He's evil, Jodi. You said so yourself."

"I did?" What was happening to me? "My blood is acting strange. I feel so confused." I rubbed my forehead.

"I think it has to do with this connection you're trying to tell me about. I don't blame you. I want to protect you from it." Finally, he looked at me. He pulled into an abandoned warehouse and parked. He cut the engine and turned to face me. "We have to get rid of him."

"Alex, I really do think we need Chase. The power between us is so strong. Maybe strong enough to fight off Hades. If that's true, we can't lose him. No matter what." I looked down at my feet. I wished I could send Chase away. Things would've been simpler, but I was the leader of the Ophi. I had to do what was best for the group, not what was best for Alex and me.

Alex sighed. "Tell me everything. Don't leave anything out. No matter how much you think it's going to tear me up inside. Got it?" His features were hard, serious.

I nodded. I told him about the way Chase's touch sent me into an almost euphoric state when he dosed me with the power in the right side of his body. How it made me feel better than alive. I also told him about the kiss. The way Chase had surprised me the day Alex had left.

"I wasn't planning on kissing him. All I cared about was you leaving. Trying to convince you to stay." I squeezed his hand, not wanting to let him go.

"I know." He looked away. "I saw it. I saw him grab you and kiss you. I also saw you kiss him back. It wasn't one-sided."

"I'm not going to deny it or try to lie my way out of this, Alex. I *did* kiss Chase. I gave in to his power. It filled me up so much I was overwhelmed by it. I loved it." I was embarrassed to admit I loved the power, but Alex needed to know. "I probably sound like a drug addict, don't I?"

"Kind of." He looked at me and brushed the hair from my forehead. "Why does he get to you like this? Make you lose control?"

"I don't know."

"Why does he make you feel so alive and…" He paused, but I knew what was coming next. "I can't?"

"I don't want you to make me feel like that, Alex. I'm scared of Chase. I'm scared of what I become when I'm with him. I lose control, and bad things happen. Everyone died when Chase kissed me. My powers went crazy, and I killed all the Ophi in the school. Medusa helped me bring them back." I swallowed hard. "All but one."

Alex narrowed his eyes. "Who?"

"Randy. He's gone. His body couldn't hold his soul in place. That zombie took a huge chunk from his shoulder and nicked a small artery. We couldn't stop the bleeding. When I brought him back, he died all over again."

Alex pulled me to him and hugged me tightly against his chest. I couldn't believe it. I thought he'd hate me for everything I'd done. For kissing Chase, for giving in to the power, for killing Randy. But he was comforting me. As much as I didn't want him to let go, I had to finish explaining what had happened.

"There's more." I pulled my head back to look at him. "When I ran away, he caught me and tortured me with his power. He can send the poisoned part of his blood to me in concentrated doses. It feels like I'm burning in a hellfire. Like when Hades stared at me. Chase can control me, Alex. He makes me hate him and crave him at the same time." I was crying now. Admitting all this to anyone was hard enough, but saying it to Alex was heartbreaking. "I'm so sorry."

"How does he control you? You have to tell me."

"I don't want to. You'll hate me. I couldn't handle it if you hated me." I squeezed him to me, afraid I was losing him again.

"I won't hate you. I'm going to hate Chase even more. I can tell. But I won't hate you."

I sniffled and looked at him. "Like I said, he can control what kind of power he transfers to me. When he sends me the life-restoring power, he can make me do anything he wants me to. My blood responds to him. I wish it didn't, but I can't stop it. When he touches me like that, I don't want him to stop."

The disgusted look on Alex's face tore me apart. He was wrong. This *was* going to make him hate me. I tried changing the subject. "Chase also stopped me from saving Lucas, one of the Ophi from Serpentarius."

"He died? How?"

So much for the topic change. "Chase kissed me again. Lucas was near us, and the connection reached out to him and killed him. It's this weird thing that happens sometimes when Chase and I are together."

"How many times have you kissed him?" Alex's face was bright red with rage.

I shook my head and sobbed. "I don't know. I swear I'm not doing it because I want to. He's making me. When I tried to bring Lucas back, Chase pretended to help me because the others were watching, but instead of transferring life-restoring power to me, he dosed me with poison. He was killing me, too. I had to break the connection and let Lucas go."

Alex punched the steering wheel. "I'm going to kill him! My God, Jodi, what he's doing to you, it's worse than—"

"Stop. Please, don't say it." I didn't want to talk about it anymore.

Alex took a few deep breaths, getting himself under control. "I found out something while I was gone."

"Where were you? Where did you go?"

"I went to see an old friend. Mason's brother, Ethan."

Ethan, the guy from the email. "Mason's brother? That would make him—"

"Chase's father. Yeah."

I'd never stopped to think about it before, but Chase called Mason Uncle Mason. That meant his father was Mason's brother, and since the only way an Ophi could have a sibling was to be a twin, it meant Mason was a twin.

"Jodi, there's something you need to know." He pulled away, just far enough to look me in the eyes. "It wasn't Ethan. It was Mason."

I shook my head. "Mason's at the school."

"No. *Ethan* is at the school. He's pretending to be Mason."

My head was spinning. Things were falling into place. "No wonder Chase was able to convince Mason to come here after I'd spent months begging him. He wasn't convincing his uncle. He was convincing his dad."

Alex nodded. "Mason told me everything. He said Chase and Ethan planned the whole thing. They made sure no one knew that Ethan would be taking Mason's place. They were going to pretend Chase had convinced him to come with the rest of the Ophi because things were going so well at the school."

"Wait, when Mason—I mean Ethan—practically demanded that Chase and I show him how our combined power worked—"

"That was part of the plan to get you and Chase together. I'm sure of it. They staged everything."

"How could I be so stupid? I fell for all of it. They used me. Manipulated me!" I was yelling now.

"You couldn't have known. I wouldn't have figured it out either if I hadn't gone looking for Ethan. I only knew he wasn't Ethan because Mason has a tattoo on his shoulder. He got it from Thayer. He was working out when I found him. I saw the tattoo and realized something was wrong. He confessed everything to me."

"Why did he go along with it?"

"Because he's got to keep Serpentarius open to keep making money. He had no idea Ethan was up to something. He thought he wanted to check things out without people knowing he was Chase's father."

"Now what? Do we confront Ethan and Chase? Do we kick them out?"

"We play along. We have to find out what they're up to." He sighed and took my hands in his. "I'm going back to the school. I'll tell everyone I got over you and that I want to go back to training. Do my part to fight Hades."

"Then we head back."

"No. I don't want you back there. Not after what you told me about Chase controlling you. You can stay at Serpentarius with Mason, the real Mason. He'll keep quiet. All he cares about is money and his precious club."

I looked at Alex, ready to risk everything for me, even after I'd put him through hell. I couldn't let him do it. "I'm going back with you. If we have to play along to figure out what Chase is up to, then I'm our best shot. I'm the closest to him."

Alex shook his head. "Absolutely not. I can't watch him control you, Jodi. I'll kill him. It will be hard enough not to tear him apart without you there."

"I know, but I have to do this. We'll go separately so Chase doesn't suspect anything. You can drive me to the path, and I'll walk back. You show up in the morning. That should be enough time apart to avoid suspicion."

"I can't let you do this. He could hurt you."

"I don't have a choice. I'm the Ophi leader. I have to do it."

He knew he couldn't change my mind. As much as we both hated it, I was going back to the school. I was going back to Chase.

Chapter 21

I leaned my head back on the seat. I couldn't believe I was doing this. Alex was right here. My old life was right here. Yet both felt so far away. I couldn't have what I wanted. I had to do the job I'd promised I'd do, and that meant facing Chase. Figuring out what his end game was and regaining control.

Alex brushed a tear from my cheek. I hadn't even realized I was crying. "What are you going to say?"

He knew I was worried about seeing Chase again. I sighed and met his eyes. "That I freaked. That I didn't like him controlling me. That if he really wants to work with me and wants my cooperation, he's going to have to stop using his power against me."

"You think that'll work?"

"I have no idea."

He shook his head. "I can't let you go in there alone."

"You have to. If you come with me, Chase will know we're up to something. He'll hurt me for sure."

"Why don't you let me go back first? I could beat the crap out of him, and you wouldn't have to worry about seeing him again."

If any other guy had said it, I would've laughed, but Alex was serious. "We should get this over with. The longer I'm gone, the madder he's going to be."

Alex grabbed me and hugged me tight. "I'm sorry I left you. Maybe I could've stopped this from happening."

I knew that wasn't true. Chase had already gotten to me before Alex left. If Alex had stayed, he would've witnessed everything, and he would've hated me for it.

I turned my face toward his and kissed him, thinking it might be our last kiss ever. I climbed over the console so I was in his lap, and I kissed him until my lungs screamed for air. I leaned back, making the horn give a short blare. We both jumped and laughed. We needed something to break the tension.

"I need you to understand that you're going to see a lot of things you aren't going to like." I didn't move from his lap. This was the only way to make sure I had his full attention. That he understood every word I was saying.

"Like him touching you?"

I nodded.

"Could you do me a favor and not play along too well?"

I fidgeted with the ring on my pinky. "That's just the thing. It's not an act, Alex. Chase changes me when I'm with him. My blood responds to his touch, and I can't control it." I lifted my eyes, forcing myself to be brutally honest. He had to know what he was in for. It was going to kill him to see me with Chase. To see me happy with Chase and craving his touch. "If he uses his blood to fill me with life, I'll want to be with him. At least, my blood will. Inside I'll know it's wrong, but I'll be powerless to stop it. The only thing that's going to get me through this is you knowing that I love you, not him."

"It's really going to be bad, isn't it?"

This was killing me. I didn't know how to make him feel better, so I went for the one thing that never failed. I kissed him. We stayed in the car for an hour, not wanting our time together to end. As much as I didn't want to, eventually I pulled myself away from him. If I didn't go now, I never would. I slid back into my seat and sighed.

Alex started the engine without a word. There was nothing to say. Nothing to make this any easier. He drove me back to the trail and most of the way to the school so I didn't have to walk too far. I looked at him through tear-soaked eyes.

"Wish me luck," I said.

"I love you." He pulled my face to his for one last kiss, and then I walked away without looking back. Losing Alex the first time was awful. The thought of losing him again was unbearable. Why was emotional pain so much stronger than physical pain? When I reached the school, I wasn't crying anymore. I was ready to face Chase. Sort of.

I walked up the back steps. It was dark and I figured everyone was probably getting ready for bed, but I heard voices out in the cemetery. I crept around the school and saw candles. A circle of them outside the mausoleum. The cemetery lights weren't at full strength yet. They took forever to really light up the place. Replacing them was on my list of things to do, but I'd kept pushing it back, not thinking it was that important.

As I got closer, I realized the candles were held by people, all sitting on the ground. They must have been having a memorial for Lucas and Randy. I figured it was best to approach Chase when everyone else was around. Between the element of surprise and having to keep his feelings in check for the sake of the group, I'd be better off. Of course, I had been hoping to get a good night's sleep and talk to him at breakfast, but my mom always told me it was better to face your problems sooner rather than later. I was about to find out if that was true.

I started down the hill as the lights gained more strength. Then I saw the corpses. They were lined up against the mausoleum. Every single one of them. I ran the rest of the way.

"What are you doing?" I yelled. "You can't raise the entire graveyard. I don't care if this *is* a memorial. Hades is going to flip!"

Chase smiled at me. Not an "I'm-so-happy-you're-back" smile. A sinister "I-can't-wait-to-get-a-hold-of-you" smile. "Jodi, right on time." He stood up and walked toward me.

"What do you mean? How could you know I was coming back?" How far did our connection go?

"How did I know? Well, when all the bodies in the cemetery suddenly came out of the ground at the same time, I figured that was your way of letting me know you were on your way."

I looked past him at the corpses. They immediately turned toward me, recognizing the one who'd raised them. I did this? It must have happened when I was kissing Alex. I thought I was happy to see him and sad to have to let him go again. My emotions were definitely conflicted, and they'd caused my blood to announce my return in true Ophi fashion—a massive raising.

"Personally, I like it." Chase kissed my cheek. "It's good to see you giving in to your powers."

He thought I'd done it on purpose, and he was taking this as a good sign. Maybe it wasn't such a bad thing, after all, if it got Chase off my back.

"We should send them back before Hades shows up. I thought you would've done that already," I added, hoping it would cover up my previous outburst about the bodies being here.

"You're right. Why don't we do it together? I've been itching to mix our blood again." He ran his hand down my arm, sending my blood into a frenzy. I wanted to throw my arms around him and pull him close, absorb all his power, but I had to stay in control. For Alex.

"I'm kind of drained. Can you just give me enough to release these guys all at once?"

"You got it." He took my hand, and a tingling slowly crept up my arm. I hated that I loved the feeling.

I forced myself to focus on the corpses. "I release—" Chase squeezed my hand, sending a shot of concentrated poison to me. I winced in pain. Apparently all wasn't forgiven.

"Jodi, I don't feel like digging all those graves this late at night," Chase said. "Have the corpses bury themselves before you release them."

The searing pain subsided, and I struggled to stay on my feet. If I crumbled or appeared weak at all, the rest of the Ophi were going to question my abilities. They had no idea Chase was the one weakening me. Maybe Tony would figure it out after our talk, but I didn't want him to lash out at Chase and ruin the plan Alex and I had come up with.

I tried to command the souls, but I was too weak now. "Please," I said to Chase. Damn it! I hated that I needed his help.

He let his power flow to me. I turned back to the corpses. "Return to your graves; once you're there, you may release your souls to where you were before I raised you."

I expected the souls to return to the graves they'd dug themselves out of, but instead, they all went in different directions with their shovels.

"What are they doing?" Leticia asked.

"Returning to their original graves," Tony said. He looked at me. "Watch your wording. Now we don't have them all together anymore."

I was okay with that. I hated not even knowing the names of the souls I was raising. It felt wrong to treat the souls as nameless beings.

"Jodi and I will train together a little harder tomorrow to make sure no more slip-ups like this happen." Chase put his arm around me, and I cringed, expecting to feel his poisoned blood enter my body. It didn't. "Won't we, Jodi?"

I nodded. "I think I need to go to bed. I'm really tired. It's been a long day."

Mason—well, Ethan pretending to be Mason—stood up. "It's been a long day here, too. You would've known that if you hadn't run away."

He was angry with me, too. That wasn't good. I couldn't let him take the others and leave.

"I'm sorry. It won't happen again."

Chase squeezed my shoulder. "Uncle Mason, I'm sure Jodi would be happy to take over the service."

"Take over the service?" I looked around at the group in confusion.

"We just started," Carol said. "We wanted to be able to say goodbye to Lucas."

"And Randy," Leticia added. "We never got to have a service for him. He deserves one."

I knew Alex would want to say goodbye to Randy too, but I couldn't postpone the service for him. I wasn't supposed to know about Alex coming tomorrow. "Of course," I said. "I'd be happy to say a few words."

The service was pretty much a blur. I rambled on about Randy, and thankfully, when it was time to talk about Lucas, McKenzie asked to speak, so I didn't have to say much. By the end of it, all the corpses were back in their graves, as I'd commanded them earlier. They released all around the same time, and I watched the souls float away. It would've been beautiful if I wasn't at a funeral and Chase wasn't hovering no more than two feet away. He stayed in arm's reach. That way, he could easily control me if necessary, I was sure. I hated him. I hated that he could hurt me so much one minute and make me want his touch the next. He was evil, and he was making me evil.

Chase walked me up to my room after everyone said goodnight. He kissed me at my door, but this time he didn't use his power on me, and I cringed. He wasn't Alex, and I resented having to put on this charade. "Want me to come in for a little while?" He tapped his finger on my door, and I struggled not to show my disgust.

"No. I'm really tired. I want to go to sleep."

"You left me, Jodi." He raised his hand to my face, letting it hover there. I knew his next touch would be filled with the burning poison of his blood.

"I'm sorry. Chase, please. This is why I left. You can't keep doing this to me. You can't keep controlling me. It's not right."

"I'm only showing you what your blood wants." His hand came closer to my face.

I closed my eyes and turned my head away. "No, you're hurting me."

"You think taking off didn't hurt me?"

I looked at him, surprised he hadn't used his power on me. We both knew he could.

"Alex never had to make you love him."

"Are you saying you want me to love you?"

"You don't have to love me, but choosing to be with me without me having to use my power on you would be a nice change."

"I can't choose you if you don't give me the chance. You're forcing me to feel things." My mind spun with ways to work Chase's insecurity into my plan. "I bet you didn't know I really didn't like Alex when I first met him. He scared me."

Chase raised an eyebrow. "You expect me to believe that?"

"It's true. He was so wrapped up in doing his job—getting me to come here because that's what his parents told him to do. He followed me around and tried to make me listen to him. I only started to have feelings for him after he backed off."

"So, you're saying that if I back off, let you decide how you feel on your own, there's a chance you'll actually choose to be with me?" He stepped closer to me, but not in a threatening way.

"I'm not promising anything, Chase, but we do have a lot of combined power. I can't say I'm not drawn to that. Maybe we could work well together and even be together like—"

"Like you and Alex were?"

Why did he have to make it so hard to lie to him? He and I could never be like Alex and I were—and hopefully would be again. But if I said that, I'd be right back where I was before. I nodded, unable to say the words out loud.

Chase laughed, but then his hand came slamming down on the door next to my head, making me flinch. "Come on, Jodi. How stupid do you think I am? You're still in love with Alex. I can tell. You have no intention of falling for me. Not unless I make you. It looks like that's exactly what I'm going to have to do."

I tried to duck under his arm, but he grabbed me. The second his skin touched mine, I felt his power. It wasn't poison like I'd been expecting. It was the energy I craved from him. He wasn't trying to hurt me—at least not physically. Before I gave in to the power, I saw Jared and Lexi at the top of the stairs. Chase must have heard them coming, and now he was using his power to make it look like he and I were caught making out in the hallway. His lips were on mine in seconds, and without being able to stop myself, my arms were around his neck.

"Damn, Chase," Lexi said, "I thought you had better taste."

"Whatever, Lexi," Jared said. "Way to go, man!" Jared must have thought Chase and I were making up.

They went to their rooms, and when both doors closed, Chase pulled away. "Why can't you let us be this way all the time?"

I could've given him a slew of answers. He was evil. He was a manipulative prick. I wasn't his little plaything. But the simplest answer, and the one I definitely couldn't say, was he wasn't Alex.

"Goodnight, Chase." I reached for the knob, but he stopped me, taking my hand in his. His touch made my blood ripple under my skin.

"You sure you're ready to say goodnight?" He moved in closer, and I almost gave in. Almost. But I saw Leticia's door closing. She'd been watching us. I twisted the doorknob with my other hand and ducked into my room, locking the door behind me. I leaned against the door and relaxed my breathing. I pictured Alex's face in my mind. He'd be here tomorrow. I could make it until then. Of course, having Alex here was only going to make all this harder on me. I was going to have to guard myself against Chase. I needed to block him, stop him from taking over my blood. I exhaled slowly, regaining control. My blood wasn't surging anymore. I'd resisted the urge to give in to Chase. All thanks to Leticia. I hoped she'd seen everything. The way my mood changed so quickly. The way Chase looked like he wanted to kill me one minute, and make out with me the next. I hoped Leticia would figure it out. She wasn't the most skilled Ophi, but she was smart.

Please, Leticia. I needed more people on my side. Before Chase took over my blood, and there was nothing left of me.

Chapter 22

Morning couldn't come soon enough. I ran to the window and pushed back the curtains. The little girl in me had been hoping I'd catch a glimpse of Alex hiding in the woods, waiting to come rescue me. Life would be so much easier if those fairy tales they tell you as a kid were actually true. But in this scenario, I was the powerful one who was supposed to save the day. I'd saved Alex before. I didn't mind being powerful. I loved it. But just once, it would've been nice to pretend I was a princess about to be saved by her prince.

"Jodi?" Arianna called from the other side of the door. "Are you awake?"

I went to the door and opened it a crack. I wanted to see if she was alone or if Chase had tricked her into getting me up so he could get his claws on me first thing.

She was alone.

"Yeah, come on in, Arianna." I shut the door behind her and locked it again, which got me a wrinkled brow from Arianna.

"Trying to avoid someone?"

She was good. She knew I was having boy issues. "Kind of."

"Sweetheart, listen to me. I know you're still crazy about Alex, so why are you hanging all over Chase?"

My God, is that what it looked like to everyone else? He was chasing after me. Forcing me to be with him. Torturing me. But it came off as me hanging all over him?

"I'm not. I don't like Chase like that. He's—" If I told Arianna the truth, would she believe me? I still didn't know if Leticia knew what was really happening. Maybe she saw the incident in the hall last night as me throwing myself at Chase. Ugh, the thought sickened me.

"Honey, you are torn. One minute you're holding onto Chase for dear life, and the next you're taking off. Don't you see you're clinging to Chase because Alex isn't here?"

I wish. If things were that simple, they'd be fixed in a matter of hours, maybe minutes, when Alex showed up.

"Ari, things with Chase are very complicated. It's hard to explain."

"I can see that. Why are you hiding from him now?"

"I'm not hiding." I opened my arms wide. "I'm in my room. It's the first place he'd look. I'm just not ready to face him yet today."

"Did you two have a fight?"

"You could say that."

"Was it about Alex?"

"Somewhat." I knew that she knew more than she was saying. "Did Leticia come to you? Did she say anything about last night?"

"No. I was in the library yesterday, and I checked the Internet log. Alex was logged in during lessons, and so were you. I'm wondering how that was possible. He's not hiding out in the woodwork or anything, is he? Because my heart can't take surprises like that."

"No." I couldn't help smiling. I wished Alex had been hiding out here all this time. "I logged in under Alex's name. I was trying to find out where he went."

"Did you?"

I hated that I couldn't completely trust Arianna, but giving away anything about yesterday was too risky. "Not really. Arianna, please don't tell Chase about this."

"Chase was under the impression you left before lessons."

"I know." I had a feeling Tony had mentioned finding me in the library and hiding me from Chase. It looked like Arianna and I were both tiptoeing around information we didn't want the other to know.

She reached for my hand. "I know I'm not your mother, Jodi, but you can talk to me. If Chase does anything to you that scares you or makes you uncomfortable, you can tell me."

Everything Chase did scared me and made me uncomfortable. "Thanks," I said.

She looked like she wanted to say more, and I couldn't help wondering about Abby and Lexi's father. Had he been abusive? Arianna had already told me he was evil. Was she trying to reach out to me because she'd been in my shoes? She exhaled a shaky breath. "Sometimes even the strongest Ophi needs a little help. All you have to do is ask."

That was all I needed to hear. I didn't know Abby and Lexi's father, but in that moment, I hated him. He'd hurt Arianna. She turned to leave. "Ari." She looked over her shoulder at me. "You're the best second mother I could've asked for. Abby and Lexi have no idea how lucky they are."

I meant it. Even though I had to hide things from her, I still loved that she was willing to do anything for me—and the others. She was an amazing mother to all of us.

"That means a lot." Tears welled up in her eyes as she left.

I got dressed and ready for breakfast. Every time I heard a noise in the hall, I expected Chase to come knocking at my door. He'd left almost too easily last night. I was sure he wasn't happy with me slipping away like I had, and I was even more sure he was going to make me pay for it.

Finally, the knock came at my door. It had to be him. I slipped into the bathroom and shut the door behind me. I couldn't remember if I'd locked my bedroom door after Arianna left. I waited a few seconds before peeking out the bathroom door that led to the hallway. Chase wasn't there. That meant he was probably in my room and the bathroom would be his next stop. I slipped out, running into Lexi.

"What's your hurry?" She brushed off her pants as if I had dirtied them by bumping into her.

"Sorry." I didn't have time to get into it with Lexi. Besides, any commotion would draw Chase's attention to the hallway. I ran past Lexi and down the stairs. I went straight to the dining room where everyone else would be. Safety in numbers. Leticia was already sitting down, and so was McKenzie. I slipped into the seat next to Leticia. Randy's old seat. It felt weird to sit there, and everyone looked at me like I'd lost my mind.

"I thought a little different scenery would be nice," I said.

Arianna met my eyes and smiled. "I agree. I think I'll sit by you, Jodi." She put the coffee on the table and sat. I was safely wedged between two Ophi who might have seen a small glimpse of the person Chase really was. I struck up a conversation with Arianna and dug into the Belgian waffles she'd made. I barely noticed Lexi and Jared come in.

"Hey, what's up with the seating arrangements?" Jared asked.

"I thought we should mix things up. Get to know different people a little better."

"Then, why are you sitting by two people you've known for months?" Lexi had an evil smirk on her face.

Before I could answer, Chase walked in. He looked at my empty seat before his gaze traveled across the table to me. "Did I miss musical chairs?"

"I talked to Jodi this morning about mixing things up." Arianna came to my defense. "She thought we should sit by different people at each meal. That way we can really get to know each other. We were falling into a rut with the old seating."

"Hmm," Chase said. "Well, actually I had just changed my seat."

Yeah, he'd taken Alex's seat to make sure he was by me.

"Well, then you don't mind changing it again." Arianna smiled. I squeezed her hand under the table.

Chase sat down in Arianna's usual seat, and I did my best to avoid his eyes for the rest of the meal. I kept glancing at the door, expecting Alex to walk in at any minute.

"Expecting someone, Jodi?" Mason asked.

"Huh?" I nearly dropped my orange juice in my lap.

"You keep looking at the door. Were you expecting someone else for breakfast?"

"Yeah, like a few corpses?" Lexi said. "You didn't raise the cemetery again, did you?"

"No, I—I was thinking about visiting Medusa before training this morning. That's all."

"I don't think that's such a good idea," Mason said. "Most Ophi only connect with Medusa once, when they first come to the school. You seem to do it on a regular basis."

"Well, my powers are a little different than other Ophi's. I have a more direct connection to Medusa, so it seems only natural." I struggled to keep my tone friendly, but that was tough considering I knew the man calling himself Mason was really Chase's father.

He stared at me, contemplating my explanation. "Well then, why don't you take Lexi, Jared, and McKenzie to the statue before training, too? They haven't been formally introduced."

I nodded. I'd completely forgotten that they had never connected with Medusa. I couldn't help smiling, remembering the first time I'd connected with the statue. "Great idea, Mason. I will." I looked up to see Chase was still eating. Now was the perfect time.

I stood up. "Well, it's almost time to start training, so McKenzie, Jared, and Lexi, come with me. I'll introduce you to the most amazing Gorgon you'll ever meet."

"Now?" Chase practically choked on his waffle.

"Why not?"

"I'm still eating, and so is Leticia."

"That's fine. You two have already met Medusa." I smiled at him, pretending everything was perfectly normal. "Come on." I waved the others along.

McKenzie came up alongside me. "Chase doesn't like to let you out of his sight, does he?" She said it like it was a good thing. Sometimes I wondered if it was nice being so naïve.

"Really?" I shrugged, pretending not to have noticed.

"It's cute how you two can't keep away from each other."

Had everyone missed the part where I took off yesterday to get away from Chase? It was like he had them all brainwashed. Well, almost all of them. I couldn't help noticing Tony keeping a close eye on Chase during breakfast, and Arianna definitely had my back.

I got to the statue and stood next to it. "This is Medusa. Or her spirit anyway. Every Ophi who has come to this school has held hands with Medusa. One hand at a time."

"Why only one at a time?" McKenzie asked. "I heard you hold both of the statue's hands."

I looked at Lexi, who was staring at the statue. I hadn't even realized this might be hard for her. Medusa had killed Abby for taking both her hands and trying to prove she was as powerful as I am.

"I'm the only Ophi who's held both her hands and lived." I made sure sympathy came across in my voice.

"Abby isn't dead," Lexi said.

"Not anymore." I matched the venom in Lexi's tone.

"Abby died?" Jared asked.

"She held both the statue's hands, and it killed her. I used Medusa's power to bring her back."

Jared started laughing. "Lexi, your bitchy sister got herself fried by a statue and then rescued by the one Ophi she hated."

"It's not funny, Jared." Lexi smacked his shoulder.

"She's right, Jared. It isn't funny." I looked at each of them. "None of you should try it. Medusa didn't want me to bring Abby back. She said Abby had disrespected her and me. I'm one of Medusa's descendents. Her blood is in my veins."

"Her blood is in all our veins," Lexi sneered.

"Not as much." Why did I feel like she was going to repeat her sister's mistake? "Listen, Lexi, I'm trying to protect you."

"Whatever," she said. "Get on with the show."

"Can I go first?" Jared asked.

"Sure." I motioned for him to face the statue. "Take her right hand first. You'll feel her life-restoring power rush through you. It's incredible. Like you're flying on a cloud and nothing can stop you."

He reached for Medusa's hand and smiled. "Awesome."

"I know." Once he'd had enough, I had him switch hands. "Don't get freaked out. It's going to feel like snakes crawling all over you."

"I like snakes," Jared said.

We went through the others the same way. They all got to feel Medusa's power. I was really glad Mason—really Ethan—had suggested it, because by the time they were finished, they were all in good moods. Even Lexi.

"Great, let's go train," I said.

"Yes, let's." Chase came up behind me and draped his arm around my shoulders. "We need to talk," he whispered in my ear. "Now."

"We have to go train. We can talk later." Even though Chase was whispering, I was talking slightly louder than normal, making sure everyone could hear us. I was tired of looking like the lovesick girl who couldn't get enough of Chase.

Chase didn't object, not verbally at least. He let his poisoned blood travel through his arm and into me. I crumpled to the floor, my blood like fire.

"Jodi?" McKenzie bent down to me.

"What did you do to her?" Leticia looked at Chase.

Maybe Leticia *had* figured it out. Maybe I'd get enough help between Leticia, Arianna, Tony, and Alex to get Chase to leave me alone.

"I didn't do anything. She fell."

"You don't seem all that concerned either," Leticia said.

"It's Jodi we're talking about. If blood's not pouring from her eyes, she's fine."

"Is that supposed to be a joke?" We all turned to see Alex in the doorway.

I fought the urge to smile at him. Chase looked back and forth between Alex and me, but I pretended not to notice.

"Alex, you're back." I tried to sound surprised. "What changed your mind?"

"Nothing. I realized this is my home. I should be here."

"I agree." I kept my voice steady.

"It doesn't mean what you're thinking, Jodi." Alex adjusted his duffle bag on his shoulder. "We're still done." I wasn't sure where he was pulling these acting skills from, but he was convincing.

I got up from the floor. The effects of Chase's touch had worn off. "Why don't the rest of you go out to the cemetery? I'd like to talk to Alex for a minute."

Everyone headed out. Everyone except Chase. I gave him a questioning look.

"What, you thought I was going to leave you two to patch things up?" Chase walked back over to me. Alex moved like he was going to stop him, but he pulled back. He wasn't supposed to defend me. He was supposed to be angry with me for having feelings for Chase. "Something you wanted to say, Alex?"

"Yeah." Alex crossed his arms, probably to keep from punching Chase in the face. "I don't like you. I get that you're with Jodi now. I can't change that, but I don't have to like it. Or you."

"Good. That's the way I'd prefer it." Chase stepped between Alex and me. "Because you were right about Jodi and me being together. We make a better pair than you two ever did. We have more power. More chemistry." Chase turned around to face me. Oh God, he was going to show off to Alex. I backed away.

"Chase, there's no need to act like a caveman. Alex gets it. Let's not rub it in his face."

"No, I think we will. I want to make sure he really gets it."

Alex's fists were clenched. He was ready to let loose on Chase. If he did, everything we had planned would be ruined. Chase would figure it all out, and we'd get no information out of him.

"Fine," I said, "but he should hear it from me. I owe him that."

Chase smiled and stepped back so I was face to face with Alex. I tried to say more with my eyes than I could ever say with words. Alex's face remained steady. He was doing his best to stay in control of his emotions. Instinctively, I reached for his hand.

"Not necessary," Chase said, before I could touch Alex. "Just because you went around holding my hand when you were with him doesn't mean I'm going to tolerate you holding his hand when you're with me."

I could hear Alex grind his teeth. He was reliving every reason why he'd left. I had to get this over with and make it as painless as possible.

"I'm with Chase now. You coming back doesn't change that. I don't love you anymore." My breath caught in my throat. Even knowing it was a lie, it was still difficult to say.

"That's right. She's in love with me now." Chase reached his hand out and touched my arm very lightly. The tingling sensation inched through my body. I tried to fight it, to resist the urge to pull Chase to me and take more of his power. The more I fought, the more power Chase teased me with. In seconds, I was turning away from Alex and throwing my arms around Chase. He smiled and kissed me long and hard while Alex watched.

Chapter 23

Chase got so into kissing me that he stopped using his power. That was all I needed to pull away from him. I pushed my hand against his chest and backed up. I gasped for air, and my eyes instantly flew to Alex. He was looking away, but I could see his jaw was clenched. I couldn't even imagine how I'd feel if I saw him kissing another girl, even if he did hate her the way I hated Chase.

"I guess we should go train." Chase's smile was much wider than necessary. He put his hand on my back and I jumped, not knowing if he was going to use his powers on me again, or which power he'd choose if he did. Alex jerked his head in my direction, ready to defend me if Chase hurt me, but Chase only pushed me toward the door. He'd done what he'd set out to. Alex was trying to put on a strong face, but I could tell he was dying inside. I had a feeling Chase knew it, too.

Training was nothing short of awful, and not just because the Serpentarius Ophi were struggling to get control over the souls. Chase wouldn't let go of me. He didn't use his powers—unless being an overbearing wannabe boyfriend was a power. Alex trained with Jared, mostly to avoid Chase and me, although he said it was because Jared was the most advanced of the newcomers. The worst part was that I was forced to combine powers with Chase and work on making our connection stronger and more manageable.

"Can we please try something less evil this time?" I stepped out from under Chase's arm, which had been draped across my shoulders since we'd walked out of the school.

"Evil?" Chase laughed. "Jodi, we're necromancers. What we do isn't exactly pretty, but it's not evil. These souls aren't alive. Besides, we're giving most of them a break from Hell. I think it's actually pretty nice of us."

Of course he did. "Yeah, well it makes me feel evil torturing them like that."

"Like what? Making them dig their own graves? Would you rather spend valuable training time digging?"

When he put it like that, it didn't seem so bad. "Okay, but no more making corpses stab themselves. That's cruel, and I don't want anything to do with it."

Chase smiled at me and cupped the side of my neck in his right hand. "When are you going to realize that what I do is a direct reflection of the way you are making me feel? When you get me angry, I do bad things. So, don't make me angry." He looked over my shoulder, and I assumed Alex was watching us because Chase pulled me to him and kissed me. It wasn't a long kiss, just enough so Alex would notice.

I didn't object even though Chase kept his power to himself. He'd made it clear that, if I upset him, he was going to make me torture more souls. I didn't want that.

"What should we start with?" he asked me. I was taken aback. Sure, I was the one in charge of the Ophi, but Chase was used to controlling me and calling the shots. Why was he asking me for direction here?

I couldn't waste this opportunity. I had to push the limits of our connection, but in a way that wouldn't get us in trouble with Hades or cause too much pain to the souls we raised. "What if we tried to raise a soul and put it in someone else's body?" I wasn't even sure where that idea had come from. Maybe it was my way of seeing if I could raise my dad again now that Hades had his body.

"Put them in the wrong bodies? That's kind of sick." Chase smiled. "I like it, babe." He put one arm around me and squeezed. "See, when you cooperate, we make an awesome team."

I stared at his hand on my arm. I hated how he scared me so much. I looked up and met Alex's eyes. He was watching me so intently. He had to stop, or Chase was going to get pissed—and I'd probably be the one he took it out on.

"I want to try to raise my dad," I said, "but I'd rather start with another soul that Hades took first. I want to make sure we can do this right before I put my dad's soul through this."

Chase looked at me, and for a second I thought he actually sympathized with me. Like he cared about me and understood why I wanted to get my dad's soul back. He took my hand in his, and this time I didn't cringe in fear.

"You're different right now," I said.

"I get that you don't want Hades to have your dad's body. It makes sense. I'll do what I can to help you get him back."

"Really?" I searched his eyes, trying to see if this was a trick, but he looked sincere.

He let go of my hands. "I'm not faking my feelings for you, Jodi, and I was serious when I said that if you choose me—really choose me—we'll make the greatest Ophi team ever." He leaned into me, and even with no power surging between us, I reached up on my toes and kissed him lightly on his lips.

"I wish you were always like this."

"That's really up to you." He turned his head slightly, and I followed his gaze to Alex, who was staring at us with hatred in his eyes. "And him."

I looked away from Alex. He'd seen me kiss Chase, and since Chase hadn't been touching me, Alex must have known I wasn't being controlled. The action was completely my doing. I wasn't even sure why I'd done it. Chase was right, though. Something about us made sense. At least in an Ophi way.

"See, but it's things like that just now, that look of shame on your face knowing that he saw you kiss me, that make me crazy, Jodi. Why do you have to make me want to hurt you?" He grabbed my wrist, threatening to use his poisoned blood on me.

"Chase, please. I can't pretend I didn't love him. That doesn't go away overnight. You came after me the second Alex said he was leaving. You didn't give me a chance to get over him."

"Being with me should be enough to make you forget him." He squeezed my wrist harder, but he still held his powers back.

Alex must have seen the fear on my face because he started walking toward us. Luckily, Chase was too focused on me to notice. I had to defuse the situation before Alex started a fight I couldn't get him out of.

My eyes welled up with tears. "Chase, don't. Be the guy that made me want to kiss him. Don't you want me to come to you without you controlling me? Give me a chance."

Chase loosened his grip on me. Alex stopped short, no doubt because I had admitted I wanted to kiss Chase earlier.

"Can we concentrate on our training, please? It'll be just you and me. The way you like it." I reached for his hand, lacing my fingers through his. For the first time, I tried transferring my power to him. He cocked his head to the side, and I knew he felt the life-restoring power I was sending him. I kept the dose light, not wanting him to react the way I usually did when he dosed me with this kind of power.

"I've never been on the receiving end before—except for when I was connected to the Medusa statue." He stepped closer to me. "I prefer the energy coming from you."

"Good. Then let's try this."

He nodded. "Any clue how we put a soul in another person's body?"

Not really, but I was hoping it wasn't too much different than returning a soul to its own body. "Let's reach out for one of the souls Hades took. Once we have him or her, we can use our combined powers to command the soul into the body we choose."

"Okay, which corpse did you want to use?"

"Any one but the one we had stab himself. I don't want to bring the soul any extra pain. I have no idea what this is going to do to it."

Chase picked another grave and stood on one side of it. I stood on the other. We reached our hands over the grave and joined them in the middle. I could feel everyone's eyes on us. They knew we were trying something different, and they were all definitely interested.

"Ready?" I asked Chase.

"Should I transfer power to you first?"

I didn't know why, but I had a feeling this would require a give and take. "We'll transfer power to each other at the same time. You push your power to me through your right hand and into my left. I'll do the same to you. The power should circle between us that way."

"Sounds cool. But what kind of power?"

"We need to mix our blood so it's at full strength."

"What do you mean? When we combine powers, we are mixing our blood."

I shook my head. "No, I mean I'm going to mix my blood before transferring my power to you. I want you to do the same."

He shrugged. "I can't. You're the only Ophi who can, Jodi. I can only give you a concentrated dose of one side of my blood."

I knew that all too well. He'd been dosing me pretty much since he got here. "You're not like other Ophi either. Have you tried mixing your blood?"

He nodded. "When I heard you could do it, I tried every day. I hoped I could do it, too. I can't." His voice was full of disappointment.

"All right. Then send me the life-restoring blood. *Only* the life-restoring blood."

"I just said I can't mix—oh wait, you don't trust me. You think I'm going to dose you with poison."

The others were still staring, but they weren't close enough to hear us. Except for Alex. He was staying in earshot. "You've done it numerous times before. This is what I'm talking about, Chase. How can I trust you or want to work with you when you're purposely hurting me? If I'm skeptical of you, it's because you've made me be this way."

His face turned crimson with anger. "If I were you, I'd help me calm down before I lose it and my blood takes over."

I narrowed my eyes at him. "Are you saying you can't control your emotions? That you haven't been hurting me on purpose? Are you blaming your blood for what you've done to me?"

"Haven't you blamed your emotions and blood for raising the cemetery countless times?" He yanked his hands down, pulling me directly over the grave. I stumbled forward, but he caught me. "We're not that different." He pressed his lips to mine, and I realized he was trying to calm down. He wasn't trying to use his powers on me. I gave in because I didn't want his poisoned blood to cripple me and stop me from raising this soul. I let him kiss me until his hands unclenched.

I pulled back slowly. "Are you okay now?"

"Fine. I hate that you can turn me into a monster."

"Funny, I feel the same way about you."

He smiled. "We're either going to make the perfect couple or we're going to kill each other, aren't we?"

I laughed it off, but inside I knew it would probably be the latter of the two.

"You two going to actually raise something today, or did you just come here to make out on top of the graves?" Alex yelled.

I jumped, and I felt Chase tense up again. Crap! After I'd just calmed him down.

"Not your problem, Alex," I called, keeping my eyes locked on Chase.

Chase smiled again. I was getting better at fooling him.

"Okay, let's try this." We joined hands and closed our eyes. "On three." I felt Chase's power already flowing to me. For a second I wanted to let him dose me with that amazing energy. I was high on it, but I knew I had to transfer my power to him. I willed my blood to mix, feeling it bubble beneath my skin. I sent him a little at first, waiting to see how he'd respond. I opened my eyes so I could watch his reaction. He threw his head back and laughed, obviously loving the feeling. I gave him a little more power before I reached out toward the underworld.

It took me a second to realize Chase wasn't helping. He was too busy enjoying the power surging through him. "Chase, I need your help. Stay with me."

"Sorry." He didn't sound sorry at all. "Is this how I make you feel? Because this is seriously awesome stuff. No wonder you throw yourself at me when I touch you."

I felt my cheeks redden. Alex and the others were watching. I hoped they were far enough away not to hear Chase.

Chase pulled me closer to him. He was acting exactly like I did when he used his power on me. He wanted to wrap his arms around me, but I couldn't let him break our connection or mess up what we were trying to do. I clenched his hands tighter and gently pushed him back.

"Focus. Reach for the soul with me."

"Only if you promise we can do this again later when we won't be interrupted by souls."

I sighed, partly because Alex was having to watch all this and I knew it was killing him, but mostly because I understood why Chase wanted to connect like this more. I wanted it, too. I had to stay focused. I had to find a good use for the power Chase and I had.

"I promise," I said.

Chase squeezed my hands, and I felt the power circle through us. He was concentrating now, helping me call out to the souls Hades had taken. I settled for the first one that answered us. It was a woman. She came with us willingly at first, which was a nice surprise. Usually the souls didn't want to come with us. But when she realized it wasn't her body we were trying to put her in, she freaked. Her soul lashed out at us. Her screams rang through my head.

Chase squeezed me tighter. He heard her, too. For the first time, he could hear the torment the souls went through when we raised them. It was good to sense him cringing. It meant he was capable of emotion. So far today, he'd shown me that side of him more than once. It was a side of him I didn't hate.

His breathing became heavy and labored. He clenched my hands so hard it hurt. He was getting angry at the soul. I worried what he'd do. What he'd make me do.

"Chase, relax. It's always like this, only you never heard or felt it before. This is what I experience every time I raise a soul. It's awful, I know, but don't let it overtake you. Push it out of your mind."

His hands and arms shook. I had to get him to calm down. I stepped closer to him without breaking our connection, not that I could with how tightly he was holding my hands.

"Chase, I'm right here. Focus on me. Focus on our power. Forget the soul. I'll handle her."

He grunted as the soul screamed so loudly I thought my eardrums would burst. She whipped around us, not wanting to get near the body we were standing above. She tried to force us apart. Chase was losing it. His anger flared up, and I felt his blood change.

"No, Chase! Don't!" He was going to poison the soul, and in doing so, he was going to poison me.

I sent more life-restoring power to him, no longer mixing my blood but forcing concentrated bursts of the energizing power to Chase. I hoped that would snap him out of it. Instead, he countered with a shot of poison.

The soul and I screamed in agony at the same time. Chase was hurting us both. I stopped transferring power to him, too weak to give him any more. His poisoned blood was taking over mine. My vision blurred. My hearing dimmed, but I could still hear the soul screeching at us. My screams stopped, turning to choking instead. I fell to my knees, my hands still in Chase's. He wasn't stopping. I coughed up blood, staining the dirt beneath me.

Then the soul stopped screaming. Chase let go of me, and I slumped onto the grave. There were more screams, and feet shuffled against the ground. Someone slid on the dirt next to me.

Alex was at my side, cradling my head in his lap. "Jodi! Jodi, can you hear me?" His hands were caressing my face.

"Did you kill her?" Lexi asked Chase, not sounding all that concerned.

I could barely see through the blood filling my eyes, but I could make out Chase staring at me.

"We did it. She's in there." He pointed to the ground beneath me.

"What, in Jodi?" Leticia asked. "You put the soul in Jodi?"

"No, in there." Chase continued to point, not paying any attention to me.

I felt something claw at my back before two decaying arms came up out of the ground and wrapped around me.

Chapter 24

I was virtually powerless. Chase had dosed me with so much poison I couldn't defend myself against the corpse. Alex pried the arms from my waist.

"Leticia, get Jodi out of here!" he yelled. Before Leticia could get to me, Chase scooped me into his arms. He sent waves of life-restoring power to me, and I instantly started to perk up. I wrapped my arms around him and leaned my head against his chest so I was touching him and soaking up his energy in as many places as possible.

"Don't release that soul," Chase said. "We fought too hard to get it here. That's not even the soul's body. Jodi is going to want to see this when she's feeling up to it."

I heard Chase command the soul to stay where it was, but mostly I was aware of how much I wanted to be close to him. He looked down at me, concern on his face. "I've got you. Take as much as you need."

Why did he have to be two such completely different people? If he was always like this, he really could give Alex some competition. But the fact that Chase had nearly killed me two minutes ago made me realize that, no matter how nice he was on occasion, he was still mostly evil.

"You can stop now," I told him. "I feel fine."

"You sure? I don't mind connecting with you again. If you think that would help. In fact, I'd love to. I'm sure these guys wouldn't mind babysitting the soul for us." He turned to Alex. "What do you say, Alex? Can you watch this corpse while me and my girl get some private time?"

"Stop it." I smacked his chest. "Put me down. I'm fine now."

He put me down, but he didn't let go of my hand. "Just in case," he said, and I knew he wasn't talking about me needing a little more energy from him. He was making sure I didn't step out of line. So much for the temporary glimpse of good I had seen.

I walked toward the corpse with Chase at my side. "We didn't have your body to return you to," I said to the soul. "Hades took it, but we need to speak with you, so we're letting you borrow this body for now. Do you understand?"

The soul practically growled at me, but she nodded her head—or should I say his head because the body she entered was a male.

"Sorry about the gender mix-up. We didn't know which soul was going to respond to our call."

She/he continued to growl at me.

"Okay, stop." I put my hand up to her/his face. "I'm trying to have a civil conversation with you. I know you went through hell to get here, but please work with me."

The corpse stopped growling, not because it wanted to, but because I'd commanded it to. I looked at Alex, trying to silently tell him that this was the kind of thing I was hoping to be able to use Chase's power for. At least this might help us. Alex only met my eyes for a second before looking away. He was in agony. I could tell. I had to figure things out quickly before this thing with Chase really did end my relationship with Alex for good.

I turned back to the corpse. "What can you tell me about where you were? Did you see Hades? Did you see the others he took?"

The soul moved awkwardly in the corpse, not at all at home in its unfamiliar body. It reminded me of those horror movies where the zombies and possessed people bend in inhuman ways. I tried my best not to cringe. After all, I'd done this to the poor soul.

"Stop playing nice, Jodi, and make the thing talk." Chase's voice was full of anger. He dug his fingers into my hand as a warning. Either I hurt the soul or he was going to hurt me.

Alex clenched his fist, but he didn't move to help me. I looked at him briefly, letting him know I was okay, that I could handle this. Truthfully, I wasn't sure I could.

"Tell me your name," I commanded the soul.

"Rebecca Ellison," the corpse said in a rather masculine voice.

"Hi, Rebecca. I know Hades has your body trapped. Tell me where he brought you and the others." I had to remember to phrase my questions as demands to ensure an answer, but I was still trying to be a little nice about it.

"Tartarus," the corpse spit out.

"What's Tartarus?" McKenzie asked.

Jared shook his head. "Really? Tony taught us all about it. It's the part of the underworld that people refer to as Hell."

Lexi laughed. "'A place of profound misery.'" I could tell she was mocking Tony.

I couldn't be bothered with them right now. We weren't supposed to be able to raise souls from Tartarus. Hades kept them protected from us. "Hades brought you to Tartarus? Tell me how he's torturing you and the others."

"Like this!" The corpse raised its arms. "Forcing us into each other's bodies. The pain is unbearable. He removes us briefly and fakes pity, only to shove us into other bodies that are not our own. I thought I was finding freedom coming with you, but you're as bad as Hades!"

I staggered backward, but Chase put his hand against my back to stop me. "My God." My voice was barely a whisper. "What have we done?" I looked at Chase in horror.

"I think this is a good thing. Hades won't be angry when he finds out we're torturing the souls the same way he is." He smiled. "I think we found the answer to our problems, hon." He wrapped me in a hug and picked me up off the ground. My arms were pinned to my sides, and my lungs tightened.

Chase put me down, and I looked at Alex. I needed to talk to someone rational, and that wasn't Chase. "Do you think he took those bodies from my room because he knew I'd try this?"

Alex shook his head and stepped toward me. Chase grabbed my hand again, but he didn't push Alex away. He let him talk. "I don't know, but it does make sense. He took your father. That pretty much bought him insurance of exactly this."

"I'm playing right into his games." I'd done what Hades had wanted me to. "All I wanted was to talk to my dad again and see what Hades was doing in the underworld. I thought he could spy for us."

"I can spy," the corpse said.

I wrinkled my forehead at her/him. "Why would you do that? You said this is torture. I'm doing the same thing to you that Hades is."

"Yes, but he does it repeatedly. It's the initial act of shoving the soul into the wrong body that is so painful. I can adapt a little once I'm here. It's still torture, but not as bad."

"Then, I could bring my dad here."

"Jodi!" Alex looked appalled. "She said it was torture. Why would you put your own father through that?"

"Because she said this isn't as bad as what Hades is doing."

"Are you sure about this?" Alex's voice was soft and full of emotion. I was waiting for Chase to notice and punish me for it. I had to avoid that.

I put my hand on Chase's arm. "I want to try raising all the souls Hades took. Every single one of them. Let's create an army of souls. Let's take back what is ours."

Chase smiled at me. "Now that deserves a reward." He leaned down and kissed me. At first, it wasn't a reward at all. I had to pretend I wasn't turned off by him, and with Alex watching that wasn't easy. But then Chase transferred his power to me through his lips, and in seconds I was all over him. The power was intoxicating, and I wanted more. Chase's arms were around me, caressing my back and sending ripples of energy through me. I moaned in response.

"That's enough!" Alex ripped me from Chase's arms. I staggered back, resisting the urge to grab Chase and continue what we'd started. Alex turned me toward him, and the pain on his face brought me back down to earth.

"What the hell, man?" Chase was in Alex's face. "Keep you hands off my girlfriend. If I want to kiss her, I will. Got that?"

"Chase." I reached for his arm, pulling him away from Alex, but Chase shot me with a dose of poison strong enough to send me flying backward onto the ground.

"Jodi!" Leticia rushed to me.

Lexi was laughing, and the others stared, looking like they wanted to intervene but not sure if they should. Chase didn't even look at me. He had no remorse for hurting me. Alex stared at me, his nostrils flaring. He was done. He'd had enough. He lunged at Chase, and they toppled to the ground, wrestling each other. Alex got in a few good punches at first, but then Chase managed to flip over, sending Alex falling to the side. Alex hit his head on a tombstone and looked dazed.

"Chase!" I rushed to him, already mixing my blood. I placed both of my hands on his chest and sent my biggest burst of power into him. He smiled and lay back down on the ground, absorbing my gift. I turned to the others. "Take Alex inside. Get him to Arianna. Go now! I can't do this for too long without getting power back in return."

Leticia nodded and went for Alex. Jared gave in and helped, along with McKenzie. Lexi shook her head and walked inside alone. She wasn't helping. I watched them bring Alex inside. My power was weakening. I didn't have much more to give. The front door of the school closed, and I let go, slumping forward onto Chase's chest.

"You dosed me," he said, sounding euphoric from my power. "I'm not saying I didn't love it, but you tried to control me."

"Like you do to me."

He laughed. "Well, look at that. I'm making your true colors come out after all."

He wanted to think he and I were the same, but we weren't. I'd only done that to help Alex. But the thought I couldn't seem to shake, the one that haunted me, was why I hadn't dosed Chase with poison. That would've shown him how much he had hurt me. Why did I give him pleasure when all he deserved was pain?

"I know what you're thinking," he said.

"Believe me, you don't." I pushed myself off him, still feeling lightheaded and weak.

"You did it because now you need me to take care of you. You like it when I take care of you, Jodi." He sat up and brushed the hair from my face.

"I'm not a pet, Chase. You can't reward me or punish me as you see fit."

"You rewarded me for keeping Alex away from you."

Did he really think that's what had happened? I mean, sure, I did give him a power boost, but it was only to distract him. Wasn't it?

He laughed again. "One of these days, you're going to learn to listen to me. I'll make sure of it."

I didn't want to piss him off and have him dose me with poison when I was already so drained, but I had to know something. "Why do you continue to hurt me? When you first came here, you tried to lure me with your good blood. That's how you got what you wanted, Chase. Not by poisoning me. Now you're driving me away. You must know that."

He reached for the back of my neck. "Then let me make it up to you." His fingers tingled against my skin, and I soaked up his power. He didn't need to pull me to him this time. I was starved of power, and I went to him willingly. I was lost in him until I heard McKenzie's voice.

"Excuse me!" she shouted.

Chase pulled away first, smiling at me as I tried to bring his lips back to mine. "We have company."

I looked up at McKenzie, and the embarrassment set in. I jumped to my feet, feeling like myself again. "Sorry, do you need something?"

McKenzie shook her head. "I came to tell you that Arianna's got Alex all bandaged up. He asked to talk to you. Should I tell him you're too busy making out with the guy who assaulted him?"

"No!" I said.

"Yes." Chase narrowed his eyes at me. "You don't need to be talking to him right now. Not after he attacked me. It's me you should be concerned about." He turned to McKenzie. "We were doing fine before you got here, so go find someone else to annoy."

Chase was losing it. Before, he'd been trying to make me look like the bad one to the rest of the group, but now he wasn't even trying to hide the evil in him.

"McKenzie," I said, but Chase grabbed my wrist.

"Don't make me, Jodi."

McKenzie backed away from Chase, clearly afraid of him.

What could I do? "Tell Alex I'm busy with Chase right now."

McKenzie looked at me, her eyes full of fear. "You can't even protect yourself. How will you ever protect the rest of us?" In her eyes, I should've been able to stop Chase. I was the most powerful Ophi. The fact that I'd become his puppet was making her think I was the worst leader ever. She walked away, not giving me the chance to explain.

"See," Chase said, "I didn't have to hurt you because you did the right thing on your own."

McKenzie was right. I couldn't even protect myself. I had to get to Alex.

"We're probably missing lunch. We've been out here for a long time."

"Then let's go to lunch. And since you seem to like musical chairs so much, why don't you and I sit together? I'll take Alex's seat. He won't be needing it, I'm sure."

I really wanted to smack him. "I'm going upstairs to wash up quickly first."

"I'll go with you, make sure you don't get lost."

Lost in Alex's room was what he meant, and that was exactly what I was planning to do. How could I get rid of Chase? I wracked my brain as I released the woman's soul. I felt awful about sending her back to Tartarus. Maybe I'd take her up on her offer to spy. Chase and I headed to the school. When we walked inside, Arianna was coming down the stairs.

I widened my eyes at her and tilted my head slightly toward Chase. Arianna reached for me. "Oh, Jodi, good. I need to borrow you for a minute." She tried to pull me away, but Chase wouldn't let her.

"What for?" he asked.

Arianna gave him the same look you'd give a dog that just peed on the floor. "Now, Chase, I know you aren't questioning me. I'm much older than you. So, you get your sorry behind into the dining room, and I'll bring Jodi there myself when I'm finished talking to her."

I gave Chase a small shrug, pretending I had no idea what this was about. He reached for my hand, no doubt to dose me with his power, but I moved toward Arianna and he only managed to graze my jeans. I felt the heat from his scorching touch. He'd been planning to bring me to my knees to stop me from going with Arianna. This guy was seriously scary.

He watched us walk upstairs, but he didn't try to stop or follow us. Arianna took me to Alex's room. "Whatever you two are planning, do it quickly," she whispered. "That boy downstairs is determined to have you, and I'm convinced he'd sooner kill you than let you go."

I wanted to break down and tell Arianna everything. How Chase had been controlling me. How much he scared me. How I wanted to get rid of him, but I needed his power so I couldn't. She didn't give me a chance to say anything. She opened Alex's door and brought me to his bed, where he was lying with a cold pack on his head.

"Are you okay?" I carefully sat next to him.

"Are you?" He turned his head slightly to face me.

"I'll let you two talk." Arianna walked to the door. "But I'm staying in the hallway. I'm going to walk you to lunch, Jodi. I'm not giving Chase any opportunities to corner you."

I smiled and nodded, and she shut the door behind her.

I wanted nothing more than to hold Alex and feel his lips on mine. But I could still taste Chase, and I didn't want Alex to know what had happened after he left the cemetery.

"Things are getting worse, Jodi. I had no idea he was hurting you like this. And the way you cling to him when he kisses you—"

"I'm so sorry. I can't help it. You know that, right? It's the power. It has nothing to do with wanting Chase. You're the one I want, Alex."

"I know, but it's hard to watch you like that. It's like you can't get enough of him. Like you're trying to devour him. You've never kissed me like that."

Alex and I had had some kisses that could stop time, so it really made me wonder what it looked like when I kissed Chase. My cheeks warmed. "I get power hungry."

He nodded, but that only made him cringe and clutch his head.

I touched my hand to his face. "Can I try something?"

"What?" He wrinkled his brow. "No offense, but you were kissing Chase earlier. You probably can still taste him. I love you, Jodi, but I refuse to kiss you until you brush your teeth. Twice."

"Just shut up." I leaned forward, pressing my lips to his. I mixed my blood and let my power transfer to him. I'd only ever tried this with Chase, but why wouldn't it work with Alex? He didn't have the extra power boost Chase had, but I wasn't taking anything from him. I was giving him energy to heal.

Alex pulled me on top of him and ran his hands all over my back. He couldn't get enough of the power. I knew the feeling. I didn't want to overdose him since he was injured, so I slowly backed off on the power and pulled away.

"Holy crap," he said with a sigh. "That was amazing."

"Now you know."

He sat up and removed his bandages. He was obviously no longer in pain from his collision with the tombstone, but his face wasn't elated anymore. His expression was worried. "That's how it feels to kiss Chase?"

"You couldn't get enough of me or my power, right? You craved it. You were helpless against it."

He moved me off him and got out of bed. "I'm not okay with this. Knowing he can make you feel that good and I can never do that for you...I'm sorry, but I don't think we can be together, Jodi."

Chapter 25

No, no, no! This was supposed to help Alex understand how powerless I was against Chase. But instead, showing him how it felt was pushing him away.

"Alex, please. I only wanted to show you it's not Chase. It's the power."

"That's not true, Jodi." He ran his fingers through his hair and sighed. "When you were kissing me, yeah I wanted more power, but I was still fully aware of you. I wanted you more than I've ever wanted you before—and that's saying something."

I knew I was blushing from that last comment. "It's not like that for me and Chase. I don't think about him when he kisses me. I'm consumed by the power. I think it's because I have more than a normal Ophi to begin with. When Chase increases that, it sends me into a frenzy. I forget everyone."

"Including me." Alex put his hands on his hips.

"Not necessarily. When Chase kissed me in front of you today, I was able to pull away from him the second he stopped transferring his power. You were the first thought that broke through. You were what stopped me."

He shook his head. "I don't know, Jodi. This is too much. I can't compete with a guy who can make you feel so much. I see the way you look at him sometimes, even when he's not touching you, not controlling you. You feel something for him. It's not all about his blood."

"I see glimpses of a nice guy sometimes, but they're short-lived. I guess I try to hold on to those moments because they make me feel less like a monster."

He reached for me, but stopped, probably afraid I'd use my power to convince him to stay with me. I'd be lying if I said the thought hadn't crossed my mind. Maybe Chase and I were alike.

"You're not a monster."

"Not by choice." I stepped toward him, but he backed up. "Alex, please. I need you." He was up against his desk now with nowhere to turn. I reached for his face. Controlling him would've been easy. One touch and he'd do whatever I said. I struggled against the urge.

Alex reached for my hand, removing it from his face. "If you do to me what he's doing to you, it will be over for good."

He was dead serious. I turned from him and sat down on the bed again.

"I'm sorry. I'm just scared to lose you."

"Like Chase is scared to lose you?"

"Are you defending him now?" My stomach clenched against the thought.

"Definitely not. I'm worried he's changing you. You have to fight his power, Jodi." He sat down on the bed next to me. "I saw what you did in the cemetery when I was hurt. I know you were trying to help me, but what I need to know is why you didn't hurt him."

"I don't know." I wanted to think it was because I'm a good person, but I knew it wasn't as simple as that.

"Is there anything you aren't telling me?"

If I said no, he wouldn't believe me. I'd lose him. I searched for something, anything. "Medusa told me something. Hades is plotting against me. She couldn't tell me much, because she's bound by the deal the Ophi made with Hades to save her spirit, but she gave me a riddle to figure out."

"A riddle?"

"Yeah. She said, 'That which has the power to save, has the power to destroy.' I don't know what it means, though."

Alex scrunched his face as he thought. "We all have the power to save or destroy."

"I know, so it can't be that simple."

"What were you talking about when she told you this?"

I fidgeted with the bottom of my shirt, anything to avoid his eyes. "Chase and how his power affects me."

"You talked to Medusa about Chase?"

I stood up and started pacing. "I had to. I'm supposed to be the most powerful Ophi, yet all of a sudden here he comes, and he can easily overpower me. It doesn't make sense. Something is just not adding up."

"Actually, it does." He stood up and reached for my arm so I'd stop and look at him. "The answer is you. You have the power to save all the Ophi, but when you connect with Chase, you have the power to destroy all the Ophi, too."

"What?" How could he say something so awful?

"Think about it. When Chase kissed you the day I left the school, what happened?"

My eyes widened, and my chest tightened. "Everyone died." Images of Tony falling down the stairs, Leticia and Lexi collapsing in the living room, and Randy's soul refusing to stay in his body flooded my mind. That wasn't even all the evidence I had. There was Lucas when he walked in on Chase and me kissing, and there was also Leticia during movie night when Chase was touching my feet. "Oh, my God, it's true. Chase could make me kill the entire Ophi race." I felt weak, too weak to stand. Alex wrapped his arms around me, and I leaned on him for support. "What do I do? I don't want to be the one who kills all the Ophi. Please, tell me how to stop this."

Alex held both my arms and pulled me back just enough to stare into my eyes. "You have to send Chase away. He can't stay here."

I shook my head. "He'll kill me if I reject him. He can dose me with poison and end me in seconds."

"I won't let him. We'll tell everyone what's going on, and we'll all fight him. I'll kill him before he hurts you again."

I clung to Alex. As much as he wanted to protect me from Chase, I knew he couldn't. He wasn't strong enough. No one here was strong enough to stop Chase. That was why I hadn't been completely honest with Tony or Arianna. I was afraid they'd get hurt trying to protect me. I was the only one who could deal with Chase. Still, for this brief moment, I felt safe in Alex's arms.

Too bad the moment had to end. A door slammed in the hallway, and someone yelled. Chase. Arianna's voice followed his, but he wasn't listening to her. She mentioned Tony's name, and I assumed she was going to get him to help deal with Chase. She probably figured I'd be safe locked inside Alex's room for the time being. I pulled away from Alex.

"He can't find me here." I could barely get the words out. I shook with fear, anticipating the punishment Chase was going to unleash on me. Would he finish the job this time and kill me?

"Stay here," Alex said. "I'll go out and talk to him."

"And say what? You and I got back together? Seeing you is going to send him over the edge."

"No, finding out you're in my room is going to send him over the edge." He kissed my forehead, and for a second I had a flashback of Matt. Perfect human Matt. He'd always kissed me on the forehead. Before I'd killed him, at least. I shook my head trying to get rid of his image. Two guys were enough to handle right now.

"What?" Alex wrinkled his brow. "Did I do something?"

"No, I'm freaked out. You didn't do anything." No way could I tell him the truth. Finding out I still thought about Matt in a "he could've been the one for me" sort of way would definitely send Alex running.

"Stay here." He headed to the door, and I wanted to call after him, but I couldn't risk Chase hearing me. He shut the door behind him, and I locked it. I pressed my ear to the door, but that wasn't necessary. Chase was so loud the dead probably heard him. Arianna wasn't back with Tony yet. Hopefully they'd get here soon to break up the inevitable fight between Chase and Alex.

"Where is she?"

"Who?" Alex said.

"Don't mess with me, Alex. Jodi missed lunch and suddenly you're not looking so under the weather. I'm only going to ask this one more time before I put you back in those bandages. Where the hell is she?"

"Hey, if you can't keep track of your girlfriend, that's your problem. I'm done with Jodi."

I cringed. Hearing Alex say that was painful, even if it wasn't true.

"I saw the way you looked at her. The way you stood up for her. Don't try to tell me you're not still into her. I'm not an idiot."

"Doesn't matter if I am into her. She's into you. She's made that clear."

I smiled. Alex was good at this. Sure, he'd slipped in the cemetery, but he was recovering nicely now.

"So, you're going to tell me you haven't seen her? That she didn't heal you?"

"Jodi's never healed anyone. She raises the dead. I'm not dead."

"Not yet," Chase said. Shoes screeched on the hardwood floor and something slammed into the wall. My guess was Alex. I knew it would mean a great deal of pain for me, but I unlocked the door and burst into the hall.

"Chase!" I rushed to him, trying to pry his hands from Alex's neck.

Alex reached his foot up and kicked Chase in the stomach. A loud whoosh of air escaped Chase's lips, and he let go of Alex. He stumbled back, looking at me. He hit the wall next to his own door and fell to the floor.

I went to Alex first, checking out the red marks on his neck. He was in pain, but he'd be okay. I'd give him another dose of my power when we were away from Chase. Alex took my hand and laced his fingers through mine. I looked down, realizing Alex was taking a stand. He'd had enough, and he was done pretending. This was ending now.

Chase glared at me. "Jodi, come here. Now!" He did his best to scream, but his voice was strained from getting the wind knocked out of him.

"She's not going anywhere with you," Alex said. "It's over. All of it. You controlling her. You hurting her. It's done."

Chase laughed, which made him cough. "You think it's that simple?"

Reality hit me hard. Chase knew something. Just like Medusa knew something she wasn't telling me. I'd been in the dark this whole time. I had to make Chase tell me.

I stepped toward him, but Alex held me back. "It's okay," I told him. He shook his head, not wanting to let me go.

"See, she wants to be with me," Chase said. "She might love you, but she can't stay away from me."

"Why?" I asked, trying to avoid the fact that what he'd said was true.

He laughed and coughed some more. "I can't believe no one told you."

Tony and Arianna rushed upstairs. I raised my hand, letting them know I was okay. I needed answers before anyone went pounding on Chase or throwing him out. The others joined us, trying to figure out what was going on. I was surprised it took them so long, considering how loud the fight had been. I ignored them and focused on Chase.

"Told me what?"

Chase got to his feet. "The real reason why I came here."

"Spit it out already, Chase. I already know Mason is really your father."

A chorus of "What?" rang out in the hall and everyone stared at Ethan.

"He's not Mason. He's Ethan, Chase's dad. He and Mason switched places. He's been lying to all of us."

Arianna smacked Ethan on the back of the head. "Damn it, Ethan. You could've told us."

"What's with all the games?" I asked Ethan.

He looked back and forth between Chase and me. "How did you find out?"

"I went to see you," Alex said.

"I told you I was out of town." Ethan glared at Alex, clearly annoyed.

Alex shrugged. "What can I say? I didn't believe you, and I needed to talk to you about Chase. I found Mason instead. He filled in the blanks for me."

I stepped toward Ethan, trying to muster all the leader power I could. "I already know you and Chase orchestrated this whole thing. Coming here so you could force me to combine powers with Chase. You manipulated me, and it ends here."

"Not quite, Jodi." Chase was right behind me now. "Dad, should I tell her the best part, or do you want to?"

"Go ahead, son." Ethan was smiling, so I knew I was in for some really bad news.

Chase walked around so he was directly in front of me. "You and I are destined to be together. It was decided before either one of us was born. Some sort of prophecy of the Ophi. Pretty cool, huh?"

My legs felt weak, and my stomach flip-flopped. Destined? It couldn't be true. I shook my head. Chase smiled and reached for my hand, but I pushed by him and the others. I ran down the steps and straight to Medusa, grabbing her hands.

"Medusa!" Forget polite greetings. She'd kept this from me. "Medusa!" Her image couldn't come quickly enough.

"My goodness, child. What has gotten into you?" She didn't look happy. Normally I would never think of talking to her like this, being so disrespectful, but I was way past my limit.

"Chase and I are destined to be together?"

She nodded. "Yes, Jodi, you and Chase are destined to be together. He's the only other Ophi who's even close to being like you. You two are meant to be."

"That is not going to happen. I can't be with Chase."

"I'm sorry I couldn't warn you. I tried to tell you to stay away from him. I thought, if maybe you never joined powers with him, you could avoid the prophecy."

"Why didn't you tell me? You could've stopped me!"

"I don't think so. His pull was much too strong, and I was bound to secrecy. Hades may not have my soul, Jodi, but he can still keep tabs on me. If I interfere with what is destined, Hades can reclaim me."

"To hell with destiny. To hell with Chase. I don't care about any of that. I'm supposed to be the leader of the Ophi, and look at what I'm doing. I'm failing miserably. I don't care about what I'm supposed to be doing, Medusa. I'm not playing by the rules anymore."

"It's not that simple. You can't change a prophecy. This isn't Chase's fault either. He's no more in control of his destiny than you are."

"Are you defending him? A minute ago you said you'd hoped I would stay away from him so the prophecy wouldn't come true."

"It was foolish of me, but you are one of mine, Jodi. I was desperate to try to protect you. Now, I see I cannot." She lowered her head, and the snakes transformed back into hair. "This is what I looked like before I was cursed. Before I became a monster."

She was beautiful, but she'd always looked beautiful to me—with the exception of the snakes.

"None of us is free from fate. This was mine." Her hair wiggled and turned to snakes once again. "Chase was no safer than you were."

"What do you mean?" She was trying to tell me something in her own cryptic way.

"It's easy for an Ophi to go bad."

"But why is that?"

"Our powers are tied to our emotions. Every emotion we experience is heightened. So if you're angry and feeling the need for revenge, that feeling is even stronger than it would be for a human."

"So, what you're saying is that Chase wasn't always evil?"

"Probably not. I didn't know him, so I can't say for sure, but most likely something happened to him. Something that caused him to be this way."

"Is that why I keep seeing glimpses of a different side of him? A kinder side of him?"

"It could be."

"Is there any possibility that the old Chase—the person he used to be before this terrible thing changed him—is still there somewhere inside, buried by his emotions?" I was shocked that I was defending Chase, but if he and I really were destined to be together, I didn't want to believe I was supposed to end up with someone evil.

"I wouldn't put all your faith in that, Jodi. Something happened to Chase. We know that. Whether or not he's strong enough to come back from it, we don't know."

"Doesn't that mean we should at least try? I mean, do we just give up? He and I have such a strong power together. How do I turn my back on that? What if his power combined with mine is the only thing that can stop Hades from killing us all?"

"What if his power combined with yours is the thing that kills the entire Ophi race? Are you willing to take that risk?"

Chapter 26

I let go of Medusa and faced the group of Ophi staring at me, waiting for confirmation. I couldn't say the words out loud, couldn't admit the truth. Alex saw the answer on my face and said, "It's true."

I ran back upstairs and locked myself in my room. Alex knocked on the door, begging me to let him in.

"Just go, Alex. I can't face you right now."

"Jodi, either open this door or I'll break it down. Either way, I'm getting into this room."

I wiped my eyes and went to the door. The second the lock clicked, Alex pushed the door open and wrapped me in a hug.

"We'll find a way around it. I promise."

"Don't make promises you can't keep."

He let go of me. "So what, you're giving up? You're willingly going to Chase?"

"I don't know, but I can't hurt you like this. I want to be with you. More than anything. But if that's impossible, then you shouldn't waste your time on me."

He grabbed my face in his hands and kissed me. He wrapped his arms around me and lifted me off the floor. Quicker than I'd thought possible, we were on my bed. I felt the full weight of his body on mine, and it made my head spin. I kissed him like there was no tomorrow, because I wasn't sure there was one for us. My blood boiled, and I was afraid I'd end up raising more souls. I made the quick decision to transfer my power to Alex. He moaned in response. He kissed me harder, and his hands ran along both sides of my body. I knew what he was feeling because I'd felt it with Chase. Chase. The thought of him created a shift in my blood. Alex pulled away from me, choking.

"Oh, God! I'm so sorry." I squirmed out from under him. I quickly willed my blood to mix again and reached for Alex, but he backed up. "It's okay. I'll heal you. I promise."

He stopped, and I touched his cheek. Instantly he stopped choking. Then he was kissing me again, as if he hadn't just been on the brink of death. He pulled away from me long enough to take his shirt off and toss it on the floor. Then he was back on top of me, his fingers inching up my shirt.

"What the hell?" Chase yelled.

I let go of Alex, but he continued to paw at me. I calmed my blood so the effect would wear off him. He looked dazed for a second before he turned to Chase and reality set in.

"Get out," Alex said. "This doesn't concern you."

"Really?" Chase said. "'Cause it looked like you were about to hop into bed with my girlfriend."

"I'm not your girlfriend, Chase." Wow, it felt good to say that.

Chase cocked his head to the side. "The prophecy says differently, Jodi. And as your future husband, I forbid you to see Alex anymore."

"Forbid me?" My voice went up an octave. "You can't forbid me from doing anything."

"I can make you do whatever I want. Don't forget that. I'm trying to be nice. I thought, once you knew the truth, you might give in and start to be the person you're meant to be. But you always have to fight, don't you?"

Alex was on his feet and in Chase's face in seconds. "Get out before I put you out."

Chase laughed. "The last time you tried that, you ended up with a concussion. I can promise I won't go as easy on you this time."

"Stop!" I said. Didn't anyone care what I had to say? "Look, this stupid prophecy is about me, so I'm deciding what's going to happen. Got that?" I looked back and forth between Chase and Alex.

Chase shook his head. "Sorry, Jodi, but you're not the only one in the prophecy. I get a say in this, too."

"Fine. Then the two of us will work this out. Find a way around the part about us ending up together."

"I'm not leaving you two alone to talk." Alex turned his back on Chase and looked me in the eyes. "I'm not giving him a chance to hurt you again."

"Alex, we can't talk with you here. You'll be a distraction."

"Too bad."

"Screw this." Chase touched Alex's shoulder. Alex's face twisted in pain as Chase dosed him with poison.

"Stop it!" I reached for Alex and pulled him away from Chase. I mixed my blood and transferred enough power to heal Alex, careful not to make him start throwing himself at me again. That would only anger Chase more. Alex breathed normally, and I turned to Chase.

"If you ever do that again, we're finished. Do you understand me? I'll personally hand you over to Hades." I stepped closer to him, letting him know I wasn't afraid anymore.

"Then get him under control. I'm not kidding, Jodi. I won't let him come between us. You had your fun with him, but now it's time to move on. He's your past. I'm your future."

"Yeah, well, last time I checked it's the present, so I'm deciding who I want to be with. I'm choosing Alex."

Chase clenched his jaw, holding back the urge to lash out at me.

"Listen, I'm willing to talk this through with you, so why don't you take a seat at my desk, and we'll figure this out."

"Only if he waits outside." Chase nodded toward Alex.

I sighed. "Please, Alex. I'll be fine. I just want to end this."

He shook his head, but instead of refusing he said, "The door stays open."

"Deal," I said, before Chase could object. Alex kissed me and glared at Chase before grabbing his shirt off the floor and leaving.

I leaned against my dresser, the farthest point in the room from Chase. "Okay, so the prophecy says we're destined, but I don't think that means we have to end up together."

"What the hell else could it mean?"

"That we're supposed to work together. Use our powers to do something great. Maybe to finally get Hades off our back."

Chase sat up straighter in the desk chair. "You want to attack Hades?"

"No. We'd never be able to defeat him. He's a god. I think we could use our powers to force him into an agreement, though. Show him that fighting us is using too much of his time and energy. That it's not worth it."

Chase nodded. "And you expect me to go along with this plan that could get us both killed, and gets me nothing in return? And on top of it, I have to watch you with Alex?"

I thought about what Medusa had said about Ophi going bad. "Chase, what happened to you?"

"What do you mean?"

"You weren't always like this. I know you weren't. Medusa knows you weren't."

"I don't know what you're talking about." He crossed his arms, guarding himself from my question.

I walked over to the bed and sat down, closing the distance between us. "Every once in a while, I see a different side of you. You're nice. Medusa seems to think that's the way you used to be, but something bad happened that made you lose control of your emotions. Now, your anger fuels your power. It makes you act crazy, mean."

He laughed. "So, I'm some loony Ophi who couldn't handle life and turned evil?" He was mocking me.

"I'm trying to understand you, to work with you, but if you're going to laugh in my face I'll stop. We can part ways and never speak again. I'm fine with that."

"Are you threatening me now?" He sat forward and reached for my hand, but I pulled it away. "Looks like I'm not the only one whose anger is getting the best of them."

He was right. I was changing. I had been since he'd arrived. That was why I had to figure out what had happened to him. I had to try to make him go back to the way he used to be. Before his anger destroyed both of us.

"I'm not playing games, Chase. Tell me what happened. Or you and your dad can leave." His dad. Of course! Why hadn't I put it together sooner? Chase was here with his dad. They'd both lied to us, and for what? There had to be a goal. I didn't know what it was, but I had an idea why they were doing it. "It was your mom, wasn't it? The awful thing that happened, it happened to her."

"Don't try to psychoanalyze me, Jodi." He tried to dismiss it, but I could tell by the pain on his face that I was right.

"What happened to her?" I wasn't letting this go.

"Why do you care? You don't want to be with me. You chose Alex, so why bother trying to make me get in touch with my feelings and be good like you seem so sure I used to be?"

"Because you weren't wrong about us." I lowered my voice, hoping Alex wouldn't hear me. I caught a glimpse of him leaning against the wall by the open door. I knew he was trying to listen in, but I couldn't give up on Chase. Not when my future, and the future of the Ophi, depended on it. "I am drawn to you, Chase. There's a part of me that does want to be with you. But I can't be with a monster, and right now that's what you are."

He leaned closer to me again. "Is this the portion of the conversation where you try to lie to me and tell me that you really do care? That you only want to help me so we can have a future together?" He laughed. "I thought you said you weren't playing games."

"I'm not. I love Alex. I'm not going to deny that. But that doesn't mean I don't feel something for you. That I don't see what the prophecy is saying about us." I reached for his hand. "Please, tell me what happened to your mom."

"She's dead. End of story." He pulled his hand away and laced his fingers behind his head. He wasn't making this easy. I could tell he was hurting, but he insisted on putting up this wall.

"Do you love me? Or am I a game to you? A prize you win if you can get me away from Alex?"

"Don't flatter yourself, Jodi. I'm here because of the prophecy. Together, we can be the most powerful beings on this planet. That's what I want."

Finally, some honesty.

"Of course, you're nice to look at, so there are other perks. Like all those times you couldn't keep your hands off me."

I caught a glimpse of Alex's black shirt. He was coming into the room. I put my hand up to stop him. "Not yet." I glanced at him briefly.

He was majorly pissed. I hadn't exactly come clean about the number of times Chase and I had made out. Alex punched my open door, which slammed back into the wall. I jumped. Alex went back into the hallway, but this time he leaned on the doorframe, staying in complete view.

Chase laughed, and I smacked him. "Knock it off. Can't you act somewhat human?"

"No," he said. "Because I'm not, and neither are you."

Not anymore. "That doesn't mean we have to act like monsters. Ophi weren't meant to be monsters."

"So you say." Chase leaned back in his chair.

"Tell me about your mom," I pressed.

"Dump loser boy over there."

"That's it!" Alex was in the room faster than I could turn around. He slammed into Chase, tackling him to the floor.

I'd had enough. I didn't want to do this, but I didn't have a choice. I summoned the blood on the left side of my body and sent each of them a small dose of poison. They immediately let go of one another and curled into the fetal position on the floor.

"I'm sorry," I said. "But I'll do it again if you two don't stop this. Fighting isn't helping."

Alex looked at me in disbelief. "It was one thing when it was an accident, but this…"

"I didn't know what else to do." I tried to let him see how sorry I was. I didn't want to hurt him. I reached out to him. "Here, let me help you."

He swatted my hand away. "No, I'm fine." He got up and walked over to my dresser without looking at me.

"Alex—"

Chase got up, too. Except he came over to me and tried to take my hand.

"What are you doing?" I pulled away.

"I'll take a little power boost. Or was the offer only for Mr. Cheap Shot over there?"

Alex ignored him, which could only mean he was beyond mad.

I glared at Chase. "Believe me, if I give you anything right now, it will be more poison."

"I doubt that, but I get that you have to hide your feelings seeing as he's here. Still, I'm proud of you for using your powers on us. That's what you should do."

"No, it's not," I said. "I was desperate. I've had to pull you two off each other enough."

"So end it. I can't give up because of the prophecy, but he can."

"You're right." Alex turned around. "I can."

I stared at him, my eyes wide. "What? Please, tell me you're not going to."

"I never thought you'd hurt anyone on purpose. I get that your emotions are out of control and that he does that to you, but this—what you just did, you stooped to his level."

That hurt. My heart felt like it was being squeezed to death. Alex thought I was like Chase. I couldn't imagine anything worse.

I walked over to him, and my blood began to mix. Oh God! My body wanted me to use my power on him. I looked down at my arms, watching the blood boil underneath my skin.

"What, are you going to dose me with the good stuff? Make me forgive you?" Alex held his arms out in surrender. "Go ahead, Jodi. Manipulate me the way he manipulates you."

I covered my face with my hands and started to cry. I was turning into Chase. How could I call him evil when I was doing the same thing to Alex that Chase had done to me? If Chase was evil, so was I.

"How does it feel to be the one in control?" Chase asked.

I looked at him, confused. "What?"

"You're in control. It's nice, right? Except he's fighting you the way you fought me. That part sucks. So, what are you going to do, Jodi? Are you going to make him give in to you? Take what you want? Or are you going to give me what I want?"

Control or be controlled. Those were my options. Both completely sucked. I couldn't force Alex to accept me like this, but I couldn't let Chase have power over me. What was left?

"You don't have to decide," Alex said. "I'm done. The prophecy is coming true. You're changing to better suit him. You aren't the same girl I fell in love with."

Something in me switched. Instead of feeling sad and confused, I got angry. "I didn't hear you complaining when you were taking my power. When you were pawing at me and taking off your clothes. We almost—" I couldn't say it, so I turned to look at the bed.

"But we didn't. All because of him." Alex narrowed his eyes at Chase.

"She'll thank me later," Chase said.

"Shut up!" My blood was boiling again. I wanted to poison Chase and use my power to make Alex stay. Every ounce of blood inside me was urging me to take control, but what would I become if I did?

"Your blood's never wrong, Jodi." Chase pointed to my arms, which rippled like snakes were crawling under my skin. If only he knew what my blood was telling me to do.

Alex shook his head. "I really wish things were different."

He was done with me. Unless I stopped him. "They can be." I rushed to him and gave him more power than necessary. He bent under the strength of my blood. Pulling me as close as possible, he kissed me.

"Apparently I was wrong." Chase ripped me out of Alex's arms.

Alex stared at me, looking confused at first and then his expression changed to disbelief. "You really did it." He shook his head and looked heartbroken. "I didn't think you would. I thought I could snap you out of this. Convince you how wrong it was, but you gave in to the power. You chose to control me."

He looked at Chase. "You can have her. She's not my Jodi anymore. She's like you now." He walked out of the room, leaving me to fall on my knees and cry.

Chapter 27

Chase picked me up and sat me on the bed. "Calm down. You're better off without him. He wasn't strong enough for you." He held me and smoothed my hair, not using any of his power on me.

After I couldn't cry anymore, I looked up at him with puffy eyes. "This is the guy I was talking about. This is who you used to be."

"I don't want to talk about that." He leaned down and kissed me, just a small peck on the lips.

"I need you to tell me about your mom."

"Shh." He kissed me again, and this time he transferred his power to me. He wasn't playing fair. He was making me forget what he didn't want to answer. He was making me feel better about Alex walking out on me again. He was making me want him. I ran my fingers through his hair and kissed him back. The tingling coursed through me until my entire body felt like a live wire. All I could think about was Chase and wanting to be closer to him.

Then the power stopped. Chase took it away, and he let go of me. For the first time, after the power connection ended, I still wanted him.

"What are you doing? Kiss me," I said.

"Is that what you really want?" He looked different, sad.

"Yes."

"What if I didn't give you my power at the same time? Would you still want me to kiss you?"

"What do you mean? Why wouldn't you give me your power?"

"I'll give you all you want after you choose me. After you swear that you and Alex are history. Nothing more than a memory."

Alex. His name brought waves of pain. Heartache. "You don't just stop loving someone."

"Jodi, we have to fulfill this prophecy, and until you commit to me, I'm cutting you off from my power."

"You won't connect with me at all? Not even to bring my dad here? We were going to spy on Hades. See what he's planning so we could be ready for the attack. I can't do that without you." I reached for his hands, sending him some of my power.

He pulled away before he could be sucked in by it. "Don't try that on me. I invented that game." He stood up. "Sleep on it. Decide who you want. Be sure. Because whatever you decide, the decision is final. If you pick Alex, you'll never see me or your dad's soul again. If you pick me, Alex goes." He walked out of the room, pausing in the hall. "Alex will never be able to do for you what I can. Remember that." He left.

I fell back on the mattress and stared at the ceiling. The decision should've been easy. Alex. I loved him. But Chase and I were destined to be together. He had the ability to be a good person. He just needed someone to help him get there, and if I didn't choose Chase, I'd have another enemy. I didn't need any more of those. But could I give up Alex? Would Alex even take me back at this point?

Sometime around three in the morning, I finally dozed off. My questions all went unanswered, yet I knew Chase was expecting an answer in the morning. I woke up drenched in sweat, feeling like I was in the middle of a hellfire. I sat up and looked around the dark room. Even without any light, I felt the presence of someone in the room. I reached for the lamp on the nightstand. A corpse was standing at the foot of my bed.

"Not again." I was about to release him when something hit me. The feeling of hellfire. Where had I raised this soul from? I got up and walked over to him. He turned so he was facing me. His movements were awkward, like the body was unfamiliar, not really his.

"What's your name, and where did you come from?"

He opened his mouth, struggling to form words. Finally he said, "Derek Colgan. Tartarus."

I had to grip the bed to stop myself from falling over. "Dad?"

He nodded.

"How did I raise you? I wasn't trying to, and you were in Tartarus. Hades has your body. It should've been too difficult to get to you without Chase helping me."

"Another soul said you were looking for me."

The woman Chase and I had raised!

"I've been waiting for you to come for me. I felt you reaching out, and I grabbed hold of you."

I wasn't used to souls being willing to come to me. "Was it painful? The woman said it's like torture to be in someone else's body."

"I'm okay. It was worth it to see you again."

I wanted to hug him. I didn't care that he was a corpse or that my seventeen-year-old father looked like a sixty-year-old man. He was still my dad.

"I have to warn you, Jodi. Hades is planning an attack. He says he's free to claim all the Ophi after all the slip-ups you've made."

I'd figured as much. "What is he waiting for? I thought he would've come for me already."

"I don't know. He's hiding something."

"What's going to happen when you return to Tartarus and he finds out you talked to me?"

He tried to smile, but it came off looking like a lopsided snarl. "He can't kill me, because I'm already dead, but his punishments are worse than death."

"Then you're not going back. You can stay here with me. I'll protect you."

"No. He'll come for you."

"Maybe not." That was it. My decision was made for me. I wouldn't lose my dad again. He'd been taken from me before I even met him. Now I had the chance to save him, and I would.

Corpses don't exactly sleep, so Dad sat in my desk chair doing nothing but staring at me while I tried to get a few decent hours of sleep. The sun came up too quickly, and after I showered to rinse the dried sweat of the hellfire from my skin, I got dressed quickly and took my dad downstairs for breakfast. I was the last one there, and we were greeted with gasps all around.

"What in Heaven's name?" Arianna said.

Lexi smirked. "I don't think Heaven had anything to do with it."

"Everyone, this is Derek Colgan…my father. I accidentally raised him in my sleep last night."

Tony dropped his fork. "Oh, Jodi, not again."

"That's not your dad," Leticia said. "He's way too old."

"Hades took my dad's body. Remember that day in my room? He took several bodies from us. I put my dad's soul into a body from the cemetery."

"Oh, dear!" Carol said, looking frightened. "This is not good news. Hades is going to come here any second."

The table erupted in a panic.

"Relax." I sat down next to Chase, who raised an eyebrow at me, waiting to hear my decision. Of course sitting by him instead of Alex wasn't enough. He was going to make me spell it out for everyone. "I have a plan." I looked at Alex who eyed me over a forkful of mac and cheese. "I'm going to fulfill the prophecy. It's the only way to save us. Chase and I are going to reclaim all the souls Hades took."

Tony shook his head and clutched his hands in front of him. "You'll be declaring war if you do that." He didn't say it, but I knew he didn't trust Chase to help me either. The only reason Tony and Arianna hadn't kicked Chase and Ethan out was because they knew I didn't want them to. They were only holding back because of me, and I could tell it was killing both of them.

"I think it's a brilliant plan," Ethan said.

"You would." Tony glared at him. "You're all about sneakiness and tempting the gods, aren't you, Ethan? Or are we still supposed to call you Mason?"

"Enough," I said. "I'm in charge. I'm making the rules." I looked around the table, waiting for everyone to get quiet again. My eyes lingered on Alex. He stared at my dad, and somehow I knew he understood why I'd made the decision to be with Chase. It didn't make it easier on him, but he knew me well enough to know I'd do anything for the people I loved. That included using my powers on him in a moment of desperation.

"Okay, here's what's going to happen. Hades is going to be seriously pissed when Dad doesn't return to Tartarus, so we need to move quickly." I turned to Chase and put my hand on top of his. "You ready to do this?"

He sent a wave of power my way. "I know the quickest way to tap into our power and get those souls."

I knew what he meant. The whole hand-holding to transfer power wasn't enough. We'd almost failed last time. We needed a better connection. We were only going to get one chance to do this before Hades interfered. I took a deep breath and nodded.

"Everyone to the cemetery," I said.

We all headed outside without another word. Everyone was scared, me most of all. This stand I was taking was either going to show Hades we had more power than he thought and he shouldn't mess with us, or it was going to get us all killed.

I stopped in the middle of the cemetery where Chase had made the souls rebury themselves in a row. I'd been upset when I found out he did it, but now I was glad to have them all together. I motioned to the line of headstones. "Okay, everyone pick a grave." I hated having to do this with an audience, but with this many souls coming our way, we needed enough of us to control them. "When the souls get here, command them to stay where they are. The woman Chase and I raised was angry and wanted to hurt us at first, but she calmed down. In the end, she preferred being here with us to being stuck in Tartarus. Hades is constantly forcing the souls into the wrong bodies. It's awful. Chase can tell you just how awful, because he felt it too."

"Got to say, I'm not looking forward to that part." He shook his head like he was trying to forget how terrible it had been.

I put my hand on his shoulder. "I know. Me neither. But this is important."

He leaned down to me. "You chose me. I can handle anything now."

I smiled at him. At the version of him I liked.

"Everyone set?" I asked once everyone was lined up in front of a grave.

"There are a few graves left down here," Jared said.

"Then everyone shift down." I waved them on. "Chase and I will get these graves here."

"If we can pull away from each other," he said with a sly smile.

He probably had a point. The connection it was going to take to pull off a raising this huge was insane. We were going to practically have to—no, I couldn't think about it. Especially since Alex would be witnessing the whole thing. I was kind of surprised he wasn't bailing on the plan. He knew what this was going to entail. Could he really be so over me already that this wasn't going to bother him?

Chase moved toward me and placed his hands on my waist. "Let's do this."

I took one last look at Alex. His eyes were glued to the grave in front of him. "Focus, everyone. Eyes on your graves and be ready to take control."

"Jodi," Leticia said. "I've never been able to control a soul someone else raised."

The others were starting to be able to control the souls they didn't raise, but it was still hit and miss, and we needed them all to hit.

"You can do this, Leticia." I kept my expression serious. I had to make her believe me.

She wasn't convinced. "How do you know?"

"Because we can't fail. It's not an option."

"You can do it, Leticia," Alex said. "I'm right here if you need help."

Leticia nodded, looking very thankful to be next to Alex. I was grateful for his help.

"Do you want to get right to making out, or should we form a more conservative connection and let the power overtake us?" Chase asked.

Lexi scoffed. "This is going to be disgusting to watch, isn't it?"

"You have no idea," Alex mumbled.

Maybe he did still care after all. I turned back to Chase, but not before meeting my dad's eyes—or at least the eyes in the body he was borrowing. "Dad, would you mind turning around? I'd rather you didn't watch this." I knew I didn't need to command him. He was going to listen to me no matter how I asked.

He nodded and faced the mausoleum.

I took Chase's hands, interlacing my fingers with his. "Let's start here."

"You know it's going to take a lot more—"

"Chase, let's start here," I insisted.

He shrugged. "Whatever. I know where we're going to end up."

I hoped he wasn't right. I closed my eyes and willed my blood to mix. I transferred my power to Chase, very slightly at first. My power was more intense than his. If I gave him too much to begin with, he'd be too consumed by it to transfer any power back to me. I waited for him to begin sharing his blood with me.

"Come on, Chase," I said.

"Sorry, just enjoying the rush. Here you go."

I felt his power flow through my fingers, up my arms, and to the rest of my body. Unlike me, he wasn't holding back. A moan escaped my lips, and I increased my power flow to him. Our blood mixed and circled between us. I needed to wait for the connection to be strong before I tried reaching the souls.

"Jodi, why are you putting this off?" Chase yanked my hands so I was right up against him. Our hands were down at our sides, keeping the circle going, but I felt the power passing between our chests now, too. He leaned his head down, finding my lips with his. I kissed him back, and our emotions heightened our power. Chase wrapped my arms around him and cupped my face in his hands.

For a moment, I was lost in him. All I wanted was him. My nails dug into his back. He picked me up and wrapped my legs around his waist.

"Do I really need to be subjected to this?" Lexi yelled.

Her screechy voice broke through, and I remembered what I was supposed to be doing. I focused on the souls I wanted to raise. I reached out with my powers, all the way to the depths of Tartarus. I knew the woman I'd summoned earlier would be eager to come, and hopefully she'd convince the others so I didn't have to work so hard to get them here. I knew I was close by the tormented screams that filled my head. Hades was torturing them, and if they didn't understand what I was trying to do, they'd see my powers as more torture and shy away from me.

"Chase." I pulled away from his lips. "Are you concentrating? I need help. They're resisting, or Hades is clutching to them. Something isn't right."

Instead of answering, he pressed his lips to mine again. I had no idea if he was trying to make the connection stronger or if he was lost in the power. It was intoxicating. I had to fight to stay in control. I assumed he was trying to help, so I reached out further. My body shook, and I had trouble holding on to Chase. My legs slipped from his waist, but he had latched onto my hands again. He wasn't letting me go.

Finally, I felt the first soul grab on. It was so much work raising them from Tartarus, and I needed a bunch more. I was losing hope that my plan was even possible. Hades was there. I could feel him, and he wasn't going to make this easy on me. I tugged at the soul, and it screamed in pain. Its body was in Tartarus, too, so it knew it wasn't returning to its home. That made me its enemy. I felt its pain, and it overwhelmed me. My blood shifted.

No, it wasn't the soul's pain I was feeling. It was *my* pain. My blood was being poisoned. I opened my eyes to look at Chase. He stared back at me, eyes filled with pure evil. What was he doing? The poison spread throughout my body. Chase stopped kissing me long enough to say, "Trust me, you'll feel amazing once the poison takes over. It only hurts at first."

His blood overtook mine; I was no longer transferring any of my power. The soul from Tartarus slipped from my grasp. Chase had tricked me! He was trying to turn me evil. He'd only pretended to go along with my plan to take back the souls Hades had stolen from us. I tried to pry my hands from Chase's, but he was too strong, and the poison was weakening me. I heard the others choking and saw McKenzie fall to the ground. She was shaking uncontrollably, so I knew she was still alive, but this connection was killing her. It was killing all of them.

Then, the pain stopped. For me at least. The poison was taking over, and it didn't hurt anymore. I felt different, but strong.

"See, I told you," Chase said. "Now kiss me, and let's finish what we started."

I stared at him, totally understanding he meant killing the others. Even his dad. We were still connected and that craving for his blood, his power, took over. I leaned in and kissed him.

Chapter 28

"Jodi," Alex said, coughing up blood. "Fight him. What you're feeling for him isn't real. You know that. I know you do."

He was right. My brain was telling me to listen to Alex. To fight Chase. But my blood was screaming for Chase, wanting to consume him and his power. Unfortunately, my blood was proving to be stronger than my brain. Chase was playing dirty. He was making me want him, and even though I was fully aware of it, I didn't care. I did want him.

"Jodi, if you give in to him, you'll lose me forever. That's what he wants. It's him or me. Hell, it's him or you—because this isn't you. Don't let him take over. Find yourself in your blood. Find Medusa."

I didn't know where Alex was getting his strength from. The others were seconds from death.

Medusa's image flooded my brain. "My child, prophecy is never what it seems. You've connected with Chase. You've chosen him. Now, you can undo it."

"I can't. This is what I'm supposed to become."

"The prophecy said you and Chase were destined to destroy the Ophi line. You're doing that right now. It's begun. Now, end it before it's too late. Before their souls leave their bodies."

I listened for sounds in the cemetery, but there were none. Everyone was dead, but their souls hadn't left their bodies yet, which meant I had a chance to save them.

"Medusa, help me, please. I'm weakened by the poison."

"No, you're stronger because of it. Use it."

"You mean on Chase?"

"Yes, you must stop him. He's trying to hold you off so you can't bring them back."

I couldn't believe this. I'd given in. I'd killed them all. Medusa was right. I had to stop Chase. He was controlling me. I gathered my power and pushed it back into him, dosing him with concentrated poison. He faltered, staggering backward and breaking our connection. I hit him with the poison again, making him go down, too weak to fight me.

I commanded my blood to mix, but there wasn't enough life-restoring power left in me. I'd given too much to Chase when I thought we were raising the souls in Tartarus, and that had only made room for him to fill me with poison. I bent down to him and grabbed his hands. Then, I did something I had never done before. I took what I wanted. I took his life-restoring power, calling it to me like I'd call a soul. It flowed into me, and my skin rippled with the power. My hair flew up behind me, and I was sure I looked like I had snakes wriggling on my head instead of long, dark hair. I took what I needed and focused on raising the Ophi in the cemetery. Even Ethan. I brought them all back. I let go of Chase, leaving him powerless on the ground. Without a visit to Medusa, he was down for the count.

Alex opened his eyes, and I rushed over to him. He spit up blood that must have still been in his throat from before he died.

"You did it," he said.

"Not really. I let you all die before Medusa convinced me I was strong enough to overpower Chase."

"You've always been strong enough, Jodi."

"You should hate me right now. You know that, don't you?"

He sat up. "Yeah, but what can I say—once a stalker, always a stalker."

I smiled, remembering how scared I'd been of Alex when we'd first met. When I thought he was stalking me. Of course, he'd been trying to help me, in his own messed up way.

The others got to their feet and stared at me. They looked like they'd all seen ghosts, but I'd brought them back before their souls had had the chance to visit the land of the dead and see any.

"Was I—were we—" McKenzie was still in shock.

"Great," Leticia said. "How many times do I have to die? I think I've had my share of death."

Jared got to his feet. "Me too. I've only been here a few days, and I've died twice."

"What's his deal?" Lexi pointed at Chase, who was breathing heavily and unable to move.

"He'll be fine. I had to borrow some power to bring you all back."

"What exactly happened to us?" Carol asked. "I thought you were raising souls."

"I was. Chase wasn't." I walked over to him and kicked his shoe. "He lied to me. Tricked me into thinking we were taking back the souls Hades stole, but really he had a different plan all along." I moved to Ethan. "A plan I thought you were in on with him, but he wanted you dead, too."

"I should've known." Ethan practically spat in frustration. "Ever since his mother was taken by Hades, he's been different. He was supposed to follow the plan. But instead, he took me down like I was one of you."

"Wait, what?" He was speaking as if I knew the whole plan. As if I knew Hades had taken Chase's mother. "Back up. What happened to Chase's mom? I knew something happened to her and that it changed him, but Hades took her? Alive?"

"No, he killed her. Rather brutally."

When Hades took an Ophi, the Ophi relived the deaths of every person they'd killed or brought back from the dead. If Chase's mom had died brutally, she must have raised some pretty awful souls in her life.

"Why did he take her? What did she do to anger him?"

Ethan scoffed. "She was Ophi. That's enough for Hades."

"Why did you two," I motioned to Chase, "team up with Hades?"

"What?" Leticia shrieked. "They're working for Hades?"

"More like doing his dirty work, I think." I got in Ethan's face. "Am I right?"

The ground shook, and we all scrambled to avoid the enormous crack that was creeping up the cemetery, splitting it in two. Alex and I were on separate sides, getting farther apart by the second. I fell backward to avoid being pulled into the abyss. I'd seen this trick before. It was Hades' grand entrance.

I wanted to tell everyone to run. I couldn't protect them from Hades. He was too powerful, and I couldn't even reach everyone right now thanks to the crack in the ground. Not that it would help. This was it. Everything I'd tried to do over the past two and a half months was worthless. I was going to die, and so was everyone else.

A swirl of black smoke rose from the darkness in the chasm. I braced myself to see Hades. Would he come out swinging or would he make me suffer? My money was on making me suffer. I willed my blood to mix. I didn't think it would really help, but it was the only weapon I had.

The smoke stilled and disappeared, leaving me face to face with Hades. He was still majorly hot. He made Chase look like the dweeby guy who sat right in front of the teacher's desk and took enough notes to fill a textbook. My blood rippled through me at the sight of him. If he wasn't completely terrifying and didn't want me dead, I probably would've been kissing his feet.

"Well, this isn't exactly what I expected to see." He looked at the others. "So many Ophi still alive, or should I say alive again?" He whipped his head around at me. "We had a deal that you would return every soul you took from me."

"You never had their souls. I brought them back before they lost their souls to you. I didn't break our deal." My voice shook, but I stood my ground.

"Hmm." He tapped his finger on his chin, mocking me with his questioning look. "I think you may have forgotten someone." He walked over to the mausoleum, where my dad was still facing away from the group like I'd asked him to.

"Dad," I mumbled. "No, Hades, wait!"

He turned to me. "Are you ordering me around, Jodi Marshall?"

"No." I frantically shook my head. "It's just that—"

"What, you were hoping that, since he's your father, I'd let this one slide?" He reached a hand out to the corpse my dad was borrowing. "Turn around and face your daughter," he commanded.

My dad turned, and the terror in his eyes was intense. He couldn't talk without being invited to. It was one of the drawbacks of being a zombie. One of the many drawbacks.

"I'm sorry." I locked eyes with my dad, but Hades thought I was talking to him.

"Sorry? What an interesting thing to say. Do you really think an apology is enough to make me forget you broke our agreement?"

What could I say? I wasn't planning on returning my father's soul. I'd been planning to take a whole bunch more.

"Funny thing." Hades walked around my dad so he was directly behind him. "I was in Tartarus today, checking up on a few things, when some of my souls started disappearing. One minute they were there taking their punishments and the next..." He touched my dad's shoulder with one finger, and the corpse collapsed on the ground. I saw my dad's soul release. "They were gone. Just like that."

"No!" My blood boiled. Hades was toying with me. It reminded me of Chase and the way he'd controlled me. I'd had enough of guys pushing me around. I stepped toward Hades.

"Uh-uh, Jodi Marshall." His voice was laced with mockery. "You wouldn't want to make me any angrier with you right now."

"You're angry?" I threw my arms out. "What about me? You sent Chase here, didn't you? You struck some kind of sick deal with him. It had to do with his mom, right?"

Hades raised his eyebrows. "When did you figure that out? Before or after you fulfilled the prophecy and killed your friends?" He laughed, a real belly laugh to show how much he was enjoying my misery.

"Why do you hate us so much?"

"Do you know what my role is in the underworld?" He stepped over my father's body and walked toward me. I resisted the urge to back away. "I see that the afterlife suits the life the soul lived."

"Then why are you torturing all those souls you took from this cemetery? I raised one of them. I know you've been shoving them into the wrong bodies, making them endure the pain of that experience over and over again. What did they do to deserve that?" I was yelling now, and I didn't care. Hades was going to kill me. He'd taken my dad away again, and I was going to be next. I might as well get out what I had to say.

"Did you think this cemetery was a peaceful resting place? Somewhere family buried their loved ones?" He circled around me like he'd done with my dad. "Think about it. Have you ever seen anyone come put flowers on one of these graves? Anyone crying over a lost loved one?"

I shook my head. "This place is hidden. Humans don't know we're here."

"Exactly. Why would humans bury their loved ones where no one could find them?" He stopped right behind me and leaned forward, his mouth inches from my right ear. "Because they weren't anyone's loved ones."

My eyes widened. Why had I never questioned who the bodies were in the cemetery? I'd raised enough of them to know they were vicious as zombies. I'd come to the conclusion that I'd been raising them from Hell because they were awful. The way that corpse had attacked Randy. The way the souls always lashed out at us. I thought back to Matt. When I raised him, there was no screaming. No anger towards me for raising him. Because he hadn't been in Hell. Matt was the nicest, sweetest guy ever. If his soul had moved on, it had gone to Heaven. That was where I'd pulled him from. None of the others had been like him.

"Who were they?" I asked Hades. "These people—how did they get here, isolated from the rest of the world?"

Hades smiled. "It's making sense now, isn't it?"

Yes, it was.

"This building you call a school was once an experimental prison. The people who stayed here were either criminally insane or downright murderers. Instead of living in cells, they were heavily sedated to keep them under control, and they were buried here, where the rest of humanity would never have to think about them again."

"My dad was buried here." I felt tears in my eyes. "What did he do wrong? He deserved better. And none of this explains why you hate Ophi."

Hades smirked. "What is an Ophi's power, Jodi?"

I rolled my eyes. He was treating me like a child. "Raising the dead."

"When was the last time anyone with a shred of humanity considered that a good thing?" He reached up and touched my face. "You are as evil as the people in these graves. You torture souls." He smacked my cheek, not hard but enough to show his disapproval. "The only reason why I didn't come after this school sooner was because you were raising souls that deserved to be punished. Others weren't doing the same, so I claimed them."

"The group in Washington?"

"Yes. Still think *I'm* the bad guy?"

"Yes," I said, being completely honest. "You killed Chase's mother. Fine, she did some awful things. I get that. You did your job and punished her, but then you made a deal with Chase. You wanted him to use his powers to help me destroy all the Ophi."

"Yes, yes, and yes."

"What made you think your plan would work? You knew I was with Alex. You saw us together."

Hades laughed and stared at Chase, still on the ground and suffering from the poison I'd given him. "Girls always go for the bad boys."

Chase was the bad boy. He was everything Alex wasn't. Sure, Alex had a little bad boy in him. I'd seen that side of him, but he was also really sweet once you got past the wall he put up. Medusa seemed to think Chase might have been different before his mom died. Before he made the deal with Hades.

I avoided Hades' eyes and focused on Chase. "Why did you do it? Why did you agree to help him? Did he threaten you?"

Hades laughed again. "Always blaming me, aren't you, Jodi Marshall?" He walked over to Chase, and the contempt he felt for him was written all over his face. "This one, he was evil from the start. He knew his powers were greater than other Ophi. With the exception of you." He turned to me. "Chase was jealous of your power. It was all his parents ever talked about. Isn't that right, Ethan?"

Ethan turned away.

"That's why your son hated you. You pushed him, forced him to use more power than he should have. Tried to make him be more like Jodi. But that backfired, didn't it?"

"Backfired how?" I asked, since Ethan wasn't talking.

"It was Chase I came for that day, not Charlotte, but she begged me to give him a second chance. To let him prove he could be of use to me." Hades bent down, getting in Chase's face. "Your mother begged for your life, putting hers up in exchange, and you let her do it. You took my deal without hesitation."

"No." I couldn't believe it. Chase had seemed tortured over losing his mother. How could he be the reason Hades took her? "Chase, what really happened?"

He was still too weak to move or talk, so I walked over and gave him a dose of my power to heal him.

"Talk!" I demanded.

Chase staggered to his feet, looking at Hades and ignoring me. "I did everything you told me to. You said you'd give her back to me."

My stomach lurched. "You did all this to get your mom back?" I whipped my head toward Hades. "You only took her temporarily?"

"That depended on whether Chase succeeded. Which he did not." He motioned to the others. "They are still alive."

"They died. It worked. I did what you said." Chase was desperate, grasping for a loophole.

That's when I realized Hades never set up a deal he couldn't win.

"We'll do it again," Chase said.

"Like hell we will!" I'd had it. Chase might be trying to save his mom, but I wasn't going to let him kill everyone else to do it. I shoved him, letting a dose of poison knock him back to the ground. If it were my mom on the line, I wouldn't have given up, either. I was sure that was something Chase and I had in common. I had to eliminate him as a threat, and poisoning him was the only way I knew how.

"Perhaps I can persuade you otherwise." Hades raised his arms out to his sides and a figure rose from the crack in the earth.

Matt. I stared, nearly collapsing. He was himself again. Not a corpse. Not a zombie.

Chapter 29

I couldn't breathe. My body was frozen in place as I looked at the first guy I ever loved—or could have loved if I hadn't killed him. I'd never forgiven myself for killing Matt. I had known I was poisonous to him, yet I'd kissed him anyway. I'd given in to my emotions and kissed him, knowing what the consequences would be. Now, he here was. Alive.

He stared at his arms, hands, and legs. He patted his chest, trying to figure out if he was real. I knew the feeling. I wanted to do the same thing.

I shook my head, still in disbelief. "How?" I asked Hades.

"I'm god of the underworld. I can even bring your father back. If you give me what I want."

"What do you want?"

Hades walked toward me, invading my personal space and making every hair on my body stand on end. "I want you to destroy the Ophi. Choose Matt and your father. You could be happy. The only thing I ask for in return is your promise never to have a child. I don't want any loopholes left open. The Ophi line ends with you."

Matt wrinkled his forehead and reached his hand toward me. "Jodi? Where are we? What's going on? All I remember is being in your backyard, kissing you. Then things got fuzzy."

Tears streamed down my cheeks. "Oh, Matt, I'm so sorry. I never meant to hurt you. I never meant for any of this to happen."

"Don't cry. I'm fine." He took his thumbs and wiped the tears from my cheeks.

"Matt, no!" But I was too late. His eyes rolled back in his head, and he crumpled to the ground. I collapsed with him, my heart torn in two. I'd killed Matt again. Hades had brought him back alive, and I had killed him for the second time.

I looked up at Hades, my blood boiling. "You lied! It's all a lie!"

Something landed with a loud thud next to me. Alex was clinging to the edge of the crack, trying to pull himself up. While I'd been wrapped up in Matt, he'd jumped over it to get to me.

"Alex!" I grabbed his arms and tried to pull him up, but he was too heavy.

Hades watched, clearly amused.

"Jodi, I can help." Chase's voice was weak from poison.

I held on to Alex and stared at Chase. I couldn't trust him. He'd try to make me kill everyone. But I couldn't save Alex on my own. I needed help, and Hades wasn't about to lend me a hand.

"Alex, hold on. I have an idea."

"He'll throw me over, Jodi. He's tricking you."

"Trust me." I locked my eyes on his, hoping he'd see how much I cared about him.

He nodded, and his face contorted in pain as I released my grip on his arms and he held on without my help. Leticia and McKenzie shrieked, obviously terrified for Alex. Tony moved like he was going to try to jump the crack and help Alex, but I held my hand up. I couldn't risk him falling, too.

I went to Chase and gave him only enough power to allow him to stand. "Let me be clear. You're going to help me, and if you try anything, I'll dose you with more poison than your body can take. Do you understand me?"

Chase glared at me. He'd obviously been hoping I was dumb enough to believe he was going to help me.

I pushed him over to Alex. Keeping one hand on Chase, ready to transfer my poison if need be, I reached for Alex. Chase grabbed Alex's other arm, and we pulled him up.

Hades clapped. "How touching."

I glared at him, wishing more than anything that I could take him on, but I wasn't stupid. He was a god, and he'd squash me in seconds, if it even took that long.

"This is what you're protecting?" Hades scoffed in Alex's direction. "You see, you really would be better off with Chase."

"Why would I believe anything you say? You lied to me and said I could be with Matt again. You know I can't be around humans."

"No, but you can be around Chase." He walked over to Chase, looking him up and down. "His power is almost as strong as yours. He's Ophi, so you wouldn't have to worry about killing him. He's the closest thing to an equal you are going to find."

"I'm not taking a consolation prize. I refuse to kill the Ophi." I stood my ground, but inside, I was shaking.

"Very well. Have it your way. I can't kill all the Ophi at once, but I can kill those who are right here." Hades reached his arms out, and the others fell to the ground. All but Chase and me.

"No!" I reached for Alex. He didn't have a pulse. His heart wasn't beating. He was dead.

"I will hunt down every Ophi, Jodi Marshall. I will kill them all. Your only chance at saving yourself is to take my deal. It would save me a lot of time if you'd end the Ophi race for me."

I looked at Chase. He was petrified. I was sure he thought Hades was going to kill him, too.

"Your answer?" Hades crossed his arms. "I don't have all day, you know."

Something inside me clicked. My emotions were out of control. I'd never hated someone so much. Hades had taken my father, made me kill Matt again, wiped out every Ophi in the school, and worst of all, he'd taken the guy I loved. I was done. My blood bubbled, and my skin looked like it was transforming. Hades stared at me, obviously surprised by the change in my appearance.

My hair whipped back as I stood. I must have looked insane. That's how I felt. I reached my arms out and summoned the souls of the Ophi lying on the ground. They came to me willingly, recognizing my power. There were no screams, and I didn't have to force them back into their bodies. They wanted to come with me. I heard them stirring on the ground, so I turned my attention elsewhere. Somewhere deeper. Tartarus.

Hades' eyes locked on mine, but he didn't stop me. He was measuring me. Seeing how much power I actually had. Not even I knew that, but I was going to find out. I didn't call out to the souls this time. I took them. I ripped them out of there. Hades had said they were evil people when they were alive, so I didn't feel bad about torturing them this way.

One by one, I forced them into the bodies lying in the graves below us. I hoped the giant crater Hades had created wouldn't make them all go plummeting back to the underworld. I saw the first set of fingers reach through the ground, and I commanded the soul to go right for Hades. I kept going, ripping souls from Tartarus and turning them on the god who'd tortured them for who knew how many years.

Hades didn't seem too worried. He stood there watching, mocking my attempt to stand up against him. I worked faster, making the cemetery crawl with zombies, and they all wanted one thing: Hades.

Still, Hades was toying with me instead of taking control of the situation. He wanted to make me suffer.

"Stop her!" Hades commanded Chase. "Destroy her with your power. Make her bend to my will."

"She's too strong. I've never seen her like this." Chase kept his distance. Wind whipped around me like a hurricane.

Hades raised his arms, and I expected an attack, but instead he brought a woman from the crack in the ground. I knew instantly that it was Chase's mother.

"Break through her powers and poison her, or your mother's soul is mine forever. I'll see that she suffers in Tartarus for all eternity."

I kept my focus on controlling the souls. Hades was beating them down and sending them away, but I raised them again. It was an unending cycle, and he was getting pissed. I'd hoped it would make him leave—retreat to the underworld, even if it was out of annoyance rather than fear. But he stayed.

Chase got as close to me as he dared, and he lowered his voice as much as he could with all the wind howling around me. "Jodi, take my hand. Together you and I are strong enough to stop him."

What? This had to be a trick. He didn't want to help me defeat Hades. He wanted to get his hands on me so he could poison me.

"Nice try, Chase. Don't get in my way, or I will take you down."

"I'm not lying." His eyes left me and went to his mom. She stood there, bound in place by Hades' power. "I can't let him take her again. I have to make it up to her. Please, let me help you."

Maybe he was desperate to help his mom. Maybe he really did want to defeat Hades. He'd failed Hades, and if he made it through this fight, Hades would kill Chase anyway because he'd failed. I knew it, and Chase knew it. I couldn't trust him. As much as I wanted to save all the Ophi, this wasn't the way to do it. Even if Chase was serious about helping me, our combined powers still weren't enough to defeat a god.

"I'm sorry, Chase. I feel bad about your mom, but I've made my choice, and it's not you." I reached my hand out and hit him with a dose of poison. I couldn't risk him doing the same to me. I knew it was wrong, but it was a poison or be poisoned situation. I wasn't dying at Chase's hands. If I was going down, it would be Hades' doing.

"Wrong choice, Jodi Marshall." Hades let out a yell, and the ground opened wider, crumbling beneath our feet.

I couldn't maintain focus on the souls. I stopped controlling them and tried to grab onto something, anything. Alex was next to me, and we reached for each other's hands as we plummeted into the black abyss.

The fall went on for what seemed like forever. I caught glimpses of the others. The Ophi, the zombies. Everyone was falling. Everyone was screaming in terror. The only one I didn't see was Hades. He was already where we were going to end up. The underworld.

I'd made my choice. According to Hades, it was the wrong choice. He couldn't let me go after that. I was a threat to him, and he wasn't having it. I clutched Alex, silently communicating an apology. I'd put him through hell these past few months. I didn't deserve him. Even just in the past hour, he'd had to see me with my human ex-boyfriend, who I clearly had unresolved feelings for. He should've hated me, but the look in his eyes said he still loved me.

I looked around, trying to get my bearings and remember what we were passing on our way to the underworld, but Hades had us surrounded in a black cloud of smoke. It carried us over the River Styx, which was barely visible through the smoke, and finally we fell at the gate to the underworld.

The zombies were obviously back under Hades' control because they got up and walked past the three-headed dog that guarded the gates and headed back to Tartartus. Leticia and McKenzie gasped and backed away from the dog as Hades appeared from behind him.

"Welcome to my world." He gave us a malicious smile and patted one of the dog's heads. "This is Cerberus. Normally, you'd be judged to determine if you belong in the Elysian Fields, the Fields of Asphodel, or Tartarus, but I already know where you're all going."

I guessed the Elysian Fields were where the good people went. Not people like us. Cerberus stepped aside so we could pass, but no one moved.

"We're not going there with you," I said.

Hades laughed. "How amusing that you think you have a choice." He stepped forward and got in my face. "You're on my turf now, Jodi Marshall. We play by *my* rules."

Everyone looked at me, their leader. Only I didn't know what to do. I didn't know much about the underworld. Tony did, but I couldn't exactly ask Hades to hold on while I had a chat with Tony to figure out how to get us out of here.

I did the only thing I could. I closed my eyes and mixed my blood, trying to summon Medusa's spirit. She'd been in the underworld before. She might be able to help us get out of it. I knew Hades wouldn't just stand there and let me do this, so I pretended to faint. I fell to the ground.

Panicked voices were all around me, including Alex's, but I tuned them out. I focused only on Medusa and calling her to me.

Her image appeared in my mind, but she looked lost. "Jodi, where are you?"

"In the underworld. Hades took us all."

"I felt a shift in the Ophi power. I knew you were in trouble."

"Is there anything you can do to help us?"

"That depends where you are. Did you cross the River Styx?"

"Yes. We're at the gate to the underworld, and Hades is going to take us to Tartarus."

Medusa hung her head, giving me a good view of her snakes. Right now they didn't seem so bad. I was sure they were nothing compared to what I was going to see in Tartarus. "Jodi, I cannot help you."

"Are you sure? There's nothing at all you can do?"

"I'm bound to this statue. You're lucky I can even access your mind in the underworld. If my blood was not in your veins, I wouldn't be able to."

It was over. I'd sentenced us all to eternity in the underworld. I'd failed. Hades was getting what he wanted.

"I'm sorry," Medusa said before her image disappeared.

I opened my eyes. Alex sighed, relieved to see I was okay. But how could I be okay? We were trapped. Worse than dead.

"Enough stalling," Hades said. "Follow me."

It was like we didn't have a will of our own anymore. Our legs moved, and we stared at them like they were completely foreign to us. This must be how the souls I forced into the wrong bodies felt. Hades had found the perfect punishment for a necromancer. Torture us the way we tortured souls.

"On your right, you'll see the Fields of Asphodel," Hades said in a "bad tour guide" kind of voice. He laughed at his joke. "This is all you will see of this place. The souls here walk around basically clueless. Not happy, not in pain. Just existing." He turned and looked at me. "Not at all the right punishment for you."

We walked on, helpless against the power that was moving our bodies for us. I tried to mix my blood and use my own power to regain control, but I couldn't. My blood was no match for Hades. Like he'd said, I was in his world now.

I caught a glimpse of a few souls wandering through Asphodel. I never thought I'd envy someone doomed to an eternity like that, but right now I did. Alex reached for my hand and laced his fingers through mine. Hades either didn't notice or didn't care. He continued to march us on.

Hades stopped when we reached an iron gate with what looked like a black pit inside it. No, not a pit. It was a portal. I remembered Tony teaching us about it. The entrance to Tartarus was a portal. All around the entrance, it was pitch black, darker than anything I'd ever seen. It was like someone had taken the black of night and multiplied it. And beyond that was fire. Flames that seemed to flow like a river. Hades gave us a minute to take it all in before turning to us and smiling. "This is where you will stay. I consider it my own maximum-security prison. Only my true enemies, and people who've committed horrific crimes, wind up here." He looked around the group, his eyes lingering when they reached me. "You all will fit in perfectly."

I wanted to run, but we were surrounded by the flames.

Hades saw me staring at them. "Ah, yes, you are well guarded by Phlegethon, the river of fire. You wouldn't get past the flames and clashing rocks, so don't even try."

He motioned us forward through the enormous portal. Tony's eyes widened at the pillars surrounding us. "Not even the gods could break through these."

Not what I needed to hear right now, Tony.

The darkness consumed us. I wasn't sure how we'd even find our way into Tartarus, but Hades held out his hand and a flame flickered in his palm. The fire illuminated the path. The walls were bronze and cold-looking. I'd expected to see hellfire and souls being burned, but this place was cold, unfeeling. This was the level of Tartarus where I'd raised most of the souls from—the ones who were buried in the cemetery at the school. Not quite the depths or level of torture we were walking into. Considering how awful those zombies had been, I couldn't even imagine what was waiting for us.

Gut-wrenching screams filled the air. Leticia and McKenzie were in tears. Neither one of them had an ounce of evil in them. They shouldn't be here.

"Hades." I tried to stop my legs from moving, but failed miserably.

He turned, and we all came to a halt.

"Oh, is this the part where you beg for forgiveness?" He smirked. "Go ahead then."

He was enjoying this. Enjoying our pain. He really did hate us. There was no point in arguing or trying to convince him to let us go. I was going to have to find another way to get us all out of the underworld. According to Tony's lessons about this place, it was nearly impossible to leave. My hopes weren't high, but I had to try.

"No?" Hades asked. "Well, then, if you've had a change of heart, let's proceed." He looked between Alex and me and smiled. "I believe you'll recognize a few faces here."

Oh, God! I'd completely forgotten. I'd sentenced Alex's parents and the other Ophi who'd turned evil to an eternity as Hades' slaves. They were here. They were the ones punishing the souls for Hades, and now they would be punishing us.

We came to a place where the light was better and we could actually see more than two feet in front of us. Hellhounds gnawed on souls, tearing them to shreds only to have the souls put back together and be put through that torture again. Leticia bent over and threw up, which started a domino effect with the others. I was too terrified to join them. I stared at the most frightening thing I'd ever seen.

The Ophi I'd banished stood in a group. Victoria, Troy, and Abby were at the front, wearing wicked smiles. They would enjoy torturing all of us. Me especially. How was I going to get us out of here? These guys were going to cause me so much pain I wouldn't even be able to think.

Abby put her hands on her hips. "Well, this should be fun."

Acknowledgements

First I have to thank Kate Kaynak and the amazing team at Spencer Hill Press for continuing to make my dreams come true. To my editor, Trisha Wooldridge, I can't say enough about how you just get this series. From your incredible insights to your fictional crushes, you've been nothing short of wonderful. And the locket you had designed for this cover is beautiful. Thank you to my team of copy editors, Rich Storrs, Keshia Swaim, and Shira Lipkin for your dedication to making sure this book was as perfect as possible. To Kendra Saunders, thank you for spreading the word and getting this book into the hands of book lovers everywhere.

As always, a huge thank you to my agent Lauren Hammond. I wouldn't be here without you. And to my agency sisters, writer friends, and YA Bound sisters your support keeps me sane. I'm so glad I have you all to share this journey with me.

I can't forget my daughter, Ayla, who is my biggest fan and means the world to me. Keep writing your own books, sweetheart. To my husband, Ryan, your support means more than you'll ever know. Thank you for helping me follow my dreams. To my mom, Patricia Bradley, you are the best beta reader, mother, and friend I could ask for. To my father, Martin Bradley, and my sister, Heather DeRobertis, your encouragement and your great ideas for getting the word out about my books is very much appreciated. Thank to my friends and family for understanding why my life gets a little crazy at times.

And many thanks and cyber hugs to the book bloggers who have supported this series. Keren Spencer and Kayleigh-Marie Gore, I owe a lot of the early buzz about this series to you both. You ladies rock. Thank you!

THE DOLLHOUSE ASYLUM

When seventeen year old Cheyenne Laurent falls for Teo Richardson, she thinks the biggest problem is that he's a little too old for her, a little too mysterious and a lot too smart. But that's before he kisses her. Before the monsters start taking over the world. Before Teo takes her.

Cheyenne wakes up on a street lined with fourteen houses—seven on each side—clueless as to why she's there. She knocks on doors and soon learns that each house is filled with another teen—seven girls on one side, seven boys on the other—and no one is allowed to tell her anything. She has to figure out the truth herself. It's not until Teo reveals his intentions that she understands. He's created his own world, Elysian Fields, where everyone has asylum from the monsters and where Teo and Cheyenne can be together.

THE DOLLHOUSE ASYLUM

MARY GRAY

Also available as an ebook • **SPENCER HILL PRESS** • spencerhillpress.com

Middle Grade Books

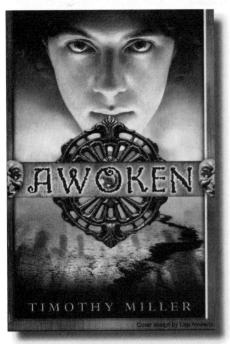

Fourteen-year-old Michael Stevens has never been ordinary; no orphan who hears music coming from rocks considers himself a typical teenager. When two-foot-tall, albino, doll-like men sneak into his room one night, transforming the harmless music into a frightening ability he cannot control. Michael finds himself in the middle of a war that could forever change the world he knows - reconstructing the very definition of humanity.

AUGUST 2013

Finn (not bleedin' Finnegan) MacCullen is eager to begin his apprenticeship. He soon discovers the ups and downs of hunting monsters in a suburban neighborhood. Armed with a bronze dagger, some ancient Celtic magic, and a hair-trigger temper, Finn is about to show his enemies the true meaning of "fighting Irish."

MARCH 2013

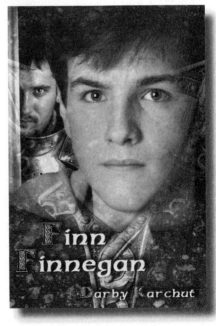

Kelly Hashway is a former language arts teacher who now works as a full-time writer, freelance editor, and mother to an adorable little girl. In addition to writing YA novels, Kelly writes middle grade books, picture books, and short stories. When she's not writing or digging her way out from under her enormous To Be Read pile, she's running and playing with her daughter. She resides in Pennsylvania with her husband, daughter, and two pets.

www.kellyhashway.com